> *"Please help us, Brynna.*
> *Please take us to Valhalla."*

Alrik's lips brushed mine as he spoke. I had an almost overwhelming desire to tilt my head up just a fraction of an inch, so his mouth would be fully pressed against mine, but a shred of dignity kept me from doing so. I never kissed men I had just met! Especially not ones who had been dead for almost thirteen hundred years. My mind did a double take. He couldn't be telling the truth. It had to be an illusion of some sort. Didn't it?

I reached up with both hands and grasped his wrists firmly. His flesh was warm and silky over steel muscles. "Now disappear," I said.

"As you wish." He leaned forward in a kiss that damn near burned my mouth, it was so hot.

Then he was gone, simply melting before my astonished eyes . . . and regretful lips.

My hands were holding nothing where a moment before Alrik's wrists had been. I could still taste him on my lips, a faintly sweet, earthy taste, like that of mead I'd once had at a Renaissance fair.

"Oh dear God," I said softly. I'd just been kissed by the most incredibly sexy man I'd ever met . . . and he had been dead for more than a thousand years.

Turn the page for praise
for Katie MacAlister

Light My Fire

"If you used just one word to describe MacAlister's magical heroine Aisling Grey, it would be 'unsinkable.' Book three in this delightful series pours on the romance big time and adds complications galore. Aisling's never-say-die attitude is mixed with a snarky humor that gives this magical saga extra zing. MacAlister's comic genius really shines through!"

—*Romantic Times*

Fire Me Up

"Unstoppable fun."

—*Romantic Times*

"Fresh, funny, and fabulous . . . *Fire Me Up* will crack you up. With so many intriguing, intelligently drawn, distinctive characters, it is no wonder [Katie MacAlister] is soaring to the top."

—*A Romance Review*

You Slay Me

"Smart, sexy, and laugh-out-loud funny!"

—Christine Feehan

"Graced with MacAlister's signature sharp wit and fabulously fun characters, this paranormal romance is wickedly sensual and irresistibly amusing."

—*Booklist*

"In the first of what I hope are many Aisling Grey novels, MacAlister shoots straight for the paranormal funny bone. Her outlandish sense of humor is the perfect complement to her sexy stories."

—*Romantic Times*

"Amusing romantic fantasy. . . . Fans will appreciate this warm, humorous tale that slays readers with laughter."

—The Best Reviews

"Katie MacAlister creates an entertaining world of demons, dragons and the people who control them. . . . Intriguing and funny."

—*A Romance Review*

"Humor, suspense, and intriguing characters . . . a real winner."

—Romance Reviews Today

Blow Me Down

"Outlandishly sexy and hilarious high seas high jinks. . . . Today's world can always use more humor and, lucky for us, MacAlister is there to deliver."

—*Romantic Times*

"A great try-it book for readers who say they don't read romances with a sci-fi twist. If that doesn't hook them, most likely the charming humor of an almost-midlife-crisis mom and a not-so-alpha hero falling head over buckles for each other will do the trick."

—*Booklist*

A Girl's Guide to Vampires

"Fantastic! It's sensual, it's hilarious, and it's a winner! Ms. MacAlister is my favorite new author."

—Reader to Reader Reviews

"With its superb characterization and writing that manages to be both sexy and humorous, this contemporary paranormal love story is an absolute delight."

—*Booklist*

KATIE MACALISTER

Ain't Myth-Behaving

POCKET **STAR** BOOKS

New York   London   Toronto   Sydney

Pocket Star Books
A Division of Simon & Schuster, Inc.
1230 Avenue of the Americas
New York, NY 10020

This book is a work of fiction. Names, characters, places, and incidents either are products of the author's imagination or are used fictitiously. Any resemblance to actual events or locales or persons, living or dead, is entirely coincidental.

First Pocket Star Books paperback edition October 2007

POCKET STAR BOOKS and colophon are registered trademarks of Simon & Schuster, Inc.

For information about special discounts for bulk purchases, please contact Simon & Schuster Special Sales at 1-800-456-6798 or business@simonandschuster.com.

Illustration by Hiro Kimura

Manufactured in the United States of America

10 9 8 7 6 5 4 3 2

ISBN-13: 978-1-4165-2493-9
ISBN-10:   1-4165-2493-2

Acknowledgments

Once again I owe tusen tack to my friend Tobias Barlind for his Swedish translations and endless help. I'd also like to thank Micki Nuding for her delightful sense of humor (and copious amount of patience), and my Senior Dog, who steadfastly snored beside me the entire time I was romping around my own versions of Ireland and Sweden.

Contents

Stag
Party

One

"My lord, do you not think . . ."

"Eh? What's that? Speak up, Stewart, you're positively mumbling."

Stewart the steward (we have many a good laugh over that) looked pointedly at the stone statue in front of me. "My lord—"

I held up my free hand. "Please, not you, too. It's bad enough having 'Most gracious lord this' and 'Oh worshipful lord that' coming from the druids, but you've known me for . . . phew, how many years now? Three hundred? Four?"

"Five hundred and twelve," the little man answered, wincing as I scratched my belly and sighed with relief. "I've always called you my lord. If not that, what do you wish me to call you?"

"Didn't we go through this last year? It's Hearne. Dane Hearne. Know it, use it, love it."

"Aye, my . . . Mr. Hearne. But . . . eh . . . is that not a bit sacrilegious?"

"Not in the least. It's the name I was born with. Well . . . in a manner of speaking. People didn't much go in for surnames back then, but that's what it would have been if they had. Nowadays, people hardly ever use my proper name. I almost forgot what it was myself until a few months ago, when I ran across an interesting online article about me."

"No, not your name. Er . . . that." He nodded to the statue in front of us.

I looked with dissatisfaction at it. "Sacrilegious because the artist depicted Taranis as standing astride the world in a position of power when we know him to be a cowardly little wimp, you mean?"

Stewart closed his eyes a moment. "No, my lo—sir. I meant the fact that you're urinating on it. Taranis is, after all, your overlord, head of all the Irish gods."

"On the contrary, I find it remarkably stress-relieving. It expresses my true inner feelings about that bastard." I punctuated the word I had written on the statue with an exclamation point before zipping up. I stretched and glanced around the yard. "So, what's been happening while I've been gone? Buildings look good. I see you've had the verge mown. The druids seem to be multiplying, though. Did you speak to them, as I asked? And why the blazes did Taranis wait until now to have me summoned?"

Stewart was a short man. Proud, and of noble birth—if on the wrong side of the blanket—but lacking in the general region of height. He trotted alongside me as I strolled around the grounds, eyeing the large square tower that made up one of two habitable parts of the castle. The tower looked as solid as ever. There was a hint of moss growing on the north side, but other than that, it looked good. Remarkable, really, considering it was older than Stewart.

"Er . . . I have no idea. I was told there was a delay. As for the druids, I tried, Mr. Hearne."

"Dane. Surely after all those long centuries of employment, you can call me Dane?"

His little round face looked vaguely shocked. "I couldn't do that, sir. It wouldn't be fitting. You are, after all, Cernunnos."

"Stewart, Stewart, still living in the twelfth century." I shook my head as I strode past the carriage house where the druids were housed, counting no fewer than three new faces in the group that was dancing around a willow tree.

"I was born in the sixteenth, sir—"

"Doesn't matter." I waved a hand at the splotches of yellow that cascaded over the crumbled stones that made up the ruined part of the castle. "Those yellow blobs there, those flowers. Just look at them!"

"Daffodils, sir."

We marched past the flower-splattered mossy ruins, following the narrow trail down to the rocky beach that dropped abruptly into the sea. "Whatever they are, they're positively bursting with life force! It's spring, man, the time of birth and rejuvenation and life! The time to celebrate being alive, not fussing around with archaic ideas and outmoded methods of speech. Live in the here and now, that's my motto, and it's never let me down. Where's Fidencia?"

"Er . . . she's not here, sir." Stewart skidded down the last of the path, and kept from falling by clutching the root of an uprooted tree that had washed ashore a few years ago.

I hopped over the tree and walked to the water's edge, breathing deeply of the fresh salt air. My position might be tied to shady woodland areas, but it was the sea I loved best. The relentless roar of the waves, the sharp tang of salty air, the piercing cry of gulls and terns as they etched great arcs into the sky—ah, yes, it was the sea that I returned to each time I was born, and it was the loss of the sea I mourned each winter when I died.

The sea air brushed away a few of the mental cobwebs that always remained after rebirth, and I turned from the view of my beloved sea to glance at Stewart. He was looking distinctly uncomfortable, shifting restlessly from foot to foot. "What's the matter with you?" I asked, feeling a momentary spike of concern. Stewart had been with me so many centuries, I couldn't imagine how I would cope without him. Had someone wooed him away from my employment while I was gone?

"It's Lady Fidencia."

"What about her? Don't tell me that she's broken that thing we started a couple of years ago. What was it?"

"A credit limit?"

"Don't tell me she blasted through that credit limit and bankrupted me again? I distinctly remember you telling me she couldn't do that anymore."

"No, sir, she has not exceeded the limit you put on her credit card—at least I don't believe she has; I haven't seen the statements for this month yet. It's something of a different nature that I believe will interest you."

I turned back to the sea, allowing its ebb and flow to soak into my soul. "I sincerely doubt that. Fidencia is so caught up in herself, she never has time for anyone else, let alone her lord and master. What's she done now? Started another artists' colony? Gone to those monks in Nepal to learn meditation again? Decided to breed more pygmy goats?"

"Alas, she hasn't, sir. She's . . . er . . ."

"Spit it out, man," I told him, not taking my eyes from the breathtaking expanse before me. It amused me to try to find the point on the horizon where the steel gray of the sea merged into the gray of the sky.

"She's gone to South America, married another god who is now a Brazilian salsa dancer, and is going to be expecting a Happy Event sometime in the near future," he said in a rush.

My blood seemed to turn to fire in my veins. I turned slowly to look at the steward. He had backed away a few steps as if he was about to bolt. "She *what*?"

He jerked at the bellow, the birds above us scattering with harsh cries of protest. I was on him in two steps, the blood pounding so loudly in my ears that it blocked the sound of the sea. The pressure in my head built until it burst forth, another roar of anger sounding against the crash of the waves. "She married someone? She can't marry someone, she's supposed to marry me in a week! She's gone and impregnated herself with some other man's child? She can't do that! I forbid her to be pregnant! I forbid her to be married!"

"You're . . . strangling me . . . sir . . ." Stewart's raspy voice pierced the roar in my ears. My eyes focused on his face, turning red as I held him by his neck two feet off the ground.

"Blast! My apologies, Stewart." I set him down carefully, straightening his tie and jacket, and watching him closely to make sure he wasn't going to swoon. "You all right?"

"Yes, sir," he squeaked, tugging at his tie. He eyed my forehead with a look of great caution. "You seem to be manifesting. Shall I fetch the swords?"

I waved away the offer. "No, no, there's no need for me to work off anger through fencing anymore. There was a new yoga instructor in my department. I spent the entire time I was dead working on anger management skills. Just let me get control again, and then you can tell me what the hell Fidencia is up to now."

Stewart looked away as I turned back to the sea, driving all thoughts from my mind but the calming rhythm of the waves. A few minutes later I was myself again, and tapped him on the shoulder before starting back toward the tower. "I think this is going to require a drink."

"Several, I would imagine."

"Take it from the beginning," I said as we walked into my study at the top of the tower. I poured brandy into a couple of glasses, sliding one toward him before moving to the window overlooking the rocky beach. The uneven stone surface that made up the entire tower was cool to the touch—it always was, no matter how hot the day. I gripped the stone windowsill, my eyes on the gray sea below.

"It was just after you left for the Underworld that she called from Rio de Janeiro. She said that she had fallen in love with Dionysus."

"Dionysus?" The named seemed familiar, but I couldn't quite place it.

"Better known as Bacchus, sir. Lord of wine and celebration. Evidently Dionysus joined a twelve-step program, has gone on the wagon, and became a salsa dancer at a hotel, which is where Lady Fidencia met him. She called soon after you died to say that she was in love, was going to marry him and go to Rio to live la vida loca."

I cast a frown over my shoulder at him. "She's living *what*?"

He made a little gesture that had his brandy splashing in his glass. "*La vida loca.* I looked it up on the Internet. Evidently it's from a popular song. It means living the crazy life."

"Life here wasn't crazy enough for her?" I asked, indignant at the thought that she felt the life I offered was lacking in any way. "She doesn't think being surrounded by neo-druids for half the year and hyperactive fitness instructors and televangelists for the other half isn't crazy? She'd have to be insane not to find that crazy!"

Stewart shrugged and sipped his brandy.

"This isn't good." I jerked the chair out from behind my desk and slumped into it. "Beltane is a week away. You know what that means—Taranis will be chomping at the bit to get a replacement for me in here. Well, I'm not going to let that happen. Get Fidencia on the phone. Maybe this is some sort of ploy to get her credit limit raised."

Stewart rose to do as I requested, but the look on his face had me worried.

He moved to the desk in the alcove that used to be a fireplace, but which was now his office space. The tower walls were several feet thick, made of local stone quarried a few miles from the castle. I looked around my study, wishing I'd had the good sense in the thirteenth century to panel the walls with wood instead of taking the advice of the local castle builder. Although the tower was the only original part of the castle to remain standing, it always had a slightly damp feel, as if the stones leeched the constant spray of water that beset the outer walls.

"Someone is going to fetch her," Stewart said, his hand over the mouth of the telephone.

I grunted and turned on the laptop on my desk, sullenly prodding a couple of buttons until the current week's schedule was displayed. "This is just what I need the second I'm reborn—a faithless consort, possible dispossession, and oh, joy of joys, what's this? Tourists? We never open the castle until June. Why does it say that we're booked for ten days starting tomorrow?"

"Sim, sim, Senhora Fidencia, por favor." Stewart covered the mouthpiece again. "I was going to tell you about that. We had an offer I didn't think you would want to refuse from one of those American travel websites. They're running an international contest for their top travel writers, and they needed several historical sites to serve as subject matter. You should be flattered they chose Bannon Castle—they skipped several others in the county. They'll only be here for ten days, and the money is quite good. You said before you went underground that the roof needed repair, and you didn't know where you were going to find the money for it—I thought this was a blessing in disguise."

I frowned and waved away his idea of a blessing. "But they will be here before Beltane! You know how disturbing I find tourists—always getting underfoot, asking questions, wanting their pictures taken with me, coveting my manly body, that sort of thing. That's why Fidencia and I go away during the summer—so we won't be bothered by them. How many rooms are they taking?"

"Just two. There's a writer who has been assigned the castle and surrounding area, a cameraman to film her, and a sound engineer. The last two are a couple, so I thought we could put them in the carriage house, and let the writer have the Tudor Room for the atmosphere. Sim? Ah. Obrigato."

"And just how are we going to explain about the druids?" I asked, exiting the schedule program with a sour expression. I disliked having my well-laid plans put awry, and now I was facing endless upheaval. "The celebration is coming up, and you know how they get—everything's a sacrifice or a ceremony, most of them conducted with no clothing on, and

many involving sexual congress. Debauchery and
pagan ceremonies is hardly how I want Bannon
Castle depicted to the world."

"I'll talk to Elfwine and tell her to keep a low pro-
file—good morning, Lady Fidencia. I have his lordship waiting to speak to you." Stewart paused for a
moment, a faint blush brightening his cheeks.

Silently, I picked up the phone on my desk and
leaned back in the chair, unable to keep the smile
from forming as Stewart was forced to listen to
Fidencia's recital of intimate woes stemming from
her pregnancy. I let her go on for a bit, but took pity
on him when she got to the part about bathroom dif-
ficulties. "What sort of game are you playing now?"
I asked, interrupting her. "You picked a hell of a bad
time to do it—I need you back here immediately.
Beltane is just a week away. We have to be married
by then, as you well know."

"Noony, darling!" Fidencia positively cooed into
the phone. "What a delight it is to hear your forceful, one might almost say *grating*, voice again. How
was the Underworld? Still filled with usurers and
adulterers?"

I scowled at the photo on my desk, that of a long-
limbed, dark-haired, sultry goddess poised seductively
on a white fur rug. *Noony.* I hated that absurd nick-
name, which was no doubt why she used it. "There
haven't been usurers since the investment advisers
fed them to the sharks. And as for adulterers—those
who live in glass houses, my dear."

Her laughter tinkled in a way that, for the three

years I had been unaccountably smitten with her, delighted me, but now just made my teeth itch. My jaw tightened in response, causing my teeth to grind.

"Darling Noony! One can't adulterate someone who isn't one's legal spouse. You died. Therefore, I was a widow and free to remarry as I liked."

"It's a symbolic death, as you very well know. Or you *would* know if you'd ever gone into the Underworld with me, as you were meant to do."

"Once was enough," she answered quickly, the shudder evident in her voice. "I've moved on since then. While you were moldering away in the Underworld, I was falling madly, wonderfully, totally, and completely in love with Dion. He asked me to marry him the very first night we met—at a samba contest, which naturally we won—and I just knew that he could offer me everything you couldn't. It was kismet, darling, kismet."

I ground my teeth some more, just for the hell of it. "You have no right to marry someone else. You agreed to the rules of the job, even if you've disregarded most of them. But you can't just brush aside the fact that in a week's time, we are to be *married*. I'm willing to overlook this indiscretion, just as I've overlooked all the other ones, but I won't have you jeopardizing my job simply because you've had it off with some Latin boy toy."

"He's actually Greek, dear heart, but I wouldn't expect you to know that. Dion gave up his licentious past, and has devoted himself heart and soul to salsa. And me, naturally. I can assure you that Dion is anything but a boy," she purred. "And as for your job—I am sorry, darling, but I've decided to quit. I've found my true métier in life—to be a wife and mother—and nothing you can say or do will change my mind."

"You can't do this to me!" I yelled, ignoring the pressure in my forehead. "You know that Taranis has been breathing down my back for the last two hundred years! The instant he knows you've married someone else, he'll take everything away from me and hand it to one of his minions!"

"I'm truly sorry, darling, but my mind is quite made up. There is nothing in the laws that say *I* have to be your wife—you'll simply have to find someone else to marry you at Beltane."

A few more layers of tooth enamel were ground off. "You can't seriously expect me to find, court, and marry a woman in a week?"

"There once was a time, many centuries in the past, when you had something approaching charm," she said thoughtfully. "I suggest you dust that off and use it. Otherwise . . . it's been nice knowing you."

The call continued in that vein for another agonizing fifteen minutes. I tried every argument I could to make her see reason, but she always was an unreasonable woman.

"Hellfire!" I swore, slamming down the phone. I then took great pleasure in jamming her photo into the trash, followed by a great many invectives.

"I take it the call did not proceed in a satisfactory manner?"

"No." I stormed around the room for a moment,

cursing Fidencia, cursing women in general, cursing the situation I found myself in. "After eleven hundred years, she suddenly decides I don't offer her enough scope. Scope! What the hell does that mean, anyway?"

"I believe, sir, it means she feels her life is going nowhere, that marriage with you is stifling—"

One glare was enough to leave him mumbling an apology.

"As if anyone could stifle her! She's the most unreasonable woman in existence, and I rue the day I ever saved her wretched neck by pulling her out of the sea before she drowned. The little witch has me by the balls good and proper. Well, I'll just show her who is lacking in scope! There is no way in this world or the next I will give up my job to one of Taranis's lackeys. Stewart! Round up every marriageable female you know. I'm going wife shopping!"

Two

"A nd this is Aoife, Lord Cernunnos," Elfwine said the following day as a shy-looking girl with a broad, freckled face stepped forward and peeked at me over the top of her thick-rimmed glasses.

I frowned.

"Just barely eighteen," Stewart whispered. "If that."

I frowned more.

"Aoife is one of our newer ovate initiates. She comes from County Clare and will be going to university next month. Her interests are herbalism, art, and nature in its purest form. She is, naturally, a virgin. Aoife, dear, take off your robe so his lordship may see your physical being better."

"That won't be necessary," I said quickly, holding up a hand to stop the virgin from stripping. "Quite charming, but as I mentioned, I'm looking for a woman with a bit more . . . experience than this young lady offers."

"Experience?" Elfwine's formidable brows pulled together in a puzzled frown.

She was an elder in the order of druids that had shown up at my doorstep six centuries ago, claiming they existed solely to worship the lord of the forest: namely, me. Elfwine was a leader in the group that set up home in what had once been the castle's inner ward. Although silver now streaked her black hair, she retained the forceful personality for which she was known. A few minutes with Elfwine always left me feeling like a bit of moss directly in the way of a rolling boulder—she had a way of sweeping everyone up before her, putting them inexorably on the path she desired. It was an uncomfortable feeling, one I avoided as much as possible by leaving Stewart to deal with her.

"How can a virgin be experienced?" she asked, fixing me with a gimlet eye. I had to steel myself not to take a step back.

"I never said my wife had to be a virgin, did I, Stewart?" I asked, desperately trying to foist her attention onto him.

Her steel-gray eyes gave Stewart a look that would have made the hair on a lesser man's head stand on end, and I congratulated myself on my cunning ability to distract her. True, it wasn't very sporting to offer Stewart up as a sacrifice, but I had much on my plate and little time to spend dodging Elfwine's all-knowing gaze.

"No, you didn't, sir, although you didn't say she couldn't be one, either," Stewart answered, and damn him, her attention returned to me.

"You are Cernunnos, lord of the hunt, lord of the dead, lord of the forest," Elfwine said slowly, each word striking me with the blow of a sledgehammer. "Nothing but a pure woman will do for your consort. You must have a virgin. As your devoted worship-

pers, as keepers of the wood of Cernunnos, it falls to
us to provide for you, and provide we will. We currently have three virgins for you to look over. There
were five—but an unfortunate brewing incident that
led to unusually strong mead caused two girls to be
stricken from the rolls."

I took a step to the side, hoping to distract her
long enough to make my escape.

"The three who are left are very nice girls, brought
up to properly worship you. They know their place,
are well seeped in druid lore, and all of them are
willing to cast aside their worldly concerns to devote
themselves wholly to you as your wife."

Escape wasn't going to happen. I straightened my
shoulders and looked down my nose at her, arranging my expression into an intolerably lofty sneer.
Elfwine had refused in the past to be intimidated by
such pitiful tactics, but I had few weapons against
her, and was forced to rely on what was at hand. "I
haven't had a virgin in the past, so I don't see why I
need one now."

"You haven't had one . . ." Her eyes showed astonishment for a moment as she chewed that bit of
information over.

Stewart blew out a breath that sounded suspiciously as if he'd said, "Fidencia will have your balls
for that."

"Furthermore," I said, raising my hand to stop
her from speaking, "I find it nerve-racking to be
around virgins. They're either skittish and giggly, or
lust-filled vixens who have an itch they want me to

scratch simply because I'm Irish, lord of the woods, or just male, depending on their particular itch. I'm looking for a woman who will spend the rest of eternity with me, a woman of intellect as well as beauty. I do not need an untried teenager who has more knowledge of the latest boy band than what it means to be my goddess."

I swear Elfwine seemed to grow. The air around her fairly vibrated as she took a deep breath. Stewart took three steps backward. I seriously considered running for the tower, but remembered in time who I was.

"You are Cernunnos!"

"Yes, but—"

"You are a god!"

"Just a minor one, really—"

"You are lord of the forest! Of the dead! Of fertility!"

"The last is purely an honorary title, to be perfectly frank—"

Her words chipped away at me like tiny sledgehammers. "You must have a virgin!"

Desperate times called for desperate measures.

"Was that the phone?" I tipped my head toward the castle, pursing my lips. "I believe it is. We'll have to continue this conversation another time, Elfwine. Or better yet, you talk it over with Stewart. That's no doubt a very important call that I must take. Good morrow and all that."

The look on Stewart's face as I raced off to the tower would have wrung the heart of the sternest misanthrope, but I simply didn't have the time to waste on the awkward, inept virgins Elfwine wished to thrust on me.

"You can run, my lord, but you cannot escape your fate." Elfwine's bellow followed me even as I ran around the stone tower, intent on gaining sanctuary. "You must have a virgin!"

"Over my dead body," I muttered. Distracted by the thought of being stampeded by a herd of thundering virgins, as I rounded the corner to the front of the tower, I collided with something warm, soft, and extremely sweet smelling. An obstacle at my feet sent me falling forward onto the something, which gave a surprised squawk as we hit the ground.

Blue eyes gazed up at me in dazed astonishment, a blue like nothing I'd ever seen before—pure, glittering blue, almost cerulean, shining with a brightness that reminded me of a sapphire I'd once given Fidencia. I stared into the eyes, my brain grinding to a halt as I watched with fascination as the astonishment faded into quick-lived amusement, followed almost immediately by vague annoyance.

"You're crushing me," the owner of the eyes said in a charming American accent.

My lips stretched into a grin. An inane one, but for some reason I couldn't stop staring into those lovely eyes. The body beneath me was soft and curved in enticing places . . . enough so that a primitive part of my brain sat up and took notice.

"Um . . . can you get off me now? Seriously, you're crushing me. There's a rock the size of Montana beneath my left shoulder, and it's really starting to hurt."

The face that went along with the eyes was equally entrancing. Eyebrows the color of dark amber honey arched upward, framed by a widow's peak of dark blondish-brown hair that was the exact color of a satinwood bureau in my sitting room. Lightly freckled cheeks that were as silky as a mare's bottom swept downward to a gently pointed chin, above which resided two rosy lips.

"Hello? Don't they speak English here? HELLO? Get off me, you great lummox!"

The lips pursed for a moment; then the world shifted suddenly and I was on my back, staring up into a sky that was pale in comparison to the woman's eyes.

"Christ on a handcar, I think one of my ribs is broken! What is *wrong* with you? I'm going to have bruises all over my back now. You know, a more litigious person than myself would consider a lawsuit for pain and suffering."

Stewart's face hove into view. "My lord, are you all right?"

"My *lord*?" the voice asked hesitantly. "You're a lord? An Irish peer?"

The woman's voice finally sank through to my brain. I sat up abruptly, smacking my head against Stewart's. He staggered backward rubbing his head, but I leaped adroitly to my feet and endeavored to make up for the temporary lapse in my thought processes. "My apologies, dear lady. Are you injured?

Should we call for a doctor? I didn't see you standing there when I came around the corner, and unfortunately something tripped me before I could stop."

"I think you gave me a concussion," Stewart moaned from where he had collapsed against the tower wall.

"I'm fine now, thank you. Did you hit your head when we fell? You looked a bit stunned for a minute or two." The woman's brow wrinkled in concern as she examined my head for signs of injury.

"It was nothing, just a little bump on the head." I mustered up another smile for her, one that I hoped displayed an urbane nonchalance tinged with a healthy appreciation for her beauty, grace, and overall wonderfulness.

Stewart's voice drifted over to us. "I'm seeing double."

"I'm Megan St. Clair," she said, offering me her hand.

I took it in both of mine, feeling an inordinate rush of pleasure in its possession before a slight tug reminded me she would probably want it back. "I'm Dane Hearne."

"I'm sick to my stomach," came a faint voice.

She sent a startled glance over to where Stewart was sliding down the wall to the ground. "Is that man all right?"

"Stewart? Absolutely. He's just winded—he'll be fine in a moment or two."

She tugged slightly on her hand. I tightened my fingers around it, not willing to give it up yet.

"You're American?" She'd pronounced her name in the American fashion, Saint Clair. A memory clicked into place. "Ah . . . you must be the Yank travel writer who's come to stay at the castle for a bit. Welcome to Castle Bannon."

Another tug, this time a bit stronger, almost had me losing my grip. "Thank you. Yes, that's me. You're the owner of the castle? Is it Lord Dane Hearne?"

"No, no, that's just one of Stewart's little ways. It's Dane, just Dane."

"I see. Can I have my hand back, please, Dane?"

A slight tense note in her voice warned me that insisting on retaining it might lead to trouble. With reluctance, I relaxed my grip on her until her fingers slid from mine.

"I'm very excited to be here," Megan continued, turning in a little circle to take in the grounds. "It's my first time abroad, my first time in Ireland, and my first Irish castle. I'm a bit of a virgin, you might say," she ended with a light laugh that was as golden as a late summer afternoon. It warmed me to my toes, spilling around and in me, lighting up all sorts of dark little corners of my soul. I felt almost drunk by her laughter, so heady was it.

"Indeed. I hope the deflowering wasn't painful," I said, reeling a bit from the smile she turned on me.

"Not at all, although the flight from the West Coast—I live in northern California—was a bit long. Could we . . . are our rooms ready?"

"We?" I asked, confused.

"Oh, I'm sorry, you haven't met Pam and Derek.

They will be filming my segments for GoWorld."

Two people whom I hadn't noticed standing behind her stepped forward. A young woman with short-cropped black hair, glasses, and a serious mien held out her hand with a murmured "Pam Russell. I'm the photographer."

I shook her hand, as well as that of the slight, bearded man who was loaded down with bulky bags. He nodded, and said, "Derek Thompson. Sound."

"Of course you all must be tired out by the journey. I think you two will find your room in the carriage house comfortable," I said, waving to the building behind them. "Stewart will show you the room. Stewart!"

"Coming, sir." Stewart stumbled over, still rubbing his head. He gave me a glare that was astonishing in its ferocity, but murmured all the correct things as he escorted the two travel people to their room.

"Your room," I said, smiling at Megan as I gestured toward the tower, "is in the oldest standing structure of the castle."

Her eyes widened as she gazed at me, some intangible spark igniting in the air around us. She blinked a couple of times, blushed, and looked away. "I'm sure it will be wonderful."

"I have every intention of ensuring it will be," I promised her, hoisting up her luggage and carrying it toward the door.

Her blush deepened, as if she knew I was speaking of something other than the accommodations.

Three

"Ah, there you are. Good man. We have work to do," I said a little while later as Stewart entered my study.

"I'm just here to get some painkillers for this massive headache you've given me," he answered as he went to his desk. "I'm not staying. I have things to do elsewhere."

"Forget them," I said as I strode across the room. I'd been pacing for the last five minutes, trying to make plans but being disturbed by the memories of Megan's eyes . . . and lips, and hair, and the deliciously round curve of her ass as displayed in a pair of tan linen trousers. The sight of it moving in a wonderfully feminine way as she climbed the stairs ahead of me had kept me speechless in rapt appreciation until we'd reached the room assigned to her.

It had taken all my strength not to drop down on one knee and propose to her right then and there, but hindsight had taught me much through the centuries. No longer would I be swayed by the sight of a beautiful woman into immediate lust and an offer of marriage. Well . . . at least not the offer of marriage.

"This time," I told Stewart, "things are going to be done differently."

"They are?" he asked, picking up the bottle of headache tablets.

"Yes. I offered for Fidencia the moment she was done vomiting up river water, and just look where that got me. This time, I will be circumspect. I will investigate before I propose. I will make sure the woman is the right one for me, one I can spend eternity with. I will take things slowly." I glanced at my watch. "As slowly as possible, given that I need to be married in six days. Three days for courtship, I think, three more for a general getting-to-know-you period that will include a determination of sexual compatibility, and then the last day for adjustment to her new role as my goddess. Yes, that should be plenty of time. I'd best get started on the courting right away."

Stewart stared at me with his mouth hanging slightly open. "Courting? Marriage? *What* woman? You don't mean the American?"

"Of course I mean Megan! Didn't you see her? She's prime goddess material! Those startling eyes, magnificent breasts, and her ass is a work of art. Add to that she's literate—she's a writer, after all—and has a sense of humor, and is obviously ready to fall into my arms."

"She is?"

"She said she liked my accent, *and* she blushed when she said it. Oh, yes, she's ripe for the plucking."

"I . . . you . . . she . . ." Stewart shook his head, winced, and poured out several pain tablets.

"That takes care of the basic pronoun situation, yes." I said, striding past him as I put my thoughts in order. "The first thing is to check into her past. A private investigator, do you think? That's so impersonal. I think I should do the investigating. I'll simply work a few investigative questions into our conversations, and that will be that. Not only will it allow me to make sure Megan is the right woman, it will prove I'm interested in her. Women love it when you ask them about themselves."

Stewart moaned and washed down his pills with a hefty splash of whiskey.

"You're not going to get drunk now, are you?" I asked with a frown.

He eyed the whiskey bottle with a look I recognized.

"I need your wits as sharp as a battleax," I said quickly, whisking away the bottle before he could take another swig from it. "You can get pissed another time. Right now your job is to keep the druids hidden from Megan and the film crew until I have a chance to explain how things are to her. And vice versa—no need to get Elfwine in a fury because there's a woman present I want over her tree huggers. While you're at it, you can put in a good word or two about me to Megan. Although it's clear she's already smitten with my manly Irish self, it won't hurt for her to see that my staff adores me."

Stewart stared at me with bleary, disbelieving eyes.

"Get to it, man! We don't have much time to pull this off! Need I remind you that if I do not marry at Beltane, I will lose this position?"

"Yes, I know. That would be a terrible tragedy." Stewart remained sitting, his expression showing anything but the stark horror such a hideous contingency should generate.

I leaned over his desk, saying very softly, "The real tragedy will be the manner in which Taranis's replacement will wreak revenge on the staff left behind. You remember the man who was Neit, god of war, about two hundred years ago? Do you know what happened to his servants when Taranis replaced him?"

Stewart shook his head mutely, his eyes widening in apprehension.

"Let's just say the things they did with a spoon and two egg cups guaranteed there would be no vengeful descendants pursuing them."

"Erp," he said, his legs tightening.

"I see you understand the truly hideous nature of the situation now," I said before heading briskly for the door. "Off you go, then. I've offered to show Megan around the grounds so she can do some preliminary work on a feature about the castle. We should be back in time for supper."

"But . . . Elfwine isn't going to listen to me—" Stewart started to say, leaping up from his chair.

I closed the door on his protestations and quickly trotted down the spiral stone staircase that ran down the center of the tower. The upper floor had been given over to my private rooms, but the two lower floors held four guest rooms, while the ground floor held the living areas. I made a mental note to point out to Megan the cunning way I'd worked the castle's original torture devices into the kitchen decor.

"Settled in? Comfortable? Finding the ambience impossible to resist?" I asked a minute later as she answered the knock on her door.

"Yes, very much so, and we'll see," she answered with a laugh as she left the room. "I appreciate your giving me the grand tour, Dane. I'm sure you have much more important things to do than drag a tourist around the grounds."

"You wound me, dearling," I said, putting a hand over my heart. "I can think of nothing I'd enjoy more."

She paused on the top of the stairs leading to the ground floor, glancing back at me over her shoulder. "Darling?"

I smiled. Women like my smile. I've been told by several lasses that I have a particularly effective smile, that there is something about green eyes and black hair, not to mention dimples, that melts their knees. Or some such nonsense—all I know is that they seem to be particularly susceptible to a full-frontal smile. I put a little extra wattage into my smile and waited for Megan to swoon.

An annoyed look flickered in her eyes. "Are you all right? Are you sure you didn't hit your head too hard this morning?"

I turned down the smile a notch or two. Maybe it was too much for her? Perhaps I was overwhelming her with my masculine charms. I would pull back a bit and let her get her footing before I blasted her with the full effect. "Thank you, I'm fine."

She turned until she was facing me, three steps below me. I could see down the front of her lacy white shirt to where her pale pink bra encased two delectable, slightly freckled mounds that suddenly had my mouth watering and my hands itching.

"Then would you mind telling me why you're calling me darling, and if you could do it while not actually drooling as you look down my blouse, that would be worth bonus points."

My penis stirred at the sight of those bountiful swells of feminine flesh, but I reminded it of the schedule—there were three days of wooing to get through before the Lively Lad had his way.

"Dane?"

"Hmm?" Maybe two days would be enough. She was clearly an intelligent girl. Two days of wooing would surely be enough to sway her.

Her breasts heaved in a wonderful, if exasperated, sigh. I wondered, just for a moment, what the color of her nipples was.

"Just like every other man . . . hello! Eyes up here!"

Then again, if I put my mind to it, I bet I could pack three days of wooing into one day. That would leave five days of bed sporting. I knew how important those things were to women—they liked to feel cherished in the bedroom, so it behooved me to give her as much time being cherished as possible before the wedding.

Her breasts bobbed enticingly for a second before they were torn from my view.

"Why are you taking your breasts away?" I heard a voice ask as she started down the stairs.

She spun around to face me, her jaw tight, her eyes indignant.

"Hell. I said that out loud, didn't I?" I asked.

"You certainly did! And I don't care how sexy your accent is, or how cute those dimples are, or the wonderful way your hair curls around your neck—I am not going to stand for sexual harassment."

I hurried down the few steps to her, taking her hand and bowing slightly over it, managing, by a feat of strength heretofore unknown in the county, to not look down her shirt again. "You have my profoundest apology, Megan. That was very ill mannered of me. I'm a bit fuzzy brained still, and it rather slipped out without my knowing."

"Don't be ridiculous," she said in a terse voice, and tried to pull her hand from mine. I tightened my grip. "You certainly had to know that you can't say things like that to people nowadays! Even in Ireland, such behavior has to be discouraged. As for you being fuzzy brained . . . well, it's not as if you were born yesterday."

"No, the day before that. Come, let me show you my favorite thinking spot. You'll like it, it's wild and untamed and utterly glorious." I pulled her after me down the stairs.

"What? What did you mean the day before? Will you let go of my hand?"

"The stairs are treacherous. I'm just trying to keep you from falling."

"My Aunt Fanny you are. You just want to hold my hand. First you called me darling—"

"Dearling."

"You see? You just did it again!"

"The word is 'dearling,' not 'darling.' There's a difference. One is romantic; the other mundane. Ah, here we are, the front hall. I'll show you the rest of the tower later, after we've had a ramble around the grounds, all right? This way."

"Dane!"

I shoved open the heavy oak door and paused on the landing, taking a deep breath of the tangy air. "Yes, it's true, I want to hold your hand. I like your hand. It's soft but strong, rather like you. Would you mind if I twined my fingers through yours?"

I suited action to words. A little tremor went through her as I rubbed my thumb on her palm.

"Now, over here used to be the inner curtain." I strode toward the large knoll that was partially visible, my firm grip on Megan's hand ensuring she would follow. "As you can see, there's nothing left of it but a long mound. Someday I'll let the archaeologists have at it, but I rather like it as it is now, all covered in those yellow flowers."

"Dane!"

"Hmm?" A gentle tug had her half-running down the grassy mound to the far side. "The outer curtain is nothing but rubble, but it's very scenic at night when we light it up. There's a path over here to the beach. Mind your step. Some of the rubble can be a bit treacherous."

"Dane, stop!" A sharp yank pulled her hand from mine. I spun around, fearing she had tripped over something and was about to fall, but she looked anything but helpless as she stood on the top of a rock, her hands on her hips, hair whipping around her in the afternoon wind, those gorgeous eyes of hers skewering me with blue fire. "Goddamn it, why won't you listen to me? I have been trying to get your attention!"

"Dearling, you have my attention—"

"Stop it!" Her hands waved in a wild dance of emotion. "Stop calling me darling, or dearling, or whatever Irish endearment you're using. Just stop it!"

"It's not Irish, actually—"

"I don't care!" Even her bellow had a melodious quality to it.

"All right, then." I thought for a moment. "How do you feel about 'sweeting'?"

Her eyes got a bit of a wild glint to them.

"I'll take that as a no. We can go with sweetheart, but that's a bit mundane, don't you think?"

Her magnificent breasts heaved as she struggled to get control of herself. "Why are you doing this? Why do you want to call me anything but my name?"

"I'm a bit of a romantic," I admitted with a wry little smile. "I've always used affectionate terms for the women I love. *Woman,* singular. That is, there've *been* women, plural, but not at the same time. I'm a monogamist, in case you were wondering."

"That's fascinating, but," she said, closing her eyes for a second and rubbing her forehead as if she had a headache, "we're not in love."

"No, of course we aren't, we've only just met."
She relaxed slightly. I took advantage of her distrac-
tion to take her hand and pull her gently off the rock.
"There's loads of time yet for that—three days, possibly one if I am especially clever. Come along; my
special thinking spot is around the point, here."

"You . . . this is a trick, isn't it? Or one of those
goofy reality TV shows where they film people in impossible situations, then air them with horrible shots
of an audience laughing at them, right?"

"You have an interesting mind," I told her, wondering what sort of television she watched. "I like it."

She said nothing for a few minutes while I
helped her over the occasional boulder or pile of
driftwood. We rounded the point to the small inlet
that was a peaceful haven in an always turbulent
sea.

When she did speak, her voice bore unmistakable signs of control. "Would you mind telling me, if
it wouldn't be too much bother, why you are under
the impression that we will be falling in love with
each other, thus making the use of affection terms
desirable?"

I had to think quickly. Women liked to know a
man found them desirable, but my somewhat limited experience the last few centuries—limited to
the few weeks I had before I married Fidencia each
Beltane—had proved that women's attitudes toward
sex had changed somewhat. It followed, then, that
their attitude about marriage had changed, as well.
Therefore, I needed to keep the ultimate goal of the

wooing quiet until she had time to get used to the idea. Say, by tomorrow.

"Dane?" She stood a few feet away from me, something about her reminding me of a deer about to bolt.

"Sorry, I was thinking about something. What was the question?"

She marched over to me and smacked me on the arm. "Why are you doing this to me?"

"You're beautiful, intelligent, and you are clearly aware of the spark of attraction between us."

"I am?" Her mouth dropped open slightly. I took a slow step forward, so as not to startle her into flight, leaning in to her until I could smell the wonderful scent of a sun-warmed woman. Her eyes dilated. "There's an attraction?"

"Oh, yes, there is." The smell of her was heady stuff, bringing my penis to life again. "Not to mention the fact that your breasts damn near bring me to my knees. Why shouldn't we give in to our primal instincts?"

"Why?" The word was spoken on a breath that fanned across my face, her lips temptingly close.

For a moment I hesitated, not wanting to press her into a response lest she take fright, but it had been too long since I had possessed a woman. Blood rushed to my head—and the lad in my pants—with a roar.

My mouth brushed against hers gently, carefully, her feminine scent wrapping itself around me until it sank into my flesh. Her lips parted, a siren "Oh!" escaping before I took possession of the sweet, tender offering. Around us, the birds cried and wheeled, the sea pounded, and my heart set up a thundering beat that drove my need.

Her eyelids fluttered shut, her body swaying against mine as I enveloped her, pulling her tighter against me, my hands shaping the enticing curves of her bum. It was heady stuff, kissing Megan, and I hadn't even swept inside her mouth, where I knew I would find the sweetest of all nectars. The thundering in my ears took on a new note, a sharper, higher note of anticipation, a primal sound that trumpeted my desire.

Megan moaned into my mouth, her tongue gently foraying forth to caress mine, and I knew that I had made the right choice. No other woman had possessed me quite like she had in only a few minutes. No other woman felt so right against me, as if her body was made specifically to fit against mine. And no other woman drove my passion to such a height that the sound of it deafened me, the sharp, rhythmic sound burrowing deep into my brain, pounding, pulsing, throbbing against me with a familiar sense of urgency . . .

I ripped my mouth from hers. Megan gave a faint whimper of dissatisfaction and confusion, but I had no time to reassure her. Beyond us, a horrible noise rent the air, a harsh rhythm that I'd somehow heard despite being wholly occupied with kissing Megan.

"Run!" I yelled, shoving her toward the washed-up tree trunk. "Take cover by the tree."

"What . . . huh?"

The noise grew closer, more strident. I spun around and raced up the path, waving toward the tree. "Now, woman! Before they're here!"

"What? Who's here? What's that horrible noise?"

"The hounds! Someone has released the hounds! For the love of the gods, woman, run to the tree lest they find you unprotected!"

"You have dogs?" she asked, nonetheless scrambling over rocks and driftwood toward the tree. I lurched up the path as fast as I could, despite the full-fledged erection that didn't understand why it was no longer nestled up against Megan.

"These aren't normal dogs, they're hellhounds, come from the depths of the Underworld. They are the bane of mortals . . . Bloody hell!"

The baying of the hounds reached a fevered climax that threatened to burst my eardrums. Just before I reached the top of the path, Stewart appeared, his hair standing on end, his eyes wild as he gestured behind him. "My lord—"

"Yes, I hear, someone has released the hounds. Get out of their way before you're torn to shreds!"

"But, my lord—"

A wave of frenzied black bodies washed over the crest of the path, white teeth flashing against savage red maws. I yelled and waved my arms, attempting to distract them from the scent of Megan's tender mortal flesh, flinging myself on top of the hellish beasts with a battle cry that hadn't been heard in four centuries. Instantly, the dogs were upon me.

I braced myself for the inevitable pain of their

first greeting, but rather than the familiar rending of flesh and abrading of tender parts by their teeth, soft, little moist dabs touched various parts of my body. I rolled onto my back and stared up in wonder.

"These are . . . hellhounds?" Megan's face came into view, her lovely alabaster brow furrowed with confusion. She held up a small, wiggling black creature.

I frowned, and pushed several similar objects from my chest, glancing at Stewart. He picked up a hound that was wrestling with his shoelace. "I tried to tell you, Mr. Hearne. Elfwine felt the previous hounds were too aggressive, so she arranged for these to be your dogs this season."

I took the small, curly-haired bundle from him, and examined it thoroughly. Despite its petite size, its voice was that of a full-grown hellhound. "Poodles. She gave me poodles. Me, the lord of the hunt."

"Toy poodles to be exact, sir."

"You Irish sure have a strange way of treating your dogs," Megan said, cuddling one of the beasts. "Hellhounds! Ha! Very funny. They're adorable, although I don't know many men who are big toy poodle fans. How many are there? Six? Shall we take them for a walk along the beach?"

The hellhound poodles abandoned me when Megan snapped her fingers, all six of the little monsters bouncing around her in a curly-haired wave of excited enthusiasm as she headed down the rocky beach.

"Toy—"

"—poodles," Stewart finished, helping me to my feet and dusting off bits of sand and dirt. "Elfwine said she was tired of your normal hellhounds killing the sheep she and the druids use for wool, so she asked Taranis for something less vicious this time."

"Poodles," I said, under my breath, and made a mental note to wreak revenge upon Taranis at the earliest possible moment.

Four

I think we need to talk," Megan said, then gave a self-conscious laugh. "Boy, I sound like I'm a girlfriend, huh? But I'm a firm believer in getting everything out in the open, and although I've been here just an hour or so, there's already some things we need to talk about. Oh, dear—is the poor thing all right?"

We were walking the perimeter of the castle grounds proper, which six hundred years ago had been a massive eight-foot-thick wall of stone, hand cut and hauled by local serfs.

"If I'd known then that the mortar used to hold the stones together would last only a few hundred years, due to the constant sea spray, I'd have done a few things differently," I said absently, picking up the poodle that had evidently stubbed its toe on a rock and was now baying loudly enough to disturb birds three miles inland. I looked at the paw it held up, removing a splinter of stone that was wedged into its pads.

"Is it all right?"

"The hound? Yes, they're remarkably indestructible," I said, putting the beast down. It bared its minute lips at me in the traditional snarled greeting before trotting over to its brethren and resuming its patrol.

"They have very . . . er . . . unusual voices, don't they? So loud and deep for such little dogs. I don't think poodles are hounds, though," Megan said slowly, giving me an odd look from the corner of her eyes. She giggled a little. "And they're certainly not *hellhounds.*"

"It's a misnomer since hell doesn't exist, as such," I agreed, and used the opportunity of helping her up a slight incline to take her hand again. I liked the feeling of her hand in mine—the fingers strong and warm, twitching slightly when I stroked my thumb across her palm. "There's Abaddon, of course, and the Underworld, but hell? It's more of a generalized idea than an actual place. Mind the ditch; it's what's left of the moat. That was another mistake, but we'll leave that story for another day."

Megan was silent for a few minutes, her eyes frequently peering up at me with an endearing expression of confusion. I smiled to myself, pleased the wooing was going in accordance with my plans.

"I think there are even more issues we need to talk about," she finally said as we stopped at what used to be the gate leading into the castle. "Those dogs, for one. And some of the things you're saying—they're very confusing. But most important is this attraction thing you seem to think is happening."

"Oh, good, I was hoping you were going to bring that up," I said, pulling her into a loose embrace. The scent of her, subtle but heady as the oldest wine, sank deep into my awareness. "I suspect the effect you have on me is going to be one of my favorite subjects."

"I'm willing to concede that you're an incredibly handsome man, and I'm flattered you seem to find me attractive as well," she said breathily, her eyes losing a bit of their focus as I fitted her to my body. "But this isn't why I'm here. I have a job to do."

If my time with Fidencia had taught me anything, it was that women liked to be nurtured in their little projects. "A job I will be happy to help you with. I know the history of the entire county. Ask me anything you'd like to know."

"You will?" she asked, her voice soft and dreamy as my lips brushed hers. A little tremor shook her as her body yielded to mine. "You do?"

"Oh, yes." The scent of her, the feel of her, the rightness of everything about her, made my senses reel. "I want you, dearling. Right now, right here in the grass. I want to lay you down and love you until your toes curl. I want to take you with the sun shining down on your hair, your cheeks flushed with arousal, your glorious breasts bared for my attention. I want to see your eyes go the same lovely misty blue they are now, and when I finally make you mine, when I take everything you have and give you back myself in return, I want to hear your cries of ecstasy mingle with the birds overhead. I want you, Megan, more than I've wanted any woman before."

"Oh, my God, you talk like someone out of a romance novel," she said, her breath as ragged as my own.

"To love, and to be loved, is the reason for existence," I murmured against her mouth.

"Who *are* you?" she whispered as I gave in to my raging desire and kissed a hot, wet path along her jaw to her ear.

"Dane Hearne, lord of the hunt, and of the fifth hour of the Underworld, also known as Cernunnos. Marry me."

"What?" she all but shrieked, putting both hands on my chest and shoving backward.

"Was that too soon?"

Her eyes had a wild cast to them that I took as a yes.

"We'll forget the marriage part for now—we have six days for that, anyway. Let's go back to what we were doing. I was just going to nibble your ear, and you were about to demand I rip off your clothes and have my manly way with you. Which, I should warn you, the schedule says I can't do until tomorrow at the soonest, but we can do everything else until then."

She stepped back, holding out a hand to keep me from sweeping her back into my arms where she belonged. "You're . . . you're insane!"

"Only half the year, and that's mostly due to trying to keep the fitness instructors and televangelists from destroying my section of the Underworld."

"Okay, this has to stop right now," she said, taking two more steps back.

I wanted nothing more than to hold her and reassure her that I wasn't quite as deranged as she imagined, but the flight instinct was running hot with her, so instead I sat down on a large boulder and gestured toward one a few feet away. "I apologize."

She took the seat, running a rather shaky hand through her glossy blondish-brown hair. "You do?"

"Of course. I overwhelmed you, which is inexcusable. I'm not normally like that, but given the circumstances . . . it's regrettable."

"I think we need to get a few things straight," she said, taking a deep breath.

"Absolutely. May I hold your hand while we're doing so?"

"No!"

I frowned. "You don't want me to hold your hand? You don't like touching me?"

"On the contrary, I like touching you all too well, but that's the problem." She took another deep breath, and spread out her hands. "I'm not what you would call a normal tourist, all right? For one, I'm here to do a job. I have to win that contest so I can quit my job and do travel writing full-time."

I held my tongue. I wanted to tell her that I would support her in whatever style she demanded, but I sensed that now was not the moment to inform her of her good fortune.

"Also, I'm not looking for a vacation fling. You're incredibly handsome, and your accent makes my legs go all rubbery, and I have to admit, the things you do and say tend to make me forget about everything else. But I am not looking for a casual relationship."

"Good. Neither am I."

Her eyes were wary. "I'm sure you use that marriage line, and all the *taking me under the sun* business,
and the mystical lord of the Underworld story with
all the tourists, but I don't put up with bullshit, all
right? When I was younger, I had ovarian cancer. I
beat the odds and survived it, but one of the results
was that I cut out everything in my life that wasn't
really important. So why don't we start over again,
and do this without all the crap, okay?"

My admiration for her rose, and with it, the cer-
tainty that this time, I had found the right woman.
She had been tried, and conquered adversity. She
was a worthy woman to be my goddess. I would
spend the rest of my life in happiness with her. Fate
had finally given me what I'd been searching for.

I knelt at her feet, taking one of her hands in both
of mine, pressing my lips to the back of it in homage. "You are magnificent. I can't wait until our first
quarrel to see your eyes spit blue fire at me, and to
watch them turn soft with desire as we make up. You
have captured me, Megan. I am yours. We will spend
eternity together learning all there is to know about
each other."

"Why are you doing this?" she said in a near wail.

"Because I am Cernunnos, and come Beltane, you
will be my goddess."

Her fingers tightened in mine. "Wait a second—
now you're saying you're a . . . god?"

"A minor one," I answered quickly, not wanting
her to get the wrong impression. "I do not possess
great powers, Megan. I am not high-level deity, de-

spite the druids worshipping me. I'm just a simple man, really, but I will make it my life's work to ensure you are as happy as I can possibly make you."

"A lot of men think they're gods, but you're the first one I've met who's actually come right out and admitted it," she said with a hint of laughter in her voice. "Tell me again who you think you are? Kerwhosit?"

"Cernunnos," I said patiently, getting to my feet and pulling her with me. Explanations of who and what I was had never been my strong point, and I was relieved this tricky part of the wooing was over. "Although only the druids use that name. I prefer Dane."

"Druids," she said, biting her lower lip as I escorted her up the slope that led to the standing parts of the castle. Her shoulders trembled beneath the guiding hand I had placed there. I wondered briefly if she was cold. "Druids worship you?"

"Not all, only one sect. Neo-druids, to be exact. You can see their camp over there."

She looked where I had pointed. Elfwine and her clan set up camp every year with a collection of caravans, tents, and two motor homes, all arranged in a half-moon around a fire pit. "Those are druids? I thought that was a camping area."

"I don't allow camping on the castle grounds by anyone but the druids. Erm . . . it may be best if you give the druids a bit of a miss until after Beltane. They're usually high strung until the wedding."

She stopped, her hand pulling in mine, and I

turned to see what was the matter. The smile had
faded from her delectable lips, her eyes back to being
wary again. "You're serious, aren't you? You believe
everything you just told me?"

"Of course. I wouldn't lie to you, Megan. There
will be no deception or falsehoods between us."

"You're . . . you're a god." She extricated her hand
and made a wide circle around me, turning so as to
keep me in front of her.

"Minor, yes."

"You're god of the hunt?"

"Exactly. It's not every woman who could take
in all of this at once, but you have mastered it quite
quickly."

"And the Underworld?"

I hesitated. If there was a part of her future I
wanted to keep hidden, it was the bit about death
and the time spent in the Underworld. "The fifth
hour, to be exact."

"Hour?"

"The Underworld is divided into twelve hours, or
sections. I rule the fifth one."

She opened her mouth to say something, shook
her head, and closed it again. She also took a couple
of steps backward.

The hellhounds galloped past, continuing their
endless patrol.

She pointed at the furry little black bodies as
they spilled down the rocks to the road leading out
of the castle. "And when you said those were hellhounds—"

"I meant it. Technically, they come from the Underworld, not Abaddon, but they've been called hellhounds for so long, it's difficult to call them anything else. Their job is to patrol the perimeter, guarding against potential attack."

One of her delicately shaped eyebrows rose in question. "You have six toy poodles guarding a castle."

"Yes, well . . . unfortunately, the druid leader takes her job too seriously. When she summoned the hellhounds, she requested they be a bit less formidable than is normal." The back of my neck itched. I ran a hand over it.

"Just out of idle curiosity," she said, giving a rueful little laugh. "I know I'm going to regret asking this—who exactly does a god have to fear attack from?"

"Anyone who wants my job," I said with a shrug. The skin between my shoulders tightened uncomfortably, and I flexed them to ease the feeling. "That bastard Taranis has tried for centuries to get one of his sons into my place, but don't let it worry you. I may only be lord of the hunt, but I protect what is mine."

She held up both hands. "Okay, I think I've reached my saturation point, because all of this is starting to sound perfectly reasonable instead of wildly insane, as it should. Clearly jet lag has left me without cognizant skills, so I think I'm going to have an early night and hit the hay."

An annoying burn ran the length of my spine, as if someone was poking red hot needles into my back—which is more or less what was happening. I

needed to get rid of Megan before the situation wors-
ened. "Why on earth would you want to hit hay?
Not that I have any—as you can see, the stable has
been converted into a dwelling."

"Sorry, an American expression. It means go to
bed."

"How very odd. Of course you must rest if you
are tired, but . . ." I cast a glance at the sky. There
were still several hours of the day remaining, and I
hated to waste them with nonwooing activities. On
the other hand, the burning and itching and tightening were become too uncomfortable to ignore. It
would be best if I got Megan out of the way for a
few hours to deal with the situation. "Perhaps a little
nap instead? I'm told dinner tonight is to be an event
you won't want to miss. Stewart excels in producing
meals which both entertain and inform visitors about
the history of the castle. You wouldn't want to miss
that."

She frowned and glanced at her wristwatch. "That
does sound like something I should see—maybe a
couple hours' nap will be enough."

"I'm sure it will be more than sufficient," I cooed,
escorting her into the house and up the first flight of
stairs. "I'll call for you at dinner, shall I? Sleep well,
dearling."

She paused halfway up the stairs, turning to look
at me. "I don't suppose you'd like to drop the love
names?"

The muscles between my shoulders jerked invol-
untarily. "I'm sorry, it goes with the job."

"You are such a strange man," she said, shaking her head as she continued up the stairs.

"Strange but intriguing," I yelled up after her. "Don't forget the intriguing part!"

Stewart came out of the dining room, where he had no doubt been arranging for the evening's event. "Did I hear a familiar bellow? Ah, my lord, there you are."

"Dane!" I snapped, hurrying out the front doors.

"My apologies, Mr. Hearne. Would now be convenient for a few words about this evening's show?" he asked, trotting alongside me as I headed for the druids' encampment.

"Not really. I'm being summoned."

He came to a stop in the middle of the road, glancing hesitantly toward the tents and motor homes. "I believe I'll wait until you're done, then. Elfwine was in a fury, earlier, when one of the maids told her you'd been seen kissing a tourist."

"When is she not in a fury?" I grumbled, and ignoring the itching and pain and discomfort, donned an austere and unmoving expression with which to face the formidable Elfwine.

I had a feeling I was going to need every ounce of my charm to deal with her.

Five

"My lord Cernunnos, I bid thee welcome to our grove," a voice said as I marched into the druids' camp.

"Might I have a word with you?" I asked, grabbing Elfwine by the arm.

Her dark eyes glittered ominously as we came to a stop on the far side of the largest motor home. "Certainly, my lord. You know I am your humble servant."

Humble, my arse. "I thought we had an agreement about the hot needles, Elfwine! You know how I feel about needles, and hot ones doubly so! Needles have *no* business being stabbed into whatever horrible voodoo doll-like object you use to summon me. In fact, needles should be nowhere near it! STEWART!"

The pull of power needed to summon Stewart made my forehead tingle, but I managed, by dint of thinking about the effects of the bubonic plague on the human body, to keep from manifesting. Stewart held a stuffed penguin in one hand and one of my old broadswords in another, and the annoyed expression on his face warned me I had disturbed him while he was busy. "You bellowed, my lord?"

"Yes, I bellowed. Henceforth, all needles, pins, and tacks are to be banned from the castle grounds."

Stewart blinked at me. His silence was profound.

"That's it," I said, giving him what I hoped was an airy wave of dismissal. I avoided looking directly in his eyes. The expression in them wasn't pretty.

"Might I inquire why you wish to have all needles, pins, and tacks banned?"

"She"—I pointed to Elfwine. "She used hot needles in one of those horrible summoning dolls she keeps of me. *Hot* needles! Down my back!"

"I should have stuck them somewhere else," she muttered, glancing at my crotch.

"Ban them!" I ordered Stewart.

"You want them banned because she used them to summon you?" he asked, obviously not getting the point.

"Yes! Summoned me rudely, without my permission, interrupting me while I was conducting important business."

Stewart pursed his lips. "Summoned you as you just summoned me, from my own not inconsiderable workload, a workload you have dumped on me with a carefree gaiety that borders on the obscene?"

"Er . . ." I cleared my throat. Elfwine's lips curled into a sour smile. "That's entirely different. I am your employer. You are my steward. I have a right to summon you whenever I like."

"May I go now?" he asked, casting his eyes skyward.

"Yes." By concentrating, I sent Stewart back from

whence I had summoned him. As lord of the hunt, I didn't have too many powers that weren't related to game, which meant those I didn't use often—like the summoning of minions—were lamentably a bit rusty. I turned back to Elfwine. "And as for you . . . no more needles!"

"You ignored my summons. I was fully justified in taking whatever means necessary to ensure your participation in the ceremony."

"You thought torturing me was justified?" I stomped around her, waving my hands to keep from throttling the annoying woman.

"You *ignored* the summons!" she repeated, both the volume and emotional intensity in her voice rising. "Yes, Maeve? What is it?"

I turned to see who it was she was addressing. One of the new druids, a young woman of probably around nineteen or twenty, stood clad in the traditional druid garb of linen and wool robe, leather sandals, and a wreath of leaves twined in her hair. I squinted, just a little. The robe seemed to be a particularly sheer one, of a pale eggshell color. If I looked hard enough, I could see the dark circles of the girl's nipples beneath it . . .

The woman's glance slid to me for a moment before quickly jerking away. "Are we having the ceremony now, or not? It's cold standing around in the ceremonial robes."

"I said we were. Get back to the altar, child. His lordship will be with you in a minute."

"Ceremony?" I asked suspiciously as the girl

bobbed a little acknowledgment and trotted off to the main part of the druid camp. "What ceremony? There aren't any ceremonies to be performed between my birth and the hunt, other than bringing forth the hellhounds, and you've already done that."

A brief, fleeting smile flickered across her lips. "I greatly enjoyed that."

"I'm sure you did." The look I gave her could have curdled milk. "We will be having a little talk about you complaining to Taranis about my dogs, but not until after the wedding. What ceremony are you planning now?"

"Why, the initiation, of course."

"What initiation?"

She gave an exaggerated sigh, and grabbing me by the wrist, hauled me the way we'd come. "The goddess's initiation, of course. Since you didn't like Aoife, Maeve has volunteered for the position. She's very sweet, and docile to the point of being submissive."

I jerked back from her. "Not another one of your virgins! I told you I want nothing to do with them!"

"Excuse me, am I interrupting?" Megan's voice cut through the madness that was a conversation with Elfwine. She stood next to the motor home, an odd smile on her face.

"Megan!" I leaped to her side, taking her hand. "I thought you were having a bit of a rest?"

"I lost the key to my room, and thought you could give me another one, but if you're busy initiating virgins—"

"No!" I interrupted, squeezing her hand in a meaningful manner. Elfwine evidently saw the gesture and took druidic umbrage with it. She grabbed my wrist again, displaying strength that would do a stevedore proud. I gave Megan my most charming smile. "You're not interrupting at all. I was just having a chat with one of the druids."

"We're just about to have a ceremony," Elfwine said briskly. "A *private* ceremony."

"Not with me, you aren't," I said, pulled against my will toward the blazing fire pit. Desperate not to lose Megan, I grabbed her by the arm and towed her behind me.

We must have made quite a sight, because the people we passed stopped and stared.

"Elfwine, this is ridiculous. Release me at once."

"Not until you've done what you must do. It's the law. You must marry by Beltane, you must have a virgin, and you must consummate the relationship under the eyes of the lord son and lady moon."

"Oh, my. It really does sound like I am interrupting . . ." Megan's voice was rife with amusement.

"You should know that by now," Elfwine continued. "We will chant while you deflower Maeve. Everyone, gather around and take your places; we will recite the druid's prayer." She dropped my hand and bent to pick up her staff.

"I have nothing to do with this," I assured Megan.

She looked around the camp. "I can see you don't. Where do they sell the I ♥ CERNUNNOS T-shirts? I'll want to be sure I get one as a souvenir."

One of the male druids by the name of Patrick was hurrying past us, but he paused at Megan's words. "Miriam handles the T-shirt sales. She also has a nice selection of mugs, mouse pads, and thongs."

I groaned and closed my eyes for a moment.

"Thongs?" Megan asked in disbelief.

I wondered if I could go back to the Underworld for another few months.

"Oh, yes. They have a picture of his lordship's face on . . ." Patrick gestured toward his crotch. "Very popular items, our Cernunnos thongs. You won't want to miss the commemorative deflowering tea towel, either. It'll have both the god and goddess on it, in a border of red to symbolize blood."

"*Blood*?" Megan imbued as much horror in the word as was humanly possible.

"Aye, from the deflowering. Goddess's blood is much prized. We hope to raise enough by selling the tea towels on eBay to finance a streaming video hookup for our grove website."

"These people are total strangers to me," I said quickly to Megan, taking her by the hand again. Her fingers sent a little thrill of excitement up my arm. "Normally I have no interaction with them at all. I don't know any of them well."

"Hi, Daneykins," a sloe-eyed, sultry-voiced woman said as she strolled past, her hips swaying provocatively. The look she gave me could have set the stone walls of the tower on fire.

I cleared my throat. "Except Jen. Er . . . that was over two years ago. She's married, now. Happily."

"Is she." Megan's lips tightened. "It really is none of my business."

"That's right, it isn't," Elfwine agreed, pushing between us. "People! It's time!"

The rest of the group came running from their various abodes, their faces shining with druidic anticipation. There were supposed to be only twelve druids in the grove that worshipped me, but over the twenty or so years that Elfwine had been elder, their ranks had grown until now there were over two dozen of them running around in robes, waving their staves, and burning bundles of sage at every possible moment.

In the center of the camp, next to the fire pit, a long piece of stone rested on several smaller supports. Although most druid ceremonies did not call for an altar, this particular order had always used it for their most sacred of acts. Laid across it now, like something out of a Botticelli painting, the virgin Maeve reclined, her eyebrows waggling at me in what was surely a come-hither look.

"I am ready for you, my lord. I am ready to become your goddess. Plant your stave of life deep within my womanly depths."

"Good Lord, I had no idea people really talked like that," Megan said, watching Maeve with a fascinated eye. "I must take some notes; this stuff is priceless. I wish Pam and Derek hadn't crashed for the night—they could get the deflowering on film."

"There will be no deflowering!" I bellowed.

No one paid me the least bit of attention. Elfwine

was directing a chorus of druids to stand in a semicircle around the virgin, Megan had a notepad out and was taking copious notes as she talked with Maeve, while another man pulled out a digital camcorder from his robes, and with a whispered "I'll get it all for the website," began filming everyone.

"It wasn't like this in the old days, you know," I told Maeve as I nudged Megan aside and held out my hand for her. Maeve glanced over to Elfwine for a moment before putting her hand in mine. "In the old days, druids knew what the word 'worship' meant. They scurried out of my sight when I rode past. They never bothered me, never demanded I do anything. They worshipped quietly, and they never, *ever* used hot needles on me. Get up."

"Get up?" she asked, confusion writ upon her face.

"Yes. Up."

"You intend to take her virginity in a standing position?" Megan asked, eyeing me from crown to toes. "How very enterprising."

"I'm not taking anyone's virginity," I said, more and more exasperated by the whole situation. This was not how I'd planned to introduce Megan to the druids, or the issue of marriage.

The tingle was back in my forehead.

"My lord, if Maeve does not please you—although I can't imagine why, she's a charming girl, has wide childbearing hips, and ample breasts—I will bring forth the third virgin." Elfwine marched toward me.

"No more virgins!" I thundered, pulling Maeve from the altar since she didn't seem to be inclined to move on her own. I set her down on her feet and gave her a gentle shove toward one of the tents. "Go put some clothes on, girl. I can see your tits through that robe."

Maeve gasped and covered her breasts before spinning around and running for a tent.

Megan's eyebrows rose as she made another note.

The tingle in my head changed to a burn and I struggled to calm myself. My heart beat a furious tattoo, sending a dull roar of blood into my ears.

"This is unacceptable!" Elfwine stood next to the altar, her anger unmistakable. "You cannot change the laws to suit your whims!"

"I'm not trying to change the laws," I answered, rubbing the increasing burn in my forehead. "I'm just not interested in any of your virgins. I've found the woman I've been looking for, and she will become my goddess."

"Who?" Elfwine shoved her face in mine. "Who is it? Who have you chosen, if not one of my virgins?"

The blood roared in my ears now. I fought to maintain control over my ever-volatile emotions, knowing now was not the time to manifest in front of Megan. "None of your damned business."

"WHO?" She bellowed, her eyes sharp little shards of onyx that seemed to pierce my very being.

"I am Cernunnos! You will not speak to me in that man—"

"WHO IS THE GODDESS?"

Elfwine's screech made me lose my temper, and we all know where that leads.

"HER!" I answered in a deafening roar, pointing at Megan. The anger I'd been struggling so long to control burst forth, manifesting in its usual method.

"Who? Me?" she asked, looking up from her notepad. "What do you mean I'm your . . . Oh my God. Oh my God! *OH MY GOD*! Are those . . . *antlers*?"

Síx

The manifestation normally startled women, a few going so far as to faint. Megan didn't look horrified as some of the other women had. She just looked startled and confused, her eyes wide with disbelief.

"You have . . . antlers . . . growing from your forehead," she said slowly, her gaze fixed on the manifestation.

"I'm Cernunnos. Lord of the hunt. Sometimes, I have antlers. Most of the time I don't."

"This cannot be," Elfwine interrupted, her face pinched and red with anger. "You cannot make her your goddess!"

"Whoa! I'm really not on board with this whole goddess business. I'm just a tourist."

I smiled at Megan to let her know I heard her, but directed my question to the annoying druid in front of me. "And why the hell can't I?"

"For one, she's American," Elfwine said.

"I like Americans."

"Thank you. I think," Megan said, her gaze still roaming over the manifestation.

"She's not a virgin!"

One of Megan's eyebrows rose, but she said nothing.

"She said she was a virgin to Ireland. That's good enough for me," I answered.

"That was just a joke, you know. Er . . ." Megan reached out a tentative hand. "May I touch it?"

"You may touch anything your heart desires, although I was wondering if you wouldn't care to go inside now? I can deal with this troublesome business on my own, if you are still feeling tired."

"Sleep is suddenly the furthest thing from my mind," she answered, lightly rubbing her fingers over part of the manifestation.

A jolt of electricity ran through me, causing me to tremble a bit.

"I'm sorry," Megan said quickly, pulling her hand back. "Did I hurt you?"

"Not at all. The manifestation is extremely sensitive. Your touching it is very . . . sensual."

"Really? How very interesting . . ." She touched it again, and I closed my eyes against the wave of arousal that washed over me.

Elfwine's voice was like a cold bucket of water. "If you're through rutting with the unsuitable American, can we return to the matter at hand?"

"She's not unsuitable, I don't care that she's American, and there's not a single thing you can do to keep me from taking her as my goddess. Now, go hug a tree or something."

The druids in the circle gasped in horror at my comment. I glanced at Megan, a bit worried that she might not like my announcing her new position be-fore I'd had a chance to finish wooing her, but luckily she seemed totally and completely absorbed in the manifestation, running her fingers along the various branches with little "Oh, wow!"s of amazement.

Elfwine drew herself up and said, "You're mad."

"Perhaps, but I'll be happily mad."

She chewed that over for a minute, then spat out, "Very well. As you've chosen, however inappropri-ately, we will simply replace the eminently suitable and pure Maeve with this tourist."

"Hmm?" Megan murmured absently, her lovely blue eyes alight with intrigue as she continued strok-ing the manifestation. It was difficult to not react to the erotic pleasure she was giving me, but I knew it was too soon to introduce her to the more primal pleasures to be had in mating.

"Nothing important, dearling. You like the mani-festation, then?"

"It's so . . . wow. So different. So fascinating. So . . . male."

I waggled my eyebrows at her. "That's not all I have that's fascinatingly male."

"I bet," she chuckled; then the smile faded from her face as her eyes met mine. Her fingers trailed from the manifestation down to my temple, and down along the line of my jaw. I leaned into her hand and kissed her palm. "You really are a god. What you said before—it's real, isn't it?"

"Very much so. It's a bit world shaking, hmm? When I first saw Cernunnos—the one before me, that is—I was a simple woodcutter. I had no idea the world encompassed so much that was hidden from mortal view."

"There was another Cernunnos?"

"Oh, yes, there've been hundreds. It's a position, not something you're born to. I am currently the third longest as far as reigns go, though."

She blinked a couple of times, the look of fascination in her eyes almost as arousing as the feel of her fingers on my face. "This is so amazing. I'm almost speechless, and that never happens to me. You have to tell me all about yourself, how you came to be Cernunnos, and . . . well, everything."

"What you do on your own time is your business," Elfwine interrupted, grasping Megan's arm and frog-marching her over to the altar. "Right now I have a ceremony to conduct. Can someone get me a proper robe? The next goddess is garbed in completely unsuitable clothing."

"Now, hold on here just one minute," Megan said, digging in her heels and refusing to be hoisted onto the altar. "I'm willing to concede that somehow, by some means I haven't yet figured out, that man over there is what he says he is."

"Your slave forever," I said, giving her a particularly charming smile. "And might I say how adorable you are when you're stubborn? It's not a trait I've admired in the past, but on you it's rather endearing."

"Stop that," she said, pointing a finger at me.

"Stop what?"

"Confusing me. I can't think straight when you smile like that."

I let my eyes twinkle at her. Her legs seemed to buckle slightly, forcing her to clutch the altar. I was pleased to see her response, but knew the battle wasn't yet won. Her body might be very interested in exploring what it meant to be my goddess, but her mind was going to be more difficult to convince.

"Now you're playing dirty," she muttered under her breath.

"Only when absolutely necessary," I answered as I strode to the altar. "This is finished, Elfwine. I have no idea why you expect me to engage in sexual acts in front of your lot of tree huggers, but I have no intention of doing anything of the kind. Megan and I will consummate our relationship alone."

"Hello, I'm standing right here! Stop making consummation plans that involve me. I told you I wasn't interested in a fling, or becoming your little antler vixen, or whatever it is you people are talking about. Oh! What's happening to the . . . er . . ."

"They disappear when my anger fades," I answered as the manifestation evaporated into nothing.

Elfwine thrust herself between Megan and me, jabbing me in the chest as she spoke. "The laws say you must consummate the relationship with your goddess in full view of the lord and lady."

"One," I said, holding up a finger and ticking it off. "It's rare for the sun and moon to be present at the same time, so right there, that tells me your laws are completely mad. And two, I haven't consummated any other relationships outside, so I'm hardly likely to start now."

She frowned. "You cannot deny the laws. You must have done so, or you would not still be Cernunnos."

"Well, I haven't, so . . ." A memory popped into my mind at that moment. A millennium and a half ago, I'd come across a drowning peasant girl, and hauled her out of the river sodden and half dead. Despite the mud, muck, and stray bits of vegetation that dotted her person, she welcomed me with open arms. Right there, on the bank, under the hot July sun . . . "Well, hell."

"I am not having sex with you outdoors," Megan said firmly, slapping away Maeve's hands as she tried pull Megan's red sweater off, to garb her in the druidic virginal robes. "Will you stop trying to take my clothes off? No, I will not put it on! Go away!"

"Never fear," I said calmly, taking Megan's hand and giving it a squeeze. "When we have sex, it will be on my bed. It's quite comfortable. You'll enjoy it. Ah, there's Stewart again. Must be time for tea. Shall we?"

Before Megan or Elfwine had a chance to protest, I herded Megan toward the tower. Elfwine spat something that sounded like an ancient curse, but I ignored it. "Tea ready?" I asked Stewart as he trotted by us.

"Hmm? No idea. I'm having a bit of a problem with the musicians, so I'm off to town to try to find some others."

"What's wrong with the ones we normally use?" I asked, frowning at the displacement of our normally well-laid plans.

"They object to the minstrels' galley."

"There's nothing objectionable about my castle! The minstrels' galley is the epitome of perfection."

"Not according to the musicians, it isn't," Stewart answered in a snappish tone. "According to them, it's unheated, cramped, and you insist on storing the output of your last hobby there."

Megan gave me a quick once-over. "Hmm . . . hobby . . . something sophisticated? Cigar collecting? Wine tasting?"

"Taxidermy. Stewart, you tell those arsed musicians that I had a look at the badger and it doesn't stink at all, let alone smell like a five-day-old dead horse in a peat bog, as one of them claimed. Be firm with them, man. Mortals respond to firmness."

Stewart rolled his eyes and headed down the hill to the car park.

"So much for Stewart announcing tea, eh?" Megan asked with a little smile that warmed me to my toes.

"I had to get you out of the druid camp. Elfwine can be quite formidable when she chooses."

"I can imagine, although I don't for one moment believe you need to resort to subterfuge to get your way. I'm still trying to take it all in, but you're a god! A real god! What does Cernunnos do? And how did you get to be him in the first place? Wait, don't answer that. Let me get my tape recorder. This will make a fascinating article."

She was off and running before I could answer her. I contented myself with ogling her fine ass as she ran, indulging in a little fantasy of how I was going to consummate our relationship. By the time tea had been ordered, and Megan had found her tape recorder and digital camera, we were settled quite comfortably on the settee in my study.

"Now, I want to hear all about how you became a god . . . and let's do it without you trying to cop a grope, all right?" she said, pushing away my questing hand with brutal cruelty.

"I would never do anything so mundane as trying to cop a grope, which I'll assume is on par with feeling you up. Which, I would like to point out, I was not trying to do. Time is passing quickly, and now that we're so comfortable with each other, I thought we might slip into phase two."

If the stony look on Megan's lovely face was anything to go by, my charm was not as effective as it had proved in the past. I turned on both the eye twinkles and deepened my dimples for added effect.

She melted into my arms.

"I'm not having sex with you, Dane," she mumbled against my Adam's apple. "You can smile those knee-melting smiles, and you can tickle my palm, and flash your dimples at me as much as you want— I'm not going to stay here in Ireland. I have no time for a relationship. I have a job to do, remember?"

"And I'm perfectly content to let you do it." I inhaled a deep breath, savoring her scent. It was the mingled aroma of warm woman, soap, and a faint woodsy scent that reminded me of the violets that blanketed the roots of an ancient oak deep in the nearby woods. It was a primal, earthy scent, one that seemed to sink deep into my bones. "I enjoy travel, as well. We can go together to the places you are sent to write about. It will be enlightening."

"Somehow, I don't think enlightenment is what you need," she answered, pushing away with both hands on my chest.

"On the contrary, I believe life with you will provide me much to think about. We will have many intelligent conversations over the centuries."

"Centuries . . ." She chuckled, then moaned as my mouth found the sensitive spot behind her ears. I was careful not to make the same mistake as before, and contented myself with stroking her back gently, rather than reaching for more intriguing parts. "I'm not a god like you. I am not going to live for centuries."

"Once you marry me and become my goddess, you will cease to be mortal. It's one of the many perks I have to offer you." I nibbled delicately on her ear. For a moment I thought she was going to pull back out of my gentle embrace, but she gave a little shudder of pleasure and allowed me to continue to press hot kisses to her neck.

"What sort of perks?"

I kissed a path to her chin, her adorable chin. "You'll live a life of comfort. I have ownership of this castle so long as I am Cernunnos. You will live in an authentic fifteenth-century castle with me, an authentic Irish god."

Megan laughed, and turned her head slightly to allow me access to the other side of her face. She wasn't returning my caresses yet, but the fact that she wasn't spurning them was a strong indicator that things would go well once our relationship took on a more intimate form.

"I'm not sure everyone would count either point as being a perk, but we'll let that go for now. What else do you have to offer a potential goddess?" she asked.

"An eternity of devotion." I paused in my nibbling, arguing with myself whether or not I should address the dark half of each year. I'd already mentioned my role in the Underworld to her once, but I hadn't gone into details. If I told her more, she'd surely be frightened off, putting in jeopardy my job, those of the people whom I employed, and even my life. Could I risk all that just to satisfy the nagging conviction that to hide any truth from her would be reprehensible?

I sighed to myself, placed a kiss on the pulse point below her ear, and pulled back just enough to look into those beautiful blue eyes. "There is one thing you deserve to know. It's about the Underworld. As I mentioned, I'm the lord of the fifth hour, which means that part of the year I spend overseeing my part of the Underworld. As my goddess, you would be required to come with me during those times."

Strictly speaking, that wasn't true, but I was taking no chances with Megan—I wanted her by my side, not gallivanting off in Brazil meeting oiled-up samba dancers.

"Hell, you mean?" she asked, her eyes still misty with passion. "You want this woman you pick out to go with you to hell each year?"

"The Underworld is not hell," I corrected her, gently brushing a loose eyelash that had fallen onto her cheekbone. She was so indescribably lovely, it made my testicles tighten just to touch her.

"Oh? What is it, then?"

"It is the first step in the journey to either Abaddon—which is what you think of as hell—or the Court of Divine Blood."

"That would be heaven?" she asked, her lips so tempting I had to struggle to keep from possessing myself of them.

"Not quite, but most people make that mistake." I couldn't help myself. I had to kiss her, I had to taste those delectable lips once again. I leaned down, my mouth just brushing hers when she slid out of my arms, leaping to her feet.

"This is . . . you're so overwhelming . . . I just can't think straight when you're so close to me!"

The last few words came out as a wail. Megan started to pace the study the way I'd paced it earlier.

"Dearling, what's wrong?"

"What's wrong? What's *wrong*? How can you sit there, a man who just a half hour ago was sporting antlers, and ask me what's wrong?"

I thought back over my most recent actions, looking for something that might have upset her. "I'm sorry about kissing you, but your lips were beckoning me, and I gave in to temptation."

"They were not! There was no beckoning! And I'm not upset about your kissing me—"

I leaped to my feet, hearing as clear a go-ahead signal as any man has heard.

"No, wait! I meant I *am* upset about that! That is . . ." She stopped pacing and ran a hand through her hair. "Oh, you have me so confused, I don't know what I'm saying. Would you believe that I'm thought to be an unusually calm, collected person? No one who saw me now would recognize me! You've cast some sort of insanity spell on me, haven't you? Admit it!"

She had ahold of my shirt and was trying to shake me. I looked down into her stormy, troubled face, confused. What was she so upset about? "I don't know of an insanity spell, although I do know one to remove warts. Do you have a wart you'd like me to take care of?"

"No!" she said, letting go to pace past me again. I sat back, content to watch her breasts and ass jiggle as she walked, her hands gesturing wildly. Evidently she was one of those people who spoke with their hands.

"It's just that . . . oh, this is so hard to explain. This morning I landed in Ireland, and the world was the way it should be. I was happy and excited and looking forward to this trip, and doing my best to win the contest. And then I came here, and you were so incredibly handsome, and you started saying the most outrageous things, and then those poodles charged us, but they weren't normal poodles because they sounded more like bulls roaring than dogs . . . what are you doing?"

My gaze snapped up to her face. "Hmm?"

She stopped to face me, both hands on her hips. "You were staring at my boobs, weren't you? I'm here baring my soul to you, trying to explain what I am feeling, and you haven't heard a single word because your whole attention has been focused on my boobs. Hasn't it?"

"No, of course not." I glanced down at the objects in question. They rebuked me for my betrayal. "Possibly I was. But to be equally fair, your ass also held my interest."

"My . . ." She stared at me open-mouthed for a moment.

"And I did hear what you were saying. I heard every word. I am capable of multitasking: I can watch both your ass and your breasts, and listen to you at the same time."

She inhaled so much air, it was a surprise there was any left in the room. "You . . . you man!" She stormed out of the study and raced down the stairs to her room.

I followed, peering down the spiral staircase to make sure she made it there safely. She shoved past Stewart, who was climbing the stairs, with a word that brought back memories of a sailing trip to Portugal a few centuries before.

"Dinner is in an hour, dearling," I called. "Don't be late—Stewart likes the musicians to start while we're still dining."

The slam of her door echoed up the staircase, disturbing the pigeons that sat outside the study window.

"Trouble?" Stewart asked as he followed me into the room.

"Not that I'm aware of," I answered, settling in my chair to take care of some business before dinner. "Why, have you heard something?"

"I take it Miss Megan was upset about something?"

I waved it away. "Nothing serious. She was a bit upset that I was admiring her assets."

"Women like that don't usually like to be ogled," Stewart pronounced, taking his seat behind his own desk.

"Women like what?"

"Intelligent."

"Ah." I thought about it for a moment or two, but there was nothing to worry about. "Megan will realize that my attentions to her were meant in a flattering rather than a lascivious way. Her little upset is nothing serious. She'll be all right after dinner, you'll see."

Stewart's look spoke volumes.

Seven

There was a naked woman in my bed when I arrived at my bedroom an hour later.

"Good evening," the woman said, moving her shoulders slightly so the sheet slid down and bared her breasts.

They were very nice breasts. I admired them for a few moments before I sniffed the air, and sighed. "Sandalwood."

"Erm . . . what?"

"Sandalwood. The druid women always wear sandalwood. I have no idea why—patchouli always seemed to me to be a much more feminine scent. I assume you are yet another one of Elfwine's virgins, here to seduce your way into goddesshood."

The sandalwood-scented druid gave me a wanton smile. "No, I'm not one of the sacrificial virgins. I just wanted to sleep with you. I like the way your trousers fit."

"I'll pass along the compliment to my tailor." I picked up the woman's robe and tossed it to her, along with various undergarments and the huaraches the druids favored in warmer months. "Thank you for thinking of me, but I'm obsessed with another woman, and getting her to the altar is taking up all my time and attention. You might try me later, after I've sated myself on her, say in . . . oh . . . five thousand years? Six? No, let's make it ten to be on the safe side."

The woman blinked at me in disbelief, confusion writ upon her attractive heart-shaped face. "But . . . you don't want to make love to me?"

I frowned, eyeing her closely, paying particular attention to her breasts, then conducted a mental examination of myself. My heart rate was steady, my blood pulsing along as normal, my breathing perfectly controlled. Not even the lad in my trousers was stirring. But let me even think of Megan naked, warm, and welcoming, writhing beneath me . . . I cleared my throat, opening the door for the druid, hoping she wouldn't see the tent pole that had started growing. "No, thank you. You could try my steward if you're in a randy mood. He's usually very obliging to women."

The druid shook her head, not moving from the bed. "I don't believe this. Everyone I talked to said you would shag anything that moved. You're rejecting me?"

I cocked my head, the echoes of a familiar noise reaching my ears. "It's difficult to believe, isn't it? But true, nonetheless. I have met the woman of my dreams, and I intend to take full advantage of the twist fate has given me. I would advise you to don your clothing quickly, before the hellhounds get here. They're on the way up the stairs now, and they don't take kindly to interlopers in my private quarters."

The deep, bell-like baying of the hellhounds rolled up the stairs. The druid froze for a second, then was out of the bed and into her clothing before I could count to five.

"You may wait in the room across the landing until I have them shut into this room," I told her. The door closed behind her just as the hellish beasts crested the stairs, pouring into my room with a frenzy of snapping jaws, bobbing curls, and the ticky-ticky-ticky noise of tiny toenails scrabbling on a stone surface.

I glared at them for a moment, opened the door, and bellowed out to anyone who could hear, "Who the hell put red bows on my hellhounds?"

Silence was the only answer I was to receive . . . and what sounded like muffled snickering from the floors below.

I dressed in the black wool trews, linen léine, and leather ionar (jacket) that made up my traditional garb, worn for the show we gave tourists the first night of their stay. The hellhounds made things a bit difficult, but in the end, Stewart and Jack the stable boy and I managed to get my boots away from the poodles' slavering jaws and onto my feet.

"Is everyone assembled?" I asked as Jack clattered downstairs. Stewart adjusted one of the leather ties on my ionar and brushed off a bit of hellhound fluff.

"Aye, my lord. All but Miss Megan. She said something about not being hungry."

"Tell her if she doesn't go down to the dining room with you, I'll consider it her statement of desire for me to visit her in her room, instead."

Stewart grinned and hurried off. I stood before my mirror, the hounds milling and snapping around my feet, and practiced a charming yet humble smile—one that said that although I admired Megan for her delicious and much anticipated body, I also valued her keen intellect, slightly skewed sense of humor, and any other character traits I could pack into the smile. Satisfied with the result, and figuring Stewart had had enough time to explain to Megan how things were, I snatched up my horn, slung a quiver and bow over my shoulder, and opened the door.

"Fag an bealac!" I bellowed, giving the traditional Irish war cry of "Clear the way!" The hounds leaped forward as the horn touched my lips, its rich, mellow sound counterpointing nicely with their deep bellows. They raced down the stairs, myself in close pursuit, since it was more visually stunning if we all arrived at the door of the dining room together. Not to mention safer for anyone who wasn't well out of the hounds' path.

Stewart stood in the doorway to the dining room, an odd expression on his face. "My lord," he called out as the hounds and I raced past him.

"Later," I called, anticipating with much pleasure the look of admiration that would fill Megan's glorious eyes when she saw me in my manly, authentic medieval Irish outfit (authentic in appearance—it had none of the lice, fleas, and itchiness of the original items of clothing). I ran into the middle of the dining room and halted the hellhounds with a sharp command, raising my hand and striking a dramatic pose to intone the traditional greeting, "Rise thee to the hunt! Cernunnos, lord of the woods, is come!"

I held the pose so Megan could have the full effect of the tight ionar stretching across my chest. Once suitable time had passed for that, I turned to face the obviously speechless woman of my dreams.

The dining room was empty of all but a group of men in kilts, clutching bagpipes and bodhrans, huddled together in the minstrels' alcove.

"Where the hell is everyone?" I asked, at the same time that Stewart said, "My lord, I tried to tell you— Miss Megan and the others went out with Taranis."

"Taranis? What's he doing here?"

"I have no idea. He was simply here when Megan and I entered the dining room. Before I could say anything, he introduced himself and took her off on a tour of the castle."

"A tour of the castle? He took my wife-to-be on a tour of my castle-that-is? Argh!" I spun on my heel and bolted out of the dining room, up the stairs to the entryway, and out the door, pausing to scan the horizon for the sight of Megan.

The hellhounds followed and lifted their heads as one, catching the scent of a newcomer. In a flash, six furry little bow-bedecked bodies were bounding over rock and earth, their voices torn from the very depths of the Underworld as they hunted their prey. They ran around the castle perimeter three times with me on their heels before I realized they were following the track of one of the barn cats, not Taranis. By the time I corrected them, and they'd set off across the rocky rubble after their proper prey, my heart was pounding, I had a stitch in my side, and was short of breath.

". . . and of course, it's all gone to ruin now, but it was a lovely castle in its prime, I'll give that much to Dane. Not that he knew what he was doing when he built it on this forsaken bit of rock, but I've always said that people learn best from their own mistakes. Which means Dane should be the most knowledgeable man on the earth, but we know just how unlikely that is," Taranis was saying with a low, intimate laugh to Megan when I finally ran them to ground. He turned to look, one eyebrow cocked as I doubled over, hands on my knees in a desperate attempt to keep from collapsing while I caught my breath. "Good evening, Dane. I was just showing this delightful young lady around Castle Bannon, giving her the benefit of my unique knowledge of history. A bit out of shape, are we?"

"Mine," I gasped, snatching her hand from where Taranis was helping her over a large chunk of granite. I clung to her hand like it was a life raft and prayed I wouldn't collapse of a burst artery right there in front of her.

"I beg your pardon?" Megan asked with a flash of her eyes as she jerked her hand from my desperate grasp.

"I was just lending her a hand over this treacherous ground," Taranis answered with an amused twitch of his lips. He was everything I loathed in a man—a high, sweeping forehead topped with glossy blond hair, its waves slicked back with some sort of smelly pomade, a frilly lace jabot that looked down-right affected, overly pleated trousers, and square-toed Milan shoes that always left me with the urge to scuff their polished perfection. His eyes, a muddy hazel, always wore an expression of near boredom, as if he could just barely tolerate his present com-pany. "If *I* owned Bannon, I would have had this mess cleared away years ago. So dangerous, not to mention unattractive. But then, you've never cared much for appearances, have you?"

"Did you say mine? As in, possession?"

"My . . . Megan . . . will . . . help her . . . over . . . rocks," I gasped, still desperately trying to get some air into my lungs. The blood pounding in my ears made it a bit difficult to hear, and I had a horrible presentiment that the extreme emotion I felt in see-ing her standing so close to Taranis was about to trig-ger the manifestation.

"I am not anyone's possession!"

"Of course you're not, my dear. Some men sim-ply do not grasp that women are their equals, if not superiors, and attempt to assert their dominance by categorizing them as something with no more worth than a cow or piece of pottery," Taranis said in his smooth, oily voice.

The manifestation burst from me at the same time as Megan gave Taranis a long, cool look. "I'm not stu-pid, you know," she told him.

The hellhounds, who had swarmed out to the far end of the field to savage the corpse of a long-deceased mole, returned with the spoils of their victory, their eyes crimson with the torment of the damned.

"Oooh, you brought your poodles!" She bent down to pat one, but it snarled and rumbled a warning that came straight from the belly of the Underworld. I threw myself forward to protect her from the vicious beast, stumbled over a rock, and ended up facedown in the dirt. Megan reached over my prostrate form and rapped the hellhound smartly on its miniature muzzle. "Bad dog! No growling! Bad!"

To my intense surprise, the hellhound retreated, a puzzled look on its face.

Megan's expression changed from haughty frost to concern as she bent over me. "Are you all right?"

"Heart attack . . . highly probable . . . must help . . . you . . . Taranis . . . bad . . ."

"For heaven's sake, sit down and catch your breath. You sound like an elderly Tarzan," she said, helping me to my knees. Her eyes widened at the manifestation, although in all honesty, it could have been the clods of earth bedecking the horns like the last few leaves on a barren tree that gave her pause. "You've . . . er . . . got something on your antlers. Shall I just remove it?"

The gentle touch of her fingers on the sensitive manifestation sent a shiver down my back. I allowed her to pluck the muddy clods of grass from the antlers, sitting when she pushed me back onto the block of granite Taranis had helped her climb over.

I glared past her shoulder at the man in question.

He stood with smug enjoyment, watching as Megan worked over me. "This is the woman you've decided to make your goddess?" he asked in Gaelic. "Quite the impression you're making on her—winded, babbling, horns bristling out of you every which way, and covered in muck."

I told him in succinct brevity what he could do with himself.

"Is that Irish Gaelic?" Megan asked as she finished with my antlers. She made a face at the mud and dirt smeared across my léine and ionar, and dabbed at them briefly with a tissue she pulled from her pocket.

"Yes, it was," I answered, having at last regained my breath. I gathered the tattered shreds of my dignity around me and rose to my feet. "Taranis told me I made quite an impression on you."

She laughed as I brushed off my trews and ionar. "That's a bit of an understatement."

"Deus, man, just look at you!" Taranis asked, waving a hand at me. "Is it any wonder the woman is in hysterics at the sight of you? What in the name of all that's holy are you wearing? Are those trews? I haven't seen those in a good three hundred years."

I gave him a level look, even though my belly was tightening to a tight wad of embarrassment. That Taranis laughed at me, I could bear. But for Megan to mock me . . . pain cut through me in a shaft as sharp as a steel blade. "It's an authentic medieval Irish outfit. It's part of the dinner presentation for the history of the castle."

"Well, it's damned silly-looking, and rightly covered in muck. Go playact for the other tourists while I tell this lovely lady the way things really were." He took Megan's arm and turned her toward the castle.

The hellhounds swarmed around my feet as I watched him urge her forward. My heart, an organ I hadn't given much consideration to in the past, contracted painfully. I wanted to rip Megan from Taranis's side, to prove to him once and for all that she was mine, but an image rose in my head of what I must look like—horny, muddy, and dressed in antiquated, if manly, clothing. The hellhounds, ever sensitive to my emotions, tipped back their heads in unison and howled their pain to the sky as I wiped the last of the mud off the knees of my trews.

A white tissue hove into view, held by a graceful hand. I looked up.

Megan stood in front of me, Taranis several yards behind her, an astonished look on his face. But it was her eyes, her gloriously warm eyes, that dashed the breath from my lungs and caused my heart to start beating again. "I think the outfit is quite dashing. It makes you look rugged, and rather primal. It's very sexy."

"I'm not normally this clumsy," I assured her, covertly searching her face for the least sign of pity.

"I'm sure you're not."

"I am known by all and sundry for my ability to walk without falling face first into the mud, as a matter of fact. People all over the county honor me for just that talent." I relaxed a little—there was no sign of pity in her face, just sympathetic understanding.

"I have no doubt they do."

"Men envy my lack of clumsiness. Women admire my grace."

"Do they, indeed." The sympathetic expression slipped a bit.

"It's no exaggeration to say that women the country over have been known to drive miles just to watch me walk without so much as stumbling," I added.

Her lips pursed.

"Too much?" I asked, reading disbelief in her eyes.

"It was the women driving across the country that pushed you over the line, yes," she answered, nodding.

"Right. It's just Taranis. I'm fine any other time, but he does something to show me up, like changing my hellhounds to pom-poms on legs, or causing the mud to slip just when I'm walking on it, and . . . oh, myriad other things I won't go into now, because you look like you need your supper."

Taranis stood with his hands on his hips as he called to Megan, "Come, little one! I will tell you about the Portuguese, and how they tried to invade Ireland."

Megan, bless her heart, ignored him.

"I had a boss who used to intimidate me so much, it made me spill coffee all the time," she said quietly, offering me the tissue again.

I took it and wiped my hands. As my anger and

frustration faded, so did the manifestation. "I'm not intimidated by Taranis. It's just that he *does* something whenever he's around."

"Megan! I have much to tell you—without a tatty little mud-splattered costume. I will be happy to take you on a tour of historically important spots in the county, but we should get started now, before the sun goes down."

"I know the feeling," Megan told me, her eyes on my forehead. She was silent for a moment before adding, "I don't think I could ever get tired of watching that. It's so . . . amazing!"

I took both of her hands in mine. "And could you ever get tired of me?"

Her gaze dropped to mine, her eyes as clear and fathomless as the most flawless aquamarine. There was caution and wariness in those eyes, but there was also an acknowledgment of the intangible something between us. I felt it, and I knew she felt it, but it worried and confused her. And I knew with a deep awareness I'd never felt for another human being that she was not ready to commit to me.

"Megan! Come away from Dane. I have limited time available, and we must get started now." Taranis's voice had an ugly edge of command that I knew would rile the woman standing before me.

I lifted one hand, then another, brushing my lips against her fingers in a caress that promised much. "Stay with me, dearling?"

She took a deep breath, her eyes never leaving mine. The question in them was clear to read.

"Tonight," I answered, wanting to ask her for more, but knowing she wasn't ready. "Stay with me tonight."

Her fingers curled in mine as Taranis stomped over to us, and she told him, "I'm sorry. A tour of the county sounds lovely, but I think I'd like to see Dane's dinner presentation instead. The castle has such a fabulous presence, I'd like to know more about its history. Perhaps I can take a rain check on the tour?"

I led her away with only one tiny triumphant glance at Taranis.

His answering glare burned holes of promised retribution into my back.

Eight

Three days later I slammed shut the door to my study before stomping over to Stewart's desk. "What do you know about women?"

"They smell nice, they don't like to be told they can't do something, and when they're naked, they hold some sort of mystical power that overrides our brains and makes us do and say things that would normally be inconceivable," Stewart answered without looking up from his laptop.

"Why aren't you married?" I demanded to know.

That made him look up. "Pardon?"

"Why aren't you married? You're such an expert on women—why haven't you plucked one out of the crowd and married her?"

"For one, I never said I was an expert, and for another, in case it's slipped your attention, I'm a steward in the house of Cernunnos, and thus immortal. I find it difficult to establish relationships with women who I know will grow old and die in less time than it takes me to grow a reasonable mustache."

I glanced at his bare upper lip and conceded his point. "There are immortal women. You have not married any of them."

"Perhaps that's because I have had a very good

example of just what happens when a man chooses unwisely."

Fidencia's face rose before my eyes, and I was forced to concede the truth behind that statement as well. "It's all very well for you to be selective, but I do not have that luxury. I've found Megan, but I am fast running out of time, and the woman whom I have chosen above all others to spend eternity at my side has spurned my every advance." I paced the length of the room, something I'd been doing a lot of the last three days.

"What's Megan done to you now?"

"Nothing. She's done nothing. And when I say nothing, I mean exactly that. She hardly speaks to me, she refuses to look at me except when she thinks I can't see her, and she insists that those two leeches in human form always be with her, preventing me from speaking to her of private matters."

Stewart leaned back in his chair, his fingers steepled. "Ah. The old 'He's not going to get me alone' ploy, is it? I wondered what she'd do after that night she almost shoved me down the staircase. That was, if I am not mistaken, the same night you reassured me that her pique was nothing to worry about, and that you had matters well in hand."

I snarled an oath. "I did. Then Taranis showed up and threw a spanner into the works, that bastard. He knows she's mine! He has no need for her, yet he's taken her out two of the last three days to see the county. *See the county.*" I sneered. "I can't believe she'd fall for that line. I know just as much about the

history of the area as him—more, since I was interested in doing more than spawning brats on every
woman within a fifty-mile radius. God knows how
many of the little blighters are roaming around, after
six hundred years of his unbridled shagging."

Stewart pursed his lips. "It can't be denied that
Lord Taranis has a rather sizable number of progeny,
but I believe your jealousy in this respect is unjustified. I have seen the looks Miss Megan throws your
way. She is not averse to you."

"Of course she's not averse to me. I had her all but
eating out of my hand the night of the presentation.
But then Taranis got his hooks into her good and
proper, and since then she's been very, very polite
but won't let me get close to her."

"Has it occurred to you that perhaps her reserve is a
natural result of the situation, rather than an interest
in Lord Taranis?" Stewart asked, watching me pace.

"It's possible, but doubtful," I said, dismissing the
idea. "I've made every effort to ensure that Megan
has all the information pertinent to the situation. I
have tried to spend every waking moment with her,
so that she will feel she knows me and be comfortable with committing herself to me for the rest of her
life. Yet she spurns me in favor of him."

His eyebrows rose slightly as I gave vent to a few
choice words about Taranis.

"She's just being obstinate, that's what it is. She
refuses to acknowledge the fact that she was meant
to be my goddess. And here we are with three days
left to Beltane, and my wooing program is far be-

hind. We should have been up to physical intimacies by this point! And what the *hell* is all that din?"

"The druids, I believe," Stewart said calmly, answering the phone.

I stomped my frustration over to the window to see what the horrible grating noise outside was. Elfwine had her druids busily erecting a giant maypole, entwined with ivy and flowers, bearing long garlands of greenery. To the left of the maypole, one of the druids was on a ladder next to a light pole that now also bore a loudspeaker, his hands over his ears as someone tried the PA system. The Beltane festival, held each year to celebrate both the coming transition of seasons and my wedding, was coming together nicely . . . with the exception of the one person vital to the success of the party.

"This is unacceptable," I told the window. "I have tried to woo her. I have made every effort to get to know her, to please her, to allow her to become comfortable with the notion that I will worship her to the end of our days, but she will not be reasonable and allow herself to be courted."

Stewart hung up the phone. "Sorry?"

"I blame Taranis for this."

"Of course you do," he said blithely. "You blame him for everything. Erm . . . would we still be talking about the situation with Megan?"

"Naturally. Except for him, Megan would be in my arms this very moment. And my bed." I recommenced pacing.

"You can hardly blame Taranis for dribbling spiced

plums down the front of your léine the other night," Stewart said, struggling to control what I suspected was a smile.

"Like hell I can't. Every time I went to take a mouthful, he jostled my arm. Deliberately!"

"Ah. Well, I'm afraid I didn't happen to see that, being busy at the time with the performance."

I paused and cast my mind back to that evening. "That brings up a question—why, for a presentation depicting the august and fascinating history of this equally august and fascinating castle, were there musicians who bore not only Scottish instruments, but who also played Scottish ballads, marches, and jigs?"

"They were the only musical group I could get, sir. The locals swore they'd rather kiss a banshee than play for you again."

"Ungrateful bastards," I muttered, and resumed pacing.

"As we're on the subject—I'm going to have to reimburse the Scottish Lads the price of one fiddle. It seems the hellhounds were unsupervised for a moment, and they attempted to slaughter the musicians. They escaped only by sacrificing a fiddle to the leader of the pack."

I waved away such mundane concerns. "Pay them whatever they want. Back to Taranis—for twopence I'd like to take care of him once and for all."

"You can't. The sovereign wouldn't allow you to usurp your overlord without repercussions."

"I know I can't, but I'd like to," I snarled. "It's his fault that I must forsake my attempts at wooing

Megan and go straight into the next stage. It is time for action, Stewart, bold action."

"Oh, lord." Stewart's head sank into his hands.

"I must end this infatuation she has with the smarmy Taranis, and bring her to see that her life will be much better spent with me."

"Sovereign help us."

The phone rang again. I used the few moments of relative peace to foment the bold actions that I was now forced to take.

Stewart hung up the phone. "That was the Talbot, this year's huntsman. He asked if you wished to use your own pack, or if he should bring the hunt's. I told him you preferred not having the druids torn to shreds, and that we'd be using ours."

"Excellent, excellent, you've things well in hand. I must go make plans," I said, striding through the door.

"But my lord!" Stewart looked down at the pile of papers, order forms, caterer catalogs, rental equipment specifications, and a dozen other items related to the Beltane celebration, his eyes taking on a panicky tinge. "Sir! Mr. Hearne! The celebration!"

I paused and looked back. "What of it? Don't try to tell me you can't cope with the celebration. You've done it every year for six hundred years, most of that time without a telephone, computer, or fax machine."

"Yes, but there are bound to be problems for which I will need to consult you. At least take your mobile phone."

I accepted the phone he shoved into my hands. "I

have full confidence that you can deal with any and all questions. I am about to undertake very delicate work, so do not disturb me for anything less than global nuclear war."

I found the object of my desire getting out of a small rental car, the two crew members with her as usual. For once, Taranis was not accompanying her.

" . . . think that went exceptionally well," Megan was saying as I approached. She looked down at her legs, which were muddy and sodden from the knees down. "Well, except for the part where I slipped into that creek. But other than that, I think it'll make an excellent piece. I'll just go change into something dry, and then perhaps we can take a quick trip out to that nature reserve north of here? I think that would be an interesting visit—hey!"

"Good morning. Are you enjoying your stay here?" I asked Pam and Derek, who were unloading their film and sound equipment.

Pam nodded and shot a quick look to Megan, whose arm I held in a firm, no-nonsense grip. "Yes, thank you, our room is lovely."

"Dane! Let go of me!"

"Excellent," I told Pam, turning to her partner. "You managed to find the local pub, I take it?"

"Dane, dammit, let go of my arm!"

Derek grinned outright. "Yes, thank you, your directions were spot-on. And you were right about the local beer—it's good stuff. I'm going to try to have some sent home."

"ARGH!"

I nodded. "It has quite a reputation. Well then, if you're all comfortable, I'll just escort Megan to her room. She seems to be a bit agitated this morning."

"Agitated? I'll give you *agitated*, you big lummox! Unhand me!"

She continued on in that manner until we got to her room, but when we were at last there and the door was closed, she spun out of my grip and turned to face me with eyes blazing and hands fisted.

"How dare you treat me like that! How dare you behave like such an . . . an animal in front of my friends!"

"Animal?" I leaned against the door, my arms crossed.

"Yes! Only an animal would grab a woman and haul her up to her bedroom." Megan moved off to the other side of the bed, a self-righteous note to her voice. "Taranis told me there was a reason you took the position of Cernunnos. He said that you had an affinity with animals."

I was startled by the change in subject. "I do."

"He also said that he felt you've maintained the position so long because you cope much better with animals than you do with people."

I narrowed my eyes. The last thing I wanted to do at that moment was talk about Taranis. "And do you believe him?"

"Well . . ." Her hands made a plaintive little gesture. "I suppose I don't about everything. Your dogs like you, even if they are a bit . . . peculiar."

"They're hellhounds. They only look like miniature poodles. They're actually quite lethal, although the little red bows on their heads lessen that appearance."

She absorbed that for a moment, then nodded. "A week ago I would have thought you were crazy, insisting poodles are hellhounds, but now I'm perfectly willing to believe it. Are you jealous of Taranis, by any chance?"

"Yes." I thought for a moment. "No. Perhaps. Can we talk about something else, such as why you've been avoiding me the last few days?"

"No. Now, go away. I wish to change my pants, since these are muddy and wet. And my shirt, since you twisted the material on the arm all around when you manhandled me."

"Did it occur to you that I wouldn't have had to take such extreme measures to get a moment alone with you if you hadn't been avoiding me?"

Her brilliant blue eyes flashed to mine for a moment before dropping to look at her hands. "We weren't talking about me, we were talking about your arrogant, out-of-control behavior."

It took only four steps to stride over to her. She gave a little squeak and backed up against the wall. I leaned in, my hands on either side of her head, pinning her against the stone with my body. "Do you have *any* idea of the self-control I am exhibiting right at this very moment?"

"Um . . . Dane, you're squishing me. Perhaps 'out of control' was too harsh—"

"It was indeed. Because if I were truly out of control, right now you would be on that bed, naked, squirming beneath me as I thrust hard into your body."

Her eyes opened wide, the pupils dilating slightly. "You would?" she asked breathily.

I ignored the delightful sensation of her breasts heaving against my chest. "Every time I see you, I want to kiss you, touch you, stroke your flesh, taste you upon my tongue. I want to know you the way a man knows a woman. I want to learn all your ticklish spots, know where your erogenous zones are, know what will drive you wild with arousal. I *want* you, Megan, in every conceivable sense of the word."

"Oh," she said on another breath, her mouth slightly opened.

It took every ounce of strength I possessed to not give in to the invitation she offered. Instead I painfully pushed myself back. "If I didn't have the self-control of a saint, I would give in to those urges. But because I pride myself on my modernity, because I watch Oprah and read Deepak, and understand that women are from Venus and men from Mars, and that females such as you like to be cherished for more than their bodies, I have attempted to show you that I am just as fascinated with the other parts of you—your interests, your desires, the things that make you laugh and cry—as I am with the more physical elements of your being."

Her mouth opened and closed a couple of times. "I . . . you have? You are?"

"But you have spurned my every attempt. Rather than spending the time together as I had planned, you have chosen to waste it on Taranis. I do not know what he has told you, but I can assure you that he will not honor you above all women, as I will do. He will not be faithful to you, either in heart or body, as I will. He will not put your needs and wants and desires above his own. He has somewhere in the region of fifteen hundred children—you'd have to check with Stewart for the exact number—and he continues to breed women like they were baby factories. I have no children, nor will I foist upon you more than you desire."

"I can't have children," she burst out. A blush washed over the delicate curve of her cheeks as her hands fluttered toward her abdomen. "I . . . I had cancer. I lost my ovaries and a few other bits."

I shrugged. "Then we will seek alternate means to have children, if that is your desire. There are always unwanted children who need homes. Unlike the promiscuous Taranis, I do not feel the need to populate the world with my progeny."

She cleared her throat, the blush fading slightly. "Well . . . good. I feel the same way."

"We are of one mind, then. Do not misunderstand me, Megan. I do not have the time a normal man would be able to give you. Beltane is in three days, and in three days I must take a wife. I have chosen you to be that wife, a goddess at my side for the length of our lives. If you do not accept that role, I will quite simply cease to be."

She shook her head. "Now you're just being melo-dramatic to get me into bed—"

"I assure you I am being quite literal. I am Cer-nunnos. If I do not marry at Beltane and take a goddess, I cease being Cernunnos. If I cease being Cernunnos, I am no longer immortal and will revert back to mortality. Do you know how long a sixteen-hundred-year-old man would last in today's world?"

Her eyes were wide with astonishment.

I nodded. "Exactly. About two seconds before time caught up to me, and then pfft! I would be no more."

"Oh my God." She sank down onto the bed, mindless of her muddy jeans. "You . . . you didn't tell me this before!"

"I didn't think I needed to. I assumed from your reaction to my kisses that you were not averse to the idea of spending a lifetime with me."

The sympathy in her voice and face boded well. I allowed an expression of heartfelt despair to play about my face, my chin held firm in manful stoicism that was sure to wring her heart.

"Oh, Dane, it's not that I don't like you—I do, despite your . . . er . . . unusual nature. And I think it's clear that I like to kiss you, and I suppose if we're going to be perfectly honest, I wouldn't mind at all getting to know you better. But I'm not really look-ing for a permanent relationship with a man right now. There're just too many other things I want to do first. When I beat the cancer, I made a promise to myself that there would be no more excuses—life was too precious and too short to not do all the things

I'd wanted to do. Becoming a travel writer is number four on the list."

"What were numbers one through three?"

"One was to reconcile myself with a couple of family members I'd been on the outs with for the last fifteen or so years. Two was to pay off all my debts. Three was to learn how to belly dance—I'm still working on that, but I started the lessons."

"Dance for me," I ordered, moving to the window where the light was better. I wanted badly to pounce on her but reined in my desire. She was open with me now, and although I knew intimacy would increase that openness, the moment wasn't yet ripe for that. I must think of her comfort and happiness before my own gratification. I owed her that much.

"What?"

"Dance for me. Show me what you've learned in your belly dancing class."

She blinked in confusion a couple of times, opened her mouth to protest, then suddenly hopped off the bed and stood in front of me, a slight smile on her lips. "You are the strangest man. I'll show you, but you're bound to be disappointed. I can only do a couple of the basic moves."

"Dearling, I doubt if there's anything you can do that would disappoint me, with the exception of refusing me outright. Dance!"

"We really need to work on this arrogant attitude you have . . . This is a belly roll. I don't do it very well because my muscles haven't yet learned how to move in sequence, but here it is."

I frowned at her belly, unable to see much. "Take off your clothes. I can't see your belly roll at all."

"You're absolutely incorrigible." She laughed, shaking her head. Her laughter washed over me like a wave of passion, igniting my own until it heated my blood. "I am not going to take off my clothes in front of you, although I will let you put your hands on my stomach to feel the movement."

No fool I, I wasn't about to turn down the offer to place my hands on her delectable person. I spread my fingers out across her belly, nodding when I felt the muscles contract and release in a rolling motion. My fingers ached to strip the cotton jersey off her, and feel her warm flesh as it rolled and undulated. I wanted to caress every inch of her, to taste her, to inhale her scent until it was imprinted on my mind—

"Do you feel it?"

I looked her dead in the eye, willing her to see my emotions. "Yes. It would be better if you were naked, though."

She laughed again. "Most things are, but we're not going there."

"Yet."

"Back up or I won't show you the hip circle."

It took a will of steel, but I resumed my spot and watched with approval as her hips circled in a seductive motion. I wondered if perhaps I should reconsider my thoughts on delaying intimacy.

"And this is a body camel. It's pretty much a belly roll, but you also use your upper torso and legs. Can you tell the difference?" she asked as she did a slow twirl, her body moving in time to some music only she heard.

The sight of her dancing before me was too much to bear. I looked at the bed behind her. I looked at the woman dancing before me.

She caught the expression in my eyes and stopped moving, holding up one hand. "Absolutely not. I don't jump into bed with men I've only known a few days."

"You will know me for the rest of eternity. Does that not compensate for the lack of time now?" I asked, taking a step forward.

She shook her head. "No sex."

"Let me kiss you, then. Just a kiss, a chaste, innocent kiss. A sign of your trust in my honor, a token of friendship, a beacon in Anglo-Irish relations."

"Smooth," she drawled, but I could tell by the misty look in her eyes that I had swayed her. "Just one kiss, all right? Nothing more."

"One kiss," I agreed, wondering what the world record for the longest kiss was, and whether we would get some sort of an award for breaking it. "I shall kiss you once, just once, and not do any of the other things I so desire to do to you."

"What . . . er . . . what things?" she asked in a shaky voice as I spoke against her lips.

"I desire to do many things to you, dearling—but I will not. I will not bare your delicious flesh, running my hands along the smooth lengths of your legs, stroking a long line from ankle to thigh."

"No, that would be . . . wrong." Her head tilted up slightly to give me better access.

My hands moved up the curve of her waist. "I will not lick a trail across your sublime belly, down to your womanly secrets, hidden away from sight but straining for my touch, aching and yearning for the swirl of my tongue against their steamy depths."

She leaned into me as I pressed my leg between hers, pulling her tighter until she all but rode my thigh. A flush of desire rose up from her breasts, causing her breath to turn as rough and short as my own. "That's . . . it's probably better if you didn't do all that."

"I shall not take the hard tip of each breast into my mouth, and suckle hard, tasting and teasing until you cry out with pleasure," I said, my hands moving to caress her cotton-covered breasts.

She moaned deep in her throat and arched her back.

"I will not mold your buttocks," I murmured into her mouth, my fingers paying homage to the delight that was her arse before moving upward to tug her shirt from her jeans. "I will not stroke the sensual curve of your back."

She was kissing me now, pressing hot, wet kisses along the line of my jaw, her hands sliding under my shirt, skimming along my ribs in a manner that raised goose bumps of pleasure. "No, no you won't do that. Don't stroke it some more."

"I will not nibble on that spot behind your ear that makes your legs tremble," I said, my arms tightening around her as her legs gave way. I bit her earlobe gently, more aroused by her gasp of pleasured surprise than I had been in centuries.

Megan's breasts burned a brand into my chest, her hips moving in a restless rhythm against my groin. I wanted her with every atom in my being, but more, I wanted her to desire me with the same fever. I closed my eyes for a moment, gathering the strength I needed to do what was right. "I will only kiss you—just one kiss, one perfect kiss that will express to you the true depths of my feel—bloody hell!"

"Maybe I was wrong," she whispered as she nipped a spot on my neck. "Maybe I was meant to be here, meant to save you from destruction . . . bloody hell? What bloody hell?"

Regretfully, I disentangled myself from the heaven of her body. The sight through the window of a car arriving below—or more importantly, one of the people who got out of the car—was enough to send me bolting from her embrace.

"Dane? What's wrong?" Megan must have heard the sound of the car doors closing. She peered out the window. "Someone's here? Is it Taranis?"

"No one important," I assured her as I flung open the door. "It's just my wife. I'll be back in a couple of minutes."

Nine

*W*ife?"
The word bounced off the stone walls of the staircase, chasing me with sharp little barbs that dug into my flesh. The echoing abilities of the tower had never been used with such force. "You have a *wife*?"

"Poor choice of words. Ex-wife is more accurate," I yelled over my shoulder. Megan was standing at the top, leaning way over to ensure her words would strike their mark—namely, me.

"You didn't tell me you had an ex-wife. Is it just the one, or are there more? How many times have you been married?" her voice echoed down to me.

I paused at the door to count quickly. "One thousand, five hundred and sixty-eight times. But don't worry, Fidencia is married to Dionysus now. He's a Greek god of wine and parties, although evidently he's now sober and salsa dancing, instead. Fidencia is pregnant," I added, hoping that would explain everything.

A shriek of wordless, maddened frustration followed.

"There you are, Noony, darling. Have Stewart bring my things in, will you?" Fidencia said, her eyes roaming over the tower as I leaped down the steps to where she stood next to the car. A petite woman, once dark-haired, but now expensively blond, she was obviously in the middle stages of pregnancy.

I did a bit of quick mental calculating, and came up with an answer that stunned and infuriated me.

"Good God, this place is just as frightful as I remembered. Taranis, would you be a love and help me up the stairs since Noony is standing there gawking at nothing? Oh, lord, he's gone manimal again."

The anger that roiled through me like a flash fire burst out in the form of the manifestation.

"I would be delighted to," Taranis answered, brushing me aside as he strode past me, muttering in a voice audible to those in a several-mile radius, "You have no self-control whatsoever, do you? You could have frightened dear Fidencia with that show of bestiality."

"Bestiality?" I asked, downright gobsmacked with incredulity. Was he insane?

"It's all right, I'm used to his ways. It's a cross, but bear it I must," Fidencia answered, posing for a moment with one hand on her breast. "What other choice do I have?"

"You poor, sweet, abused goddess," Taranis murmured.

I almost vomited, so sickening was their display. "What the hell are you doing here, Fidencia? Where's your god of hangovers? And why did you bring *that* with you?"

Taranis straightened up when I gestured toward him, his usual sneer firmly in place. "I am here because she called me for assistance, because we both knew that despite her delicate state, you wouldn't lift so much as a finger to help her."

"*Help* her? She doesn't need help! She chews men up and spits them out for fun!"

From behind the tower, a druid named Daniel appeared, hauling a coil of speaker cable. He stopped at the sight of Taranis assisting the pregnant Fidencia up the stairs. "Lady Fidencia is back? I'll go tell Elfwine."

"Don't bother," I said quickly. "Nothing has changed."

"Dear Elfwine," Fidencia said, her voice soft with emotion despite the fact that she and the druid leader loathed each other with a passion only exceeded by competing football clubs. "How I've missed her. What does the merchandise look like this year? I'm sure it won't be as good as the ones with me on them, but I feel obliged to look things over."

"I'm afraid Elfwine hasn't done any merchandise," Daniel answered.

I turned to look at him. "That's not like her."

"I wondered about it myself, but she said we could run off of last year's stock if we had to. Still, I should tell her that Lady Fidencia has returned—"

"You'll do nothing of the sort!" I fixed Daniel with an uncompromising look. "Fidencia is *not* here. Not in that sense."

"I see you hired a new maid," Fidencia drawled as Megan appeared in the doorway. "You, girl, take my bags upstairs to Lord Cernunnos's room. It'll take me weeks to make it habitable, no doubt, but I refuse to give in to savagery as some people have done."

"Girl?" Megan bristled, her eyes so bright with

anger they damn near shot blue-tinted laser beams.

I hurried up the steps before she could incinerate Fidencia. "Dearling, did I not say I'd be right back? Why don't you go inside and change out of your damp things? I'll be along to explain things as soon as I can."

"Dearling?" Fidencia burst out laughing, and gave Megan a scornful once-over. "Oh, lord, don't tell me he's pulling that ancient line on you. And you're falling for it?"

"Your *wife* appears to be under a misconception," Megan answered, biting off each word with a savagery that would do the hellhounds proud.

"Ex-wife," I hurried to correct. "She's married to Dionysus the Greco-Brazilian dancer now."

"He *was* a dancer, but no doubt he finds it difficult to dance with two broken legs. As if he thought I wouldn't notice that little whore he was keeping on the side—but that's a story for another day." Fidencia smiled an artificially bright smile, beaming it at everyone but Megan and me. "I have returned to my rightful place, just as darling Noony knew I would."

"Like hell I did. And I don't want you here. I have Megan now," I said, pulling her close.

She elbowed me in the gut. "You might be able to charm your wife into accepting you, but there is no way in hell I'm going to now! You and your one perfect kiss! I can't believe I was going to let you—" She stopped, looking around at the others.

"But, dearling—"

"Don't you dearling me!" Megan snapped, her eyes delightfully incensed.

For a moment I had been worried that she was truly angry about Fidencia, but then I realized she was jealous! She was deliciously, wonderfully jealous! It was a new experience for me to have a woman jealous, and I wanted to revel in it, to explore it fully. I wanted to dance and sing with the sheer joy of knowing Megan cared enough to be jealous.

"You are not going to be able to get around me like you obviously are her!"

I grinned. I couldn't help myself. "Not even if I let you touch the manifestation?"

Her eyes went immediately to the antlers. Her fingers twitched slightly. "Um . . ."

I took her by the arm, gently pulling her down the stairs. "Come, my dove, we shall go to my thinking spot, and you will caress the manifestation while I explain to you about Fidencia."

Her hand was halfway to my head when she realized what she was doing, and froze, her face turning suspicious again as she sucked in a hissing breath. "You have a wife! No, wait, you said you'd been married thousands of times! You've had *thousands* of wives! You're worse than him and his thousands of children!"

Taranis smiled. "I can't help it if I have exceptionally potent seed."

"Had," I told Megan, ignoring him. "The key point to remember here that I *had* a wife. *One* wife, whom I married one thousand, five hundred and sixty-eight times. That is infinitely better than impregnating anything with two legs, like some people I could mention."

"One or a thousand, it makes no difference! You had a wife and you didn't tell me!"

I cocked an eyebrow at her. The ladies love it when I do that and I watched Megan closely for signs of weak knees or swoonage, but she was obviously made of sterner stuff. "I've told you that I must be married on Beltane, or I lose my position. How did you believe I came to exist now, if I hadn't been married in the past?"

"I . . ." She frowned for a moment, thinking about my question. "I guess I didn't . . . um . . . Very well. I'm willing to let the point go that you had a wife and didn't tell me, since you're right: I should have realized you couldn't be here now if you hadn't married in the past."

I claimed her hand and kissed her fingertips. "Have I mentioned how much I admire your intelligence?"

She was about to answer, but when I sucked the tip of her finger into my mouth, and swirled my tongue around the pad before gently biting it, her eyes got that familiar misty look. A little tremor shook her hand as I moved to another finger. "Come with me. We'll . . . talk."

"Talk," she said on a sigh, her free hand gently touching the tip of one antler. It was such a sensual feeling, I closed my eyes for a moment to struggle with the need to claim her, body and soul.

"So amazing," she said, her eyes on the manifestation, oblivious to the fact that I was escorting her away from the distractions of Fidencia and Taranis.

"Yes, you are. We'll talk about that, too."

"Sir, a question has arisen regarding the bonfire procession this year, since Lady Fidencia will not be present to lead the . . . good God. Lady Fidencia." Stewart emerged from the tower looking just as stunned as I had felt upon seeing Fidencia get out of the car.

"Steubbings," Fidencia said, nodding at him as a druid, carrying three huge suitcases, staggered up the stairs past her.

"It's Stewart, my lady. The same as it has been the last five hundred years."

"Just so," she said, waving an airy hand. "See to my bags, would you? These druids are such primitives, and I won't have my delicious Corinthian leather scuffed."

"Sir! Mr. Hearne!" Stewart called, as I hustled Megan down the path and around the side of the tower. "There are questions—"

"Deal with it! We'll be back later. Perhaps."

"Does it hurt when it pops out like that?" Megan asked as we followed the dirt path to the beach.

For a moment I thought she was talking about the lad in my pants, but realized that she was speaking of the manifestation. "Not painful, no. And it fades once the anger that triggered it goes away."

"I see. Do you mind if I use both hands?" She stopped and turned to face me. "I know it probably sounds crazy, but I've never seen anything like it, and for some reason, I like to touch it."

I grabbed her hands before she could suit action

to words. "Actually, I do mind." The hurt look in her eyes was almost unbearable, and I hurried to correct her false impression. "Dearling, don't for one moment imagine I don't want you to touch me. There's little else I can think of, to be honest. But the sensation of your hands stroking along the manifestation is more than I can bear right now."

Her brow furrowed. "I thought you said it didn't hurt?" Her eyes widened as she realized what I meant, glancing quickly at my groin before blushing slightly. "Oh. I'm sorry, I had no idea. It's . . . er . . . erotic when someone touches you there?"

"Very," I said, pushing from my mind the sensation of her fingers stroking me.

"Dane . . ." She bit her lip.

I very much wanted to take up where we'd left off earlier. "Come with me. There is a mediation spot I use sometimes; we'll be private there."

She allowed me to lead her to a small inlet, sheltered by an overhang of rock. It was protected on three sides and open only to the sea—the ideal spot for hiding, one that I used when the strains of life got to be too much for me.

"You've been here before," she said with amusement as I pulled a plastic waterproof cooler on wheels out from behind a boulder. In it were two blankets, towels, and a change of clothing.

"I told you, it's my meditation spot." I laid out two of the blankets, then took a quick peek along the shore to make sure we hadn't been followed.

The hellhounds milled around, two of them brutally decapitating a bit of seaweed, the others snarling at the gulls overhead.

"Guard!" I told them, then took a seat next to Megan on the blanket. She was sitting with her arms around her legs, her chin resting on her knees as she watched the hellhounds take up their positions.

"Comfy?" she asked as I reached for her. She held me back with one hand.

"Extremely. May I kiss you now?"

"No." She shook her head. "I absolutely cannot think when you kiss me, so just like touching your antlers is out, so is kissing me. I really want to talk about this whole situation."

I sighed and leaned back against the rock wall. The manifestation melted away to nothing as I relaxed, enjoying the sensation of being with Megan in one of my most beloved spots. "I've told you—Fidencia is my ex-wife. Not just ex in the sense that I am not married to her this year, but ex in that I no longer desire to spend time with her. I don't want her for a wife. To be brutally honest, I'd be giddy with delight if she'd just leave me once and for all."

"Let me make sure I have this straight in my mind. Every year at the beginning of May, you get married."

"Beltane, yes. It normally falls around May fifth."

"And for the last fifteen hundred years—" Megan stopped, shook her head, and went on. "For the last fifteen hundred years, you've married Fidencia every year. And that act of marriage is what kept you alive for another year."

"Yes. It kept both of us alive, as a matter of fact. She is as old as I am—if she refused to be my goddess, time would catch up with her, too."

"But isn't that what she *did* do?"

"Yes. But only after she'd married Dionysus and become his goddess."

"Gotcha." She wrapped her arms around her legs again. "So she doesn't love you?"

I snorted. "I doubt if she ever did. I will admit that when I became Cernunnos and knew I must take a wife, I fell sway to Fidencia's charms. But close association with her soon made the scales drop from my eyes."

Megan drew a little doodle in the sand at the edge of the blanket. "I take it that means you fell out of love with her?"

"By the second year, yes." A thought struck me, an unwelcome and unpleasant thought. "Have you been married?"

"No. I was engaged once, but we decided that it wasn't going to work out. He wanted kids, and I . . . well, you know about that." She threw away the stick she'd been drawing with and turned to me, her eyes curiously vulnerable. "That really doesn't matter to you?"

"No," I said magnanimously, looking her straight in the eye to let her know I was speaking the truth. "Not in the least. If you are willing to overlook the fact that I've been married fifteen hundred plus times, I can overlook a failed engagement."

She laughed and punched me lightly in the arm.

I wanted to wrestle her to the ground and cover her with kisses.

"No, silly, I meant the fact that I can't have kids. It's not something that you'd end up missing?"

I thought of all the sadness I'd seen over the centuries—starving peasants struggling just to survive, children dead of famine, disease, and the victims of war. I thought of the plague years, and how helpless I'd felt at protecting the people in my castle from its devastations. I heard the countless sobs of mothers mourning lost husbands, sons, daughters. Time had eased some of the pain of those memories, but it would never erase them.

I shook my head, watching the water with blind eyes. "No, I do not feel the need to bring new life into the world. There are enough lives now that are not sufficiently cherished."

"You look so sad," she said, moving a smidgen closer to me. "Have I said something wrong?"

I tore my gaze from the sea to look at the woman next to me, and realized, really realized, what I was asking her to give up. Everything she'd known, everything she might have experienced as a normal mortal woman, would slip away from her if she accepted me. I knew I could seduce her to my plan. It would be no great work, and certainly a pleasure to do so, but I couldn't live for the rest of my life knowing I'd taken something from her without her consent.

It was my life, or hers. Which mattered more?

Ten

I am a civilized man. I also pride myself on being
a modern one. Thus, rather than deciding I knew
what was best for Megan without any regard to her
feelings, I put her life before mine.

"I would like to tell you about my life," I said
simply, and proceeded to do so for the next hour and
twenty minutes. I told her what I remembered of life
before I'd met the Cernunnos before me, how I had
gladly accepted the job without knowing fully what
it entailed, the pain of seeing my family age and pass
away while I remained as I was. I told her briefly
about Fidencia, but left out the heartache of knowing
the woman I'd chosen wasn't for me. I told her about
the castle, about the people who lived in the town.
I told her about the wars I'd gone off to fight, the
friends I'd buried, the kings who had risen and fallen
in the passing of time. I told her about the loneliness,
of the women whose lives had briefly touched mine,
then drifted away with little left to show but yet another memory.

"It's so very sad," she said, taking the handker-
chief I'd offered to mop up her eyes. "All those
people you've lost. All those friends and lovers and

family you watched grow old and die. How did you survive it all?"

I shrugged. "How did you survive cancer? It's what we do—survive. There were good times as well as bad. I clung to hope whenever there was any to be had, I had Stewart, and occasionally Fidencia appeared and distracted me with some outrageous demand or another. I had other friends, as well. I lived for the moment. That's all we can do."

She took my hand and squeezed it, tears making her eyes glisten. "I had no idea. I never really thought about what you've gone through, the history you've seen, the events you've lived through. It makes this all seem so . . . insignificant."

"On the contrary," I said, pressing my lips to the back of her hand. "It is for this simple joy that I have lived."

She laughed even as she rubbed tears off her cheek. "You survived all that just to sit here and hold my hand?"

"Yes." I sat back, her hand clasped tightly in mine as it rested on my leg. I was happy at that moment. My soul was content. "I have lived sixteen hundred years just for this moment, to be spent with you."

Tears spilled over her eyelashes. "That is the most beautiful thing anyone has ever said to me. But Dane, what you're asking me to do—I don't know if I can do it. To live forever . . . to watch people I love grow old and die . . . I just don't know if I can do that. I don't have any close family—I was an only child, and my parents both died young of cancer—but I have friends I care about."

"The choice must be yours," I told her. "Tonight the festivities begin with the hunt. It is confined to local folk, but tomorrow will be the fire procession. Even now, people are arriving from all over Britain to celebrate it with us. The following day is Beltane, and the wedding. I wish it was different, dearling, but you must decide by Beltane whether or not you will become my goddess."

"And if I decide I can't do it?" she asked, gently disengaging her fingers from mine. "Which of the druid virgins will take my place?"

I felt the loss as if it was a blow. "There is only one who can be my goddess, and you are she. If you refuse, then I will retire from the position and allow Taranis to fill it with someone of his choosing."

Her gaze shot to mine, startled. "But you'd die."

"Yes." I stood up and held out my hand for her.

She looked at it curiously for a moment before looking upward at me. "Are you saying you . . . love me?"

She made it so very easy. But damn and blast my conscience, I just couldn't do it.

"I don't know," I told her, grabbing her hand and hauling her to her feet. "I like you very much. I like being with you, and talking to you. I want you physically quite badly, to the exclusion of all other thought. I want to share things that happen to me with you. I want to share my life with you. But it's been so long since I've felt romantic love, I'm no longer certain if that's it or if I'm just desperate."

Her full-throated laugh made me smile with the sheer joy of hearing it. "Here you should be on your knees before me, telling me you love me above all else and that you'd be lost without me, and all you can say is that you're not sure if what you're feeling is love, or a mild case of lust."

"It's not mild in the least," I said, brushing my thumb against her lower lip.

She sucked in her breath.

"Would it help if I did those things?"

"No."

"Would it help if I kissed you?"

She swayed into my arms, just as I'd prayed she would. Her body was warm and soft and melted delightfully against me. "No. But I'll let you do it anyway."

"I don't want you to *let* me do it," I murmured, sliding my hands up the delicious curve of her hips to the underside of those magnificent breasts. "I want you to be a willing participant."

"Mmmrowr!" she said, suddenly lunging at me. I wasn't expecting full-frontal lunging and we both fell backward, across the blanket.

My forehead connected with hers with an audible "clunk!"

"Ow," we said simultaneously.

Megan, who lay across my chest, rubbed her nose against mine and grinned. "Sorry. I just wanted to show you that I was very willing."

"So I see."

"Don't you like aggression in a woman?" she asked, licking the corner of my mouth.

"It depends wholly on the woman. You have my full-fledged approval."

"Oooh, does this mean I get to seduce you out of all sensible thought for a change?" She wiggled against me, her hips rubbing sinuously on mine.

My eyes came close to crossing. "Oh, yes! Seduce me! Please, if you have any mercy, seduce me!"

She laughed as she kissed me, pushing my hands, busily working their way under her shirt, back to the ground. "All right, but you have to let me do this my way."

"This isn't going to end with you demanding I call you Mistress Megan, is it?" I asked, delighted with the wicked glint to her eye.

"No, of course not."

"Good. I don't mind taking turns being the aggressor, but I am not a submissive man by nature."

"It's Mistress Sadistica," she said, biting my lower lip.

I gawked at her for a moment before noticing the laughter in her eyes.

"Wench," I said, relaxing as she kissed along my jaw.

"Devilishly handsome Irish rogue," she countered, unbuttoning my shirt.

"Are we getting naked now?" I asked hopefully, helping her remove my shirt.

"I haven't decided yet. I just like your chest, and want to see it in all its manly glory."

"I like yours, too," I pointed out. "I'd like to see it in all its feminine glory. In fact, I'd like it rubbing up against me."

"This is supposed to be a kiss," she reminded me, scattering light little kisses across my chest. "Not foreplay. Not sex."

"But foreplay and sex are good."

"Just a kiss. With your bare chest. You've earned a kiss with all your enlightened Oprah and Deepak awareness."

When she squirmed on top of me, I grimaced and tried to shift her. "Imminent castration threatens."

"Oh. Sorry." She removed her knee from my groin, and moved slightly to the side.

"Perfect," I said, clamping both hands around her ass, giving it a quick grope before nipping at her lower lip. "Resume your seduction, vixen."

"I thought I was a wench."

" 'Vixen' has a nicer ring to it."

"Such astuteness must be rewarded," she said just before her lips descended upon mine.

It was a novel experience, allowing her to take the aggressor's role. I've allowed women to take the lead before, but I've never been entirely comfortable with a woman in that position. Yet with Megan, I trusted her completely. I spent a few idle seconds wondering why that was so, when I'd known her such a short time, but then her tongue snaked its way into my mouth and I lost all ability to reason.

"Mmm," she said. "You taste like . . . cinnamon? Cloves?"

"Gingerbread for the celebrations," I answered, sliding my hands up her ribcage.

"No, you have to lie there and let me make you as mindless as you make me," she ordered, pushing my hands away from where they badly wanted to touch her breasts.

"Dearling, that'll take all of three seconds."

"Mmm," she repeated, one hand gently tweaking my nipple. It was a struggle to not react to the insistent urges my body was making of me, and she certainly wasn't helping matters with her little wiggles, and kisses, and touches, and the amazingly sinuous dance her tongue did around mine, but I am nothing if not resolute. I knew this was important to her, that she needed to know that she could trust me, too. So despite every atom in my body demanding that I take her right there under the sun and gulls, bedewed by the occasional drift of sea spray, I told my instincts to take a holiday, and simply enjoyed the moment.

"All right," she said, coming up from a kiss that came close to igniting my trousers. "This isn't working. I'm just as mindless as ever, and you're not even trying to seduce me. It's your mouth, isn't it? You have a magic mouth that drives women's wits away?"

"It's you," I answered, sucking on her lower lip. "It's me. It's us together."

"Oh, God, I am so lost," she moaned, kissing me again with a passion that matched my own.

"Megan," I said, nearly at the limit of what I could endure.

"I know. Me too. I've changed my mind, you were right. Let's get naked. No! Wait! Someone could see us!" she said, rearing back to pull her shirt off over her head. "Oh, to hell with it. Yes! I want you, too. Right now, right here!"

Her hips wiggled against me in a manner that had me damn near bursting into song. I rolled her over, pinning her to the blanket. "I have sieged many a castle in my day, m'lady, but my attack on your keep will be the sweetest of all."

She giggled as I kissed every inch of her face. "Oh, we're doing medieval now? Okay, I can do that. I've been to a Renaissance Faire. Avast ye varlet! No quarter!"

"That was piratical, dearling, but we'll go with it if you like. Lower your gangplanks and prepare to be boarded!"

"No, no, medieval is fine," she said in a breathy voice, moaning as I sucked the sweet spot behind her ear. Her hands were frantic on my chest and back. The scent of her, the taste, the feeling of her fingers dancing about my flesh, drove me wild. "Tell me something medieval to say."

I reared back as her hands slid lower, down to my fly. "How about 'Is that a siege engine in your trousers, or are you just happy to see me?' I'm more than happy to see you, but if you keep doing that, I just may expire of happiness."

I helped her to remove my trousers, then went mindless as she explored my penis with a thoroughness that I couldn't help but commend.

"Condoms?" she asked, suddenly pulling back.

I lunged for my trousers, thanking my foresight that morning, and I almost lost control as she unrolled it onto me.

"Siege me!" she commanded, pulling me down onto the lush paradise of her body as she thrust her hips up.

I swear I saw stars as her body tightened around me when I sank into her. There was so much to do—her lips begged for kissing, her breasts demanded attention, and I had a deep, unexpected need to tell her what she meant to me—but the only thing I could do was drive myself into her body, reveling in her moans of passion and the look of bliss in her eyes.

She clawed at my back as she climaxed, and I gave in to my own body's demand, oblivious to everything but the woman in my arms. If I had any doubts before, they were long since destroyed. She was right. She was good. She was the one woman I was meant to have.

"Dane?"

Something nipped my shoulder. "Hmm?"

"You fell asleep. Er . . . on top of me."

Megan's eyes, while still misted from our lovemaking, also bore a slightly amused look.

"Gods, so I did." I rolled onto my side, pulling her back tight against my chest. "I'd make an excuse, but—"

"You're a man. That's pretty much all the excuse you can make."

I smiled into her hair, and kissed the top of her

head. Was there any woman so perfect as Megan?

"That was . . . wow. 'Siege' is a good word. Was I siegeworthy for you, too?" she asked.

I pulled her tighter, throwing a leg over her just in case she had thoughts of moving. "You wore me out, woman. I have no mind or body left. I'm just a man-shaped lump of exhausted, extremely sated flesh."

"Ah. So if I did this, it wouldn't do anything for you?"

She turned in my arms to face me, dipping her head down to suck one of my nipples into her mouth.

I damn near came off the blanket with the jolt that zapped through me. "Again? Right now? Before I've had my post-coital nap? Very well, you insatiable wench."

I was about to kiss the breath right out of her when the hellhounds set up an unearthly baying.

"What the— Bloody hell!"

"Someone's coming?" Megan swore under her breath, grabbing her clothing.

I muttered a few invectives of my own as I hurried into my trousers and shirt. She was just tidying her hair, and I was pulling my shoes back on, when a most unwelcome voice reached us.

"Down! I said down, you fiendish beasts! Know you who I am? Back, you beastly curs! Well, there you are. Quite a little love nest you have here," Taranis said as he marched around the outcropping of rock that hid us from view. "Megan, my dear, I have come to rescue you from this uncouth knave, and his no doubt crude attempts to paw your lovely self. We have a bird sanctuary visit scheduled for this morning, if you remember."

"What are you doing here, Taranis? What is this horrible place? And the stench, my God! Get those filthy beasts away from me. Good lord!" Fidencia lurched into view, clutching the arm of the druid named Roger. She straightened up, looking down her nose at us as she pointed at Megan. "What is that woman doing here with my husband?"

"Ex-husband," I said, frowning. "Go away. Megan was about to seduce me a second time."

"Dane!" Megan gasped, pinching the back of my arm in a meaningful way.

I remembered Oprah, Deepak, and that women were from Venus, and worked quickly to amend my error. "She was *not* about to seduce me a second time. Go away, regardless."

"Just who do you think you are?" Fidencia asked, releasing the arm of the druid to march over to Megan. "An upstart American trying to take my husband from me! Have you no shame? Have you no mercy? How can you possibly even think of taking from my poor, innocent babe the love of a father?"

"Are you deaf, woman, or just living in your own reality?" I asked, moving over to protect Megan. "You left me. You walked right out on me, as you've done for the last fifteen hundred years, except this time you married someone else and got pregnant by him.

"I have accepted that all those centuries of putting up with your abuse, infidelities, and general indifference were a penance I had to pay in order to finally have Megan, but if you think I'm going to give her up for you, you're madder than I thought. Go take your poor, innocent babe back to its rightful father, and work on having a real marriage for a change!"

"Come, my dear, I shall take you away from this unpleasantness." Taranis smoothly insinuated himself between Megan and me. "There is no need for you to put up with the sort of abuse Dane generates."

"Abuse! Me? You're the one who bloody well brought her here," I said, pointing to Fidencia.

"Remove that woman from the castle grounds," Fidencia ordered, shoving the druid toward us.

"Over my dead body," I said, narrowing my eyes at Roger.

He backed away, a distinctly worried look on his face.

"We shall go see the birds and think pleasant thoughts," Taranis said, steering Megan past the seething Fidencia.

I wanted to knock him down, whack his blasted head right off his shoulders, but Megan had to make her own decision.

"No," she said suddenly, stopping and twisting out of Taranis's grip. She walked over to me, leveled me with a look that stripped away everything, and said simply, "You'd better be worth this."

"I fervently hope you find me so," I said.

She took my hand, turning to face the others.

"I'm sorry, but the bird sanctuary visit will have to wait for another time. As for you," she told Fidencia, who looked faintly startled, "you had your chance, and you chose to give him up. I'm not going to be so foolish. I, Megan St. Clair, hereby accept your proposal of marriage, Dane."

"Actually, I don't believe I've formally pro—"

"I hereby accept your proposal of marriage!" she said in a louder voice, giving me another intense look.

"Ah, yes. *That* proposal. Excellent. And I, Dane Hearne, lord of the hunt, lord of the fifth hour, lord of all sorts of other things that only Stewart can remember, do hereby accept you as my goddess. So mote it be."

Eleven

My heart was light, brimming with joy and happiness and everything good it could think of. Just the memory of our interlude in the cove was enough to keep a smile on my face for the next decade. Possibly two.

I beamed at my new bride-to-be as I escorted her back to the castle. "You will be happy. I swear to you that I will make you happy."

Her gaze dropped from mine. "Er . . . yeah. We'll talk about that later, shall we?"

That hesitation was a tiny little blot on my otherwise cloudless existence, but I didn't let it worry me. I'd read in an issue of *Cosmo* that many brides had second thoughts. No doubt Megan had a case of bridal cold feet. I leered slightly to myself as I thought of the many ways I'd warm her up.

"What are you doing?" she asked, a puzzled look on her face.

"Leering slightly to myself. Why?"

"Oh. I thought you might have had a painful gas bubble or something. Um . . . Dane, are you sure we should leave them?"

She glanced back at where I had ordered the hellhounds to stand guard, effectively trapping Taranis,

Fidencia, and the druid, allowing me to escort Megan back to the castle in privacy.

"Of course we should leave them. They interrupted us. They can stay there and think about that sin while I take you back home."

"But, the poodles—"

"Hellhounds."

"The hellhound poodles look a bit . . . I can't believe I'm going to say this about a toy poodle . . . they look a bit menacing. Are you certain they won't harm the others?"

"I'm fairly certain Fidencia is safe. She is a goddess, albeit no longer mine. They will respect that and not cross the line to violence against her. Unfortunately, the same can be said about Taranis."

"Wait a minute—he's your boss, isn't he? Wouldn't your hell poodles know that?"

"Taranis has no authority in the Underworld," I answered. "Thus he has no authority over them, although they would be hard pressed to tackle him. The druid, however . . ." I stopped and looked back.

"What about him?"

"He has no such protection." I cupped my hands around my mouth, and called up the hellhounds. "Better to be safe, I suppose," I told Megan as the poodles thundered down the beach to us, Taranis in hot pursuit. Fidencia wasn't so much clinging to the arm of the druid as she was dragging him along in her wake; the look on her face was one that could strip paint.

Megan smiled at me, a gesture that warmed

my blood down to my toes. I wanted to kiss her on the spot, but the hellhounds were almost to us. She glanced at the approaching people and asked quickly, "About this wedding . . . just how big is it going to be?"

"It is the culmination of the Beltane celebrations. Have I not told you of them? Tonight is the hunt, tomorrow the fire procession, and the following day is the wedding. Neo-druids from all over the UK are arriving to take part in the celebrations. The wedding vows are spoken twice—the first time is at the fire procession. The more formal version follows the next day, at the Beltane events. Did you not notice the tent city on the far pasture?"

Megan shook her head as she looked. "No, we went in the other direction this morning. Wow, that looks like a whole lot of people. How many do you normally get for the holiday?"

"You'd have to ask Stewart for the exact attendance numbers," I answered as Taranis arrived, puffing slightly. "The hunt usually garners a hundred or so participants; double that will be here for the fire procession tomorrow. Possibly triple for the wedding. Ah, there you are, Taranis. A bit out of shape, are we?"

He completely missed the irony.

"You bloody fool," he snarled, pulling up to an abrupt stop, one eye on the milling hellhounds. "You could have injured dear Fidencia with those filthy beasts of yours! I've half a mind to send them back where they belong."

"By all means, go ahead," I answered with an insincere smile. "It would give me great pleasure to go before the Court with a complaint of interference by my overlord."

Megan gave a surprised gasp at Taranis's response, made as he stormed off without a backward look at Fidencia. "Wow. That's not anatomically possible, is it?" she asked.

"Not without a winch, two pounds of unsalted butter, and four spotters. Shall we go in before the lovely but toxic Fidencia reaches our side? Ah, too late. We're in for it now. Run and save yourself, dearling. I will stand here overflowing with manly determination as I brave the ravages of the Madwoman of Brazil."

Megan giggled. It was a delightful sound, one that brought joy and an odd sense of peace to my heart.

"Noony!" Fidencia bellowed as she steamed up to us. The druid collapsed on the ground with a great heaving of his torso as he sucked in air. "How dare you abandon me! How dare you send your beastly little curs to attack me! How dare you go off with that woman and leave me behind!"

I glanced at the woman at my side. "I'm sorry, dearling, I must touch her."

I grasped Fidencia firmly by her shoulders, then tightened my fingers to let her know I meant business. "You are another man's wife! You are fat with child—a child that is not mine. You have no claim on me anymore, nor will you ever in the future. I have made my choice of wife, and you are not she. Do you understand all this?"

"Oh, that wasn't good," Megan said, shaking her head, and covering her mouth with her hand.

"What?" I asked her as Fidencia sucked in approximately half the available oxygen in Ireland.

Then a roar broke over me with such force that I staggered backward, instinctively throwing out my arms to protect Megan.

"Fat!" Fidencia screamed, her hands curling into talons. "I am not fat!"

She lunged toward me, her hands outstretched.

I held her back with one hand. "What on earth is your problem, woman?"

"You called me fat!"

I looked from her to Megan, confused. Megan still had a hand over her mouth, her eyes twinkling in the most delightful manner. I wanted to ravish her on the spot and thought seriously of doing so before I remembered Oprah, Deepak, and all those "how to understand the mystery that is woman" books, and acknowledged that she wouldn't enjoy the ravishing if it was performed right there on the steps to the tower, surrounded by a half-dead druid, a maniac pregnant goddess, and six snarling hellhounds.

"I am not fat!"

I turned back to the hellcat fighting to get at me. "I said you were fat *with child.* It's an expression you must have heard over the last six or seven hundred years, and one which I chose with great care because it's historical, and sure to appeal to Megan."

Fidencia screamed with frustration. "You called me fat to make THAT WOMAN happy?"

"Of course I did, you deranged person. It's my duty to make her happy. She likes the history of this area, so I take special care to work into common conversation as many historically accurate terms as I can. I could just have easily have said you've got a bun in the oven, but it wouldn't be nearly so historical as stating you're fat with child."

"*Great* with child, you unfeeling historical bastard!" Fidencia snarled, freeing one hand to punch me in the chest. "The term is *great* with child! As in, I am great! Not fat!"

Megan was laughing outright now.

"I do not have time to discuss the etymology of historical terms relating to deranged pregnant women," I said with much dignity. "The hunt is tonight, and Megan is a demanding vixen who no doubt has many needs and desires that she wishes to enact upon my poor body before that time. I will have Stewart arrange transportation back to the airport, so you can rejoin your lawful husband."

"I . . . am . . . not . . . leaving," Fidencia hissed, and marched past me to the tower.

"Fine, but I'll have to charge you the off-season rates for a room," I called after her. As the gesture she made was wholly unnecessary—not to mention unsuitable for a woman of her standing—I decided the best thing was to ignore it.

"Oof," Megan said as I scooped her into my arms. "Dane! You can't do that right here, out in the open!"

"Why not? This is my castle, you are my wife-to-be, and your lips have been singing a siren song I've been unable to resist. Not that I've tried very hard."

She squirmed out of my grasp, the laughter fading from her eyes. "Yes, well . . . er . . . I think we need to talk."

"Again? Excellent. Let's get naked while we're doing it again. In fact, let's make love while we're doing it." I threaded my fingers through hers and started to pull her up the stairs.

She grabbed the stone lion at the bottom and held on for dear life. "Dane! We can't!"

I stopped and frowned down from two steps above her. "Why can't we? We did so quite successfully at the cove, and I assure you, we will get better the more we practice. Or is there some quirk in your makeup that you only desire me outdoors? If so, I'd like to remind you that I am an enlightened, modern man who is more than happy to put up with all sorts of kinky demands you might make, not that making love outside is particularly kinky, but say you had other kinky desires, such as ones involving role play, feather dusters, or economy-size containers of dessert topping, why then, I would be perfectly happy to indulge your wildest desires without the slightest word of complaint."

"No," she said, the beginnings of a smile at the corners of her mouth. "That's not it at all. Feathers *and* dessert topping?"

I gave her my best leer. "Oh, yes. At the same time."

Her eyes did that soft, slightly-out-of-focus thing that sent a little thrill of passion zipping down to my groin. "Good Lord. Perhaps I could make the time . . ." She interrupted herself by shaking her head. "This is ridiculous. I can't even have a conversation with you without indulging in the most detailed fantasies. And no, that wasn't an invitation," she added, holding up her hand as I leaped down the stairs to her side. "I really do want to talk to you about these ceremonies.

"For one, I'm not happy about the idea of a hunt. I know it's your country's tradition to hunt foxes, but I'm very much opposed to blood sports, and I absolutely won't participate in one. It's probably too much for me to ask you to not do so as well, but if there was any way I could convince you—"

I covered her mouth gently with my hand, thought for a moment, then replaced my hand with my mouth.

"Relax, dearling," I said as I gave her bottom lip a quick nibble, just to let her know I cared. "It's not a fox hunt. There will be no blood, unless one of the virgins gets out. The traditional Beltane hunt has human prey. Damn. There's Stewart, and he's looking as if he'd like my head on a platter. I'm afraid your wonderful seduction is going to have to wait, sweet one. After the hunt? Yes?"

I gave her one more kiss, then another after that because she looked so delightfully befuddled, before going to see what problem had cropped up.

"But . . . humans? Dane!" Megan grabbed at the back of my shirt. "Stop!"

"You insist on the seduction now?" I sighed, leaning over the edge of the staircase to yell up to Stewart, "It'll just have to wait an hour or two, Stewart. Megan insists on having her way with me right now. I know, you have need of me as well, and don't think I wouldn't like to go slave away over a hot computer, rather than have Megan seduce me. But I am nothing if not a man of my word, and I promised her she could."

"No!" Megan pinched me. "I don't insist on anything of the kind! I . . . I don't quite know what possessed me out at that secret spot of yours, but . . . well, we're here now, and sanity has thankfully returned to me. Or what I think is sanity—I'm a bit doubtful if I'm a qualified judge anymore. Regardless, we are not going to make love again."

A little whimper may have escaped me at that point; I'm not exactly certain. "We aren't?"

"No." She crossed her arms over her chest. "And you can stop looking like your dog just died, because that heart-meltingly lost look isn't going to sway me."

I took a step down until I could peer into her lovely, if stormy, eyes. "You break my heart, dearling, you truly do. You know that above all else, I yearn to make love to you again. And again. And again after that. You're rejecting me because you think I don't value you beyond the almost overwhelming desire to bury myself deep inside you, in the heat of you, in your fiery, soft depths, plunging deeper and deeper until that moment of absolute ecstasy overtakes us, and we transcend beyond the thrusting, pounding, and taking absolute possession that defines mankind. It's because of the fact that I ache with a need that is beyond painful to know every square inch of you that you are spurning me, is that not so?"

Megan blinked a couple of times before she cleared her throat and shifted her weight. "Er . . . no."

"Ah! Then it's because you want to have a traditional wedding night! You wish to keep yourself until then." It almost killed me to do so, but I nodded. "I understand. And despite the fact that I am a man, with a man's need to possess you as only I can, by plunging, thrusting, and pounding into your feminine depths, not to mention appropriate worship of breasts that are so beautiful they bring a tear to my eye and tightness to my groin, despite all that, I am willing to give you this gift of my understanding and support and affection. I will honor your desire and not make love to you until after the wedding. The one tomorrow night, that is—because it might just kill me if I have to wait until after the Beltane vows are spoken."

"Er . . ." Megan looked a bit dazed. I put it down to her unspoken admiration for my understanding of her true self. "All right. No! Wait, that's not it at all. I just need a little time to myself—"

I leaned in to kiss her, and stopped with my lips barely brushing hers. "And you shall have it, dearling."

Her eyes crossed as I plundered briefly before running up the stairs to my study. I had to get away from her before I went back on my word and ravaged her right there on the stairs.

"Dane! Wait a minute! About this hunt tonight—"

At the top floor I leaned over the balustrade and yelled down, "Wear something dark. It'll be harder that way for anyone to spot you."

Twelve

I looked out at the gathered audience, satisfaction filling me. The evening's activities were about to begin, Megan was present—although it had taken some quick explaining to get her there, since she'd sworn she wouldn't step foot out of her room until she knew for a fact that no one was going to be harmed in the hunt—the druids were massed and ready to go, and the local hunt group was getting quite drunk on their traditional stirrup cup.

The only blots on my existence were the presence of Fidencia, who huddled pathetically in a soft woolen shawl I'd plucked from the gift shop with the intention of giving to Megan, and the smarmy man who stood next to her.

"Why the hell did you let Taranis in?" I asked Stewart. "He's just here to cause trouble. You've seen the way he's ogled Megan."

"He's your overlord. I couldn't very well refuse him when he showed up."

"There's nothing in the laws that govern us that says I have to put up with him at a Beltane celebration. I'll throw him out."

"You'll do nothing of the kind," a soft, feminine voice said from behind my left shoulder.

I turned to her. "But, dearling—"

"Despite your unjustified jealousy, which I have to admit is a bit flattering, I can assure you that there is nothing Taranis can do that will make me go back on my word to you. Don't you trust me?"

"Of course I do. Absolutely and completely. Have I not committed myself heart and soul to you? That wouldn't be possible with someone I don't trust. Taranis, however, is another matter."

Megan's eyes turned curious. "Heart and soul? Really?"

"He has no soul, darling," Fidencia drawled as she moved toward us. "And his heart is a blackened, shriveled up pea. How else could he treat me in such an appalling manner?"

"Guests are not allowed up on the platform—" I started to say, but she took the microphone with both hands.

"People of Bannon, I bid thee welcome!"

"That's my job!" I tried to take the microphone from her, but she growled at me. Growled!

"No doubt you are all wondering why a strange woman's face is on the few pieces of merchandise which Elfwine made available," Fidencia said, gesturing toward a nearby stand. "I know you're all extremely disappointed that the official Fidencia items aren't available this year. Who among you could be happy with that woman's face on your underwear? I sympathize with you, I truly do."

I made a play for the microphone, but Fidencia is not a woman who takes well to having something removed from her possession.

"What did she say?" Megan asked in a whisper.

I wrapped an arm around her and pulled her close. "For protection," I told her when she raised an eyebrow. "You never know when Fidencia might go barking mad and try to assault you or something."

Megan rolled her eyes before asking, "What did she mean about my face on someone's underwear? I thought there wasn't going to be any merchandise?"

"Stewart had a word with Elfwine, and she came up with a few things."

A female shopper at the merchandise booth held up a garment to the man next to her, eyeing it critically.

Megan's lips thinned as she watched the couple. "I'm not sure I'm comfortable with the placing of my face on the men's boxers . . ."

"Many of you have asked why Cernunnos has cast me aside for another. Just a few minutes ago, a very sweet young druid girl flung herself at my feet, and looked up at me with imploring eyes. 'Lady Fidencia,' she said, 'why are you not our lady again this year, as you have been for the last one thousand years? Why have you been forsaken?' And beloved people of Bannon, I could not answer her."

"Oh for God's sake . . ." I got one hand on the microphone, but Fidencia tried twisting out of the way in order to retain her grip on it. I had enough fingers on it, however, so that by angling my head, I was able to speak into it. "It was over fifteen hundred years ago, you daft woman, and in case there's someone out there who doesn't know the truth, you left me for your Greco-Latin boy toy. If there was any forsaking to be done, you were the one doing it!"

"Oh!" she shrieked, and tried to bite my arm. "You beast!"

"I'm not the one trying to bite! That's it, I've had enough!" I wrapped an arm around her to hold her in place while trying to pry the microphone out of her hand. "Stewart, a little assistance here, if you please."

"What would you like me to do, knock her out?" he asked, his lips pursing as he watched our struggle.

"You wouldn't dare!" Fidencia shrieked even louder, possibly piercing my eardrum.

I had a horrible idea of the picture we made—a pregnant goddess and myself in traditional hunt wear fighting for control of the microphone—and shot Megan a reassuring smile. "I'll be with you in a moment, dearling."

The corners of her mouth twitched.

"How dare you call her that while you're holding me!" Fidencia yelled, and lunged for my shoulder, her teeth catching the edge of my leather jerkin.

I leaned my head out of the way of her snapping teeth, which luckily was toward the microphone. "Welcome to Bannon Castle," I managed to get out, smiling at the people standing in stunned silence. Even the hunt club had stopped the inflow of alcohol to watch with wide eyes. Fidencia tried to knee me in the groin. I managed to block that, but just barely. "And welcome to the annual Beltane Hunt. We're having a slight technical difficulty, but things should be starting in just a moment."

"You see the way he treats me! He is abusing me! He is harming the precious child I carry!"

"On the contrary," I said through my teeth, "I'm being very careful not to hurt you, which is more than can be said for you! Stop biting me! Stewart!"

My steward of many centuries just stood there wringing his hands. "I would help you if I could, sir, but I don't wish to harm Lady Fidencia—"

"Oh, for goodness sake, I'll do it," Megan said with something that sounded very much like a snort. She marched over to where Fidencia and I were locked in battle and started prying Fidencia's fingers off the microphone.

I smiled at her over the top of Fidencia's head. Could there have been a more supportive, more perfect woman in the world? "Have I told you today how much I worship you?"

Fidencia screamed a word that had even Stewart looking shocked. Megan was working on the last finger when a bellow emerged from the depths of the crowd.

"Take yer filthy 'ands off me wife!"

The crowd parted to allow a man through. He was of medium height, with dark, curly hair and darker eyes.

"Your husband, I presume?" I asked Fidencia.

"Dion?" she whispered, looking startled for a moment before her eyes flashed with fury. Her bellow was almost as impressive as his. "You dog! You mangy cur! You beast of the darkest depths of Abaddon!"

"Sounds like a husband to me," Megan said with a

smile, releasing her hold on Fidencia. I did likewise, moving over to stand next to Megan.

"Aw, now, me lovely one, don't be sayin' such cruel things to me," Dionysus said as he leaped onto the platform. He held open his arms, clearly expecting Fidencia to fling herself into them. I, having been around her much longer than he had, snatched the microphone and stand out of her reach before she could brain him with them. "Ye're lookin' ravishin', me beauty."

"You married a Cockney?" I asked Fidencia. "I thought he was Greek."

"He learned English from a Cockney," she answered, narrowing her gaze at him. If he had been made of mortal flesh, he'd have been sliced into shreds by that look. "The filthy, lying dog! What are you doing here? I told you I never wanted to see your two-timing face again!"

"She's a feisty one, she is," Dionysus told me with a fond smile toward his wife. He paused, frowned at me, and added with much menace, "Ye had yer hands all over me wife. I don't 'old with that, ex-'usband or no. She's mine now, and ye'll be keeping yerself to yerself where she's concerned, ye got that?"

"By all means, take her," I said, gently shoving Fidencia toward him. I beamed at Megan. "I have my own bride-to-be."

Megan looked faintly worried.

"Get away from me!" Fidencia shrieked, trying to disengage herself from the grasp of her husband. "Get your horrible womanizing hands off of me!"

"I think everyone has had just about enough of that for one night," I said, reclaiming the microphone. "If you wouldn't mind continuing your histrionics elsewhere? Thank you. Good evening, everyone! Thank you for bearing with us during our little difficulty. We are now ready to commence with the Beltane Hunt."

A cheer rose from the crowd, rather ragged to begin with, but increasing as people watched Dionysus handily move Fidencia off the platform and over to a quieter spot near the tower door.

"Although I'm sure everyone knows how we do this, I'll go over the rules quickly for any newcomers. The hunt is divided into two groups, hunters and prey. Who do we have as hunters tonight?"

Most of the hunt group raised their cups. Two of them belched. A handful of druids, male and female, did the same.

"Excellent. Stewart will hand out the bindings to the hunters. And who will be prey?"

Two female members of the hunt club and most of the women druids raised their hands, all giggling.

"Good, good. And may I say that the druids have outdone themselves this year with their costumes? I like the touches of faux fur on the leather bikinis."

Normally the druids ran as prey in brown and green robes, meant to blend into the woods. Evidently the younger women had persuaded the hunt committee to design an outfit that had one sole purpose—to inflame the appetites of those around them. With bits of fake fur clinging to the minute scraps of leather covering their breasts, bums, and genitalia, they'd added ribbons bedecked with ethnic beads, twigs, and leaves, and splashed their exposed flesh with sparkling powder. The effect was a strange mixture of earthy and tacky glamour.

"Right. Prey have a five-minute head start. Hunters must tag their prey before they are considered claimed. Ready? Off you go!"

Stewart lifted a curved horn to his lips and blew a note that sounded like the hacking of an emphysemic moose. The druids whooped and scattered, the prey taking off for the woods on the other side of the crumbling wall, while the hunters swarmed Stewart to get one of the thin strips of red cloth marked with the Beltane symbol.

"Er . . . I know you said that this is all benign, and a way for people to hook up for a bit of . . . well, you know . . . but isn't this whole thing a bit barbaric? Even if it's disguised as a mating ritual, you're still hunting people," Megan said, watching with a thoughtful furrow to her brow as the hunters snatched up their markers and ran to their horses. "And why do the hunters get horses, but the prey don't? That doesn't seem very fair to me. We won't go into the fact that all the men are dressed, and the women are running around in practically nothing . . ."

"Dearling," I said, cupping her face as I gently kissed her. "You're wasting time."

"I am? How so?" Her eyes widened as she took my meaning. "You don't expect *me* to go run out there like one of those half-dressed druids—"

"You are my goddess. It is part of the Beltane tradition that I must hunt and claim you for my own. Much as I'd love to see you in nothing but a bit of tatty fur and glitter, I have to admit I approve of your dark trousers and jacket. It wouldn't do having someone else catch my goddess and claim you, now, would it?"

Megan shook her head. "This is too bizarre. You can't be serious."

"Quite so," I answered, glancing at my watch. "You have three minutes left."

She put her hands on her hips. "If you think I'm going to run around in the dark like a deranged fool, you can just think again!"

"You don't have a choice, I'm afraid. It's a mandatory part of the festival. Which means it's really a matter of my life or death."

"You have got to be kidding. How is it life or death?"

"One: You, as my wife-to-be, have to participate in the hunt. Two: I must be the one to catch you. Three: If I do not catch you and mark you as mine, then the wedding is off. If the wedding is off, I die. Life and death, do you see? I knew you would." I kissed the tip of her nose and gently pushed her toward the crumbled wall. "Off you go, then."

"Wait a second," she said, stopping to shake her head at me. "Okay, I accept the silly rule about your needing to claim me via the hunt. Why don't I just run a few steps and let you catch me? Why do I have to go out into those woods?"

I looked at my watch again. "Two minutes. You have to go because the second you start running, you're fair game, and *any* of the hunters will be able to catch you."

"You've lost me." She looked confused.

"Do you see those people, there?" I pointed to the herd of mostly males who were mounted on horseback. The horses moving restlessly as Stewart stood on the podium, a large clock at his side.

"As soon as the initial five minutes are up, they will take off after the prey. And since you are here, a few feet from them, you will be the first one caught. Do you notice Taranis in the midst of them? Do you remember my saying that he wants to replace me with someone of his own choosing? Can you think of a better way to do it than claiming you before I can?"

She didn't stay to answer, bless her adorable mind. She simply turned and bolted for the trees. I marched over to where a hunter held one of the extra horses. The horse was smaller than I was used to, a glossy chestnut half-Arab gelding with twitchy ears and a rolling eye.

"Erm . . ." I said, looking him over. "He's a bit small for me. I'll take another one if you don't mind."

"Sorry, this is all we have left. His name is Emir. He's a bit frisky," the hunter told me. As I approached the horse, he tried to bite me. "You'll want to watch him around the others."

"I will, thank you." With no other choice, I mounted up and let the gelding dance a few paces until I was near enough to Taranis, mounted on the back of a long-limbed Thoroughbred, to say, "We both know I can't forbid you from participating in the hunt, but there's no way on this green earth that I'm going to allow you to catch my goddess. You've never caught my prey before, and I'm not about to let you start now."

"She's not yours yet," he answered with a smile.

"Thirty seconds," Stewart called out. "Everyone behind the bales of straw, please."

"Oh, she's mine. And no one, not even you, can change that fact," I said.

Emir tried to bite Taranis's horse. Much as I would have liked to see Taranis bucked off, I tightened the reins and got my mount under control.

"All right, my lad, let's have it all, everything you have," I told my mount. "I guarantee you a life of comfort and ease for the rest of your equine days if you outrun that blasted hack over there. The one with the idiot on his back."

Emir shook his head, mouthing the bit as I nudged him forward with the group of hunters. We were herded together behind a barrier of straw bales, intended to keep any one hunter from getting a head start.

"Ten seconds!"

"I'll throw in a lifetime of high-quality oats and apples, all right?"

The horse reached around and tried to bite my boot. I moved him forward a step, leaned over his neck, and slid a glance over at Taranis. He was

in a similar position, a look of anticipation on his
wretched face, the bastard.

"Go!" Stewart yelled, hitting the button on an air
horn to warn the prey that the hunters were off.

Emir leaped forward without any prompting,
skimming over the bales of straw and the piles of
rubble that marked the edge of the castle wall. Strip-
ling trees flashed past us, and the flickering lights of
the torches lining a path to the forest were blurs as
we pounded down the turf, the sound of pursuit immediately behind us. I took a quick glance behind us,
and saw Taranis was nowhere to be seen at the front
of the pack. I smiled to myself. "Good lad. I knew
with that deep chest you had some speed in you.
Now to find my dearling!"

Megan hadn't had time to hide deep in the forest, and she'd want me to find her, but not at the
expense of someone else seeing her first. Emir leaped
a downed log, then gave a frustrated whinny when I
pulled him up so I could think. If she didn't go deep
into the forest, where would she hide? Up a tree?
I scanned them, but none were sufficiently leafy to
hide a person. I mentally ran over the landscape, but
didn't come up with any hidden hollow. She hadn't
been in the woods before and wouldn't know the
territory; where had she gone? What sort of hiding
spot would she know of?

"Ha!" I yelled to Emir, digging in my heels and
leaning forward over his neck. He leaped forward,
clods of dirt flying as we raced out of the forest and
headed for the sea. All around us were the sounds of

the hunt—men calling to their prey, women laughing and yelling taunting replies, urging their hunters on to find them. The sounds faded as we sped along the beach, the light of the nearly full moon illuminating the ground. My heart beat wildly in my ears as I calculated whether Megan would have had a chance to double back and reach the hidden cove. Waves crashed along the shore as our shadow flashed along it, Emir's harsh breathing and grunts the only sound as he hurtled rocks and large pieces of driftwood.

"Please be there, please be there," I chanted in time to the rhythm of his hoofbeats. We passed the main part of the castle and headed down the far side of the beach. Surely by now I should see her. Could she have made it beyond this point on foot? Just as my blood turned to ice with the thought that I might have been mistaken, I caught sight of a dark shadow racing along the hard-packed sand. "That's my girl," I shouted to the night, the tightness in my chest easing at the sight of her.

"You have to catch her first!"

Leaping down the path from the castle, a huge black horse hove into view. He hit the beach about ten feet ahead of me, his head low as Taranis urged him on.

I swore and leaned lower over Emir's neck. "Come on, lad! I know you're getting winded, but I need you to do this for me."

Ahead of us, Megan glanced over her shoulder. She stumbled as she realized there were two horses pursuing her—and who was on the lead horse. Smart woman that she is, she spun off to the left toward the looser sand, where the large boulders and the trunks of washed-up trees lay. She darted in and out of the shadows, impossible to see as she ran close to the edge of the cliff side.

"She's done what she can. Now it's up to us," I told Emir. His ears went back as his head dropped, his breath loud and labored now. Beneath my legs, I felt his great lungs heaving as he tried to give me more speed, his legs a blur as he raced around the larger obstacles. Taranis's Thoroughbred might have had more speed and stamina, but Emir was a son of the desert, bred of a long line of horses known for their nimbleness and, most of all, heart.

Megan flashed into view, her hair a wild mass around her white face as she looked back to us. Taranis was closer to her now, just a few yards away. She scrambled over a rock and disappeared into an indentation along the cliff. His horse flew over the rock, Taranis's joyful shout of triumph filling the air. Megan raced out toward the water, yelling something incomprehensible as Taranis closed in on her, leaning down with the red silk marker in his hand, just a few scant feet away from marking her.

For a moment, I swear the world stopped turning. Birds in the trees, fish in the ocean, life forms everywhere held their breath as I imagined what life would be without Megan. I would never know what she looked like in the morning, when I roused her to kiss every inch of her body. I would never be privy to all those interesting thoughts that went on in her mind. I would never get to see the world through her eyes. Life wouldn't exist for me—not because I would die once and for all, but because she wouldn't be mine. I would never be able to tell her I loved her.

"No!" The scream was ripped from my throat as Taranis's hand was about to grab the back of her sweater. Megan threw herself down into a roll, sprang up, and ran in the opposite direction, straight toward me.

Taranis swung his horse in a circle and started toward her. I swung my leg over Emir and leaped to the ground, my arms open as I staggered toward her. Running flat out, she hit me head on, knocking us both backward into the sand. She was sobbing, her breath as ragged as mine, her face wet as I wrapped my arms around her and held her tight.

"You're safe now, my love, you're safe. I have you. It's all right, I have you."

"My . . . God . . . I didn't think . . . you were go-ing . . . to make it . . . in time . . ." Her body shook as she gasped in great lungsful of air.

"I know, love, I know. But it's all right now, I have you. I've claimed you." I spoke those last words look-ing straight into Taranis's eyes as he sat a few feet away, his face impassive as he watched us. "No one can take you from me now."

"That's good . . . you bastard! Making me . . . run like that . . ." Megan pulled back and glared at me with murderous eyes. "I don't know whether to kiss you or punch you out!"

I laughed with the sheer relief of having her in my arms, of knowing she was mine, of loving her.

"Kiss me," I said.

Taranis turned his horse and walked off into the night, his expressionless face giving me much to think about.

Thirteen

"My dearling! My love! Goddess above all women! You look ravishing as ever," I declared the following morning as I entered the dining room.

"Thank you. I feel much better now that Dion explained the unfortunate situation with the poor, misguided dancer who flung herself at him without any justification whatsoever, and humbled himself properly to me," Fidencia answered placidly.

I dragged my eyes off the vision of Megan sitting in a pool of sunlight, calmly eating a plate of eggs and toast, and squinted at the two other people at the table. "Fidencia. You're still here?"

She helped herself to the pot of marmalade just as Megan reached for it. "Silly Noony. Of course we're here. It's our honeymoon, after all."

"You have to give her credit," I told Megan as I sat in the chair next to her, then poured myself a cup of coffee. "She went from abandoned wife to honeymooner in less time than it takes most women to make up their minds."

Megan cocked an eyebrow at me. "Was that a slur upon my sex?"

"Unintentional, I assure you. It was mostly a dig at Fidencia's fickle nature."

"I'm not in the least bit fickle, am I, darling?" She positively cooed as she fed Dion a piece of marmalade-covered toast.

He lowered the newspaper he was reading—*my* newspaper—and nodded. "Of course ye are, me beauty."

"Aren't, darling."

"Of course ye aren't, me beauty. Pass the tea, will ye?"

"Did you sleep well?" I asked Megan, taking enormous pleasure out of simply watching her eat breakfast. The faintest of blushes colored her cheeks as she set down her fork. "Yes. Thank you for . . . er . . ." She cast a glance toward Fidencia and Dion, but they were otherwise occupied. Her voice dropped to an intimate whisper that sent a shiver of arousal down my back. "Thank you for your kindness after the hunt. I know you wanted to go to bed, but I'm still getting used to this whole thing, and I'm afraid it was all a bit too much for me last night."

I nodded. I couldn't deny that it had been difficult to leave her be—I had a feeling that it wouldn't have taken much persuading to topple her into my bed—but I had promised to let her have the space she needed, and I was going to keep that promise if it killed me. Which it might, if she didn't resolve her issues pretty damned quickly.

"Besides, I was worn out from the race along the beach. I hadn't realized how out of shape I was until I had to run on sand."

"I like your shape exactly as it is," I said, allowing a hint of leer to show.

"Oh, that race," Fidencia said, waving her hand dismissively. "What an obnoxious tradition. Noony used to make me go to one particular tree that was hidden behind a boulder. Did I see Taranis in the hunt?"

"Yes. The bastard tried to catch Megan, but she outsmarted him." I beamed at her, still filled with happiness at the thought of how she had avoided capture by him. "I'm sure he got the message that she had sworn herself to me for all time."

Megan's smile faded a little as she pushed the remainder of her breakfast around her plate.

"Taranis was always so . . . feral," Fidencia said dreamily, stirring half a cup of cream into her tea. She slid a quick glance toward her husband, but he was still engrossed in the paper. "Not that I like that in a man, but there was a certain thrill to knowing you were pursued by a man who would have no mercy when he caught you."

My gaze turned to Fidencia. "Are you saying that Taranis hunted you?"

"Once or twice, yes. It was thrilling, really, not at all like standing around a stupid old tree for half an hour waiting for you to fetch me. With Taranis it was so very . . . primal."

I gawked. "Are you daft, woman? When did Taranis hunt you?"

She scooped out a spoonful of marmalade and sucked it off. "Hmm? Oh, a few years ago. So hard to remember exact times, don't you find? I believe it was the year after the appalling rainstorm that ruined the celebrations. No, I take it back—the first time was the year I started the goat farm."

"That was . . . twenty-two years ago," I said slowly, trying to fit things together. "The *first* time? He's hunted you more than once? And caught you?"

She nodded.

"How is that possible?" Megan asked me. "You told me that you had to be the one to find me first, or else . . ."

"I'd die," I answered. "Taranis couldn't have hunted and claimed her. If he had, he would have booted me out of the job and watched with great pleasure as I turned to dust."

"Noony, darling, you don't know everything." Fidencia complacently ate another spoon of marmalade. "I said he hunted me and caught me—I didn't say he claimed me. He never did that. He knew it would mean your destruction if he claimed me, so he contented himself with simply finding me before you did."

"I find that extremely difficult to believe."

"That's because you're a man. Men always expect the worst of other men. Except my darling Dion, of course." She blew a few kisses at the newspaper. It rustled as Dionysus made the appropriate abstracted acknowledgment.

"Maybe you were wrong about him?" Megan asked, placing her hand over mine. I cherished both the gesture and the warmth it gave me.

"Perhaps, but I suspect there's some other explanation for it. It's not like him to be in any way generous where I'm concerned."

"Come, my darling, let us go allow the druids to enjoy our visit. Elfwine will be delighted to see you again," Fidencia said, tugging the newspaper out of Dionysus's hands.

He frowned for a moment. "Elfwine?"

"The druid elder, darling. You remember her—she's the one who organized the Harvest Festival where we met."

"Ah, yes." He nodded and allowed himself to be led out of the room.

I paid them little mind as I tried to puzzle out the mystery of Taranis's behavior. "He had to have a motive."

"I'm sure you'll figure it out," Megan answered as Pam and Derek entered the room. "You guys were out early. Did you have breakfast?"

"Yes," Pam said, smiling at me. "You do such fabulous breakfasts here, Derek and I thought we'd take a walk to work some of it off. Are you ready to go, Megan?"

"You're leaving?" I asked, inexplicably hurt.

"We're booked on a canal boat to film a segment on canals. We should be back by dinnertime."

"We'll go get the equipment and meet you at the car," Derek said.

I allowed a slightly hurt expression to play over my face, and Megan's lips twitched as she looked at me.

"That is just about the most pathetic look I've ever seen. But it's wasted on me—if I want to have time for the fire celebration tonight, I have to get this segment done today."

Tonight we would speak the first set of vows. Tonight I would pleasure her beyond her comprehension. If I wanted that, I'd have to let her go now. "Very well, do your filming today. The fire procession won't start until after nine p.m."

"Great. We'll be back long before then." She rose, hesitated, then pressed a slightly off-center kiss to my mouth. "Dane, I think . . ."

"You think what?"

Her gaze dropped to her hands and she twisted a small garnet ring that she wore on her right hand. "I'm not having cold feet, but . . . does it occur to you that things might not work out between us? We really don't know much about each other, so I was thinking we might try something along the lines of what you had with Fidencia, without the animosity. What they used to call a marriage of convenience—we could get to know each other a little more before deciding whether or not we had something permanent."

My heart contracted into a leaden black ball of misery. "You don't want me? You don't wish to be my goddess? You don't want to spend the rest of your life giving me endless pleasure and getting endless pleasure from me?"

"I said I'd marry you, and I meant it. I'm not going to back out of that," she said in a reassuring tone of voice that did nothing to lighten the dead thing in my chest that was my heart. "I won't let you die."

How could she not see how much I had to give her? How could she imagine that I would not spend every waking moment filling her life with ecstasy? After last night, how could she not realize that we were destined for each other?

"Oh, Dane, don't look like that . . ." Her voice broke as she knelt before me, her hands on my knees. "You make me feel like the worst sort of monster when you look at me like that. I don't mean that you're not the most droolworthy man on the planet—because you are. You're so handsome, it makes my teeth hurt. You're sexy, and you have the strangest sense of humor that for some reason greatly appeals to me, and I really, really like you. I'm just not absolutely, 100 percent certain that I'm the woman you are waiting for."

I just looked at her, stunned by the realization that she was motivated by pity to marry me.

She bowed her head for a moment, her eyes swimming. I felt like crying myself. "Maybe I'm wrong. Maybe I'm being unreasonable. Don't you have any qualms about me?"

"No," I said, the word ripped from my heart and soul. "I know without the slightest doubt that you are the woman who will complete me. You are my life, Megan. Without you, I simply would not exist."

A lone tear swelled over her eyelid.

I looked deep into her beautiful eyes and said simply, "I love you."

"The problem is"—she bit her lip, her hands fisted on my knees—"I don't know if I love you. I like you a lot. But love . . . I just don't know. It's too soon."

The pain in my heart eased. Could it be that commitment issues were all that stood between us and happiness? I covered her hands with mine, smoothing out her tight fists. "I am wise in the ways of Oprah and Deepak. They would both say that you need more time to establish the full depth of your feelings for me. I cannot give you that time outside of marriage, but if you will trust me, you may take as long as you need inside our marriage to understand our relationship."

She leaned her cheek onto my hand. "You really are an amazing man. I don't know what I've done to deserve you."

"I have many books that will help you understand your emotions," I said helpfully. "I particularly liked the one called *How to Make Love to a Man*."

She laughed as she rose to her feet. "That's a sex manual, not a relationship guide. And if yesterday was anything to go by, you certainly don't need any help there. Well, I'd better get going or we won't be back in time for the fire thing tonight. Um . . . what exactly happens at the ceremony? Am I going to be chased in any way, shape, or form?"

"Not unless you wish to play errant sheep and randy shepherd ahead of time," I said, happiness returning to my heart.

She needed more time, that was all. Women didn't understand their emotions as easily as men, and she simply needed to explore the idea of our perfection as a couple for a while before seeing reason. "It's part of the marriage ceremony—the ancient part. The wedding tomorrow is just a civil ceremony, with a feast to follow. Tonight's event is the heart of the Beltane celebrations. I think you'll like it. There are Red Men, White Women, you as the May Queen, and myself as the Green Man. You get to kill me at the end—ritualistically, of course."

"That doesn't sound too promising for the wild wedding night you promised me," she said, laughing.

I grinned. "You also get to bring me back to life. The impassioned, steamy wedding night follows after that."

Outside, a car horn honked impatiently.

"Damn, I'd better scoot. I'll want to hear more when I get back, okay? Especially the part about the wedding night."

"I'll fill you in on the entire proceedings," I said, a warm glow filling me at the heated look in her eye.

"Thanks. See you later. Hi, Stewart. Bye, Stewart."

Stewart bade her hello over his shoulder and toddled into the room.

"She loves me," I told him with much satisfaction, helping myself to some breakfast.

"She does?"

"Of course she does. A woman like her wouldn't couple with a man unless she had a strong emotional bond. And she wouldn't eat me up with her eyes and all but rip my shirt off me unless she loved me. She's a bit resistant to understanding the true nature of our bond, but that should clear itself up soon."

"Ah." He didn't say anything else, but there was a distinctive look of doubt in his face.

"You'll see. Tonight, after the fire procession, Megan will realize what true happiness really is—and that it can be found only with me."

Fourteen

I'm so sorry! I know we're horribly late, but I tried to call and couldn't get through—the line was constantly busy. The canal boat broke down in the middle of nowhere, and we had to swim to get out of the canal. It took us hours to get back to the car. Am I too late? I see bonfires everywhere—has the ceremony started?" Megan was breathless as she burst out of the car that had pulled to a sharp stop.

Pam and Derek called apologies as they ran to their room, clearly bent on changing into something less wet.

"Is it too much to ask that a goddess honor the ancient ways?" Elfwine snapped, emerging from the tower to grab Megan.

"You're not too late, dearling, although you've cut it a bit fine. Elfwine and her virgins are here to dress you."

"Oh, I don't need any help—"

"It's not an option," Elfwine snapped, hauling Megan by the arm up the stairs.

I followed, wanting to make sure that Megan wasn't harmed in the druid's haste to have her in place on time.

"I'm so sorry. We intended to be back hours ago.

Wow, Dane, that's a great outfit. You look like something out of *The Lord of the Rings* what with those leather leggings and the jerkin."

"Movie or books?" I asked, opening the door to her bedroom.

"Movie."

"Viggo? Or the skinny elves?"

She grinned, her eyes bright with humor and a little bit of lust. "Viggo. Definitely Viggo. Maybe with just a touch of Sean Bean."

"I'll accept that. I'll leave you in Elfwine's capable hands—"

The door was slammed shut in my face.

"Is she here?" Stewart asked, leaping down the stairs from my study.

"Just got here." I frowned at the door. "I'm a bit worried about Elfwine—"

"She knows what she's doing. Come along, sir, we have to get you into place." Stewart, dressed in identical leather boots, leggings, and jerkin, with a green linen léine that was a plainer version of the gold and black embroidered one I wore, and armed with one of the several walkie-talkies used to coordinate the event, hustled me down the stairs.

"It's not her proficiency in readying the May Queen that worries me. It's something else. Have you noticed anything different about her?"

"Different how?" he asked as we wove in between the bonfires that dotted the grounds.

"She seems more unhappy with me than is the norm. As if she's dissatisfied."

"Perhaps she's about to hand over her position to someone else," Stewart offered before turning to one of the druids. "Daniel, are the hellhounds ready?"

"Hmm. Possibly." But Elfwine had always been a borderline rabid druid—dedicated body and soul to the religion.

"Yes, and I'll be thankful to get rid of the little bastards. We had a hell of a time getting the horns onto them." Daniel stepped aside to reveal the mass of hellhounds, decked out in the traditional Beltane celebration of spiked collars and strap-on horns.

Stewart pursed his lips as he looked at them. The standard horns, set into a padded leather base that was bound to elastic that went around the ears and under the hellhound's throat, were far too big for the toy poodles. Evidently Daniel had taken a hacksaw to the antlers and cut off all the points, leaving only two pronged appendages that sprouted out of each hellhound's head.

"Wasn't there a cartoon along these lines?" I asked.

Stewart nodded. *"How the Grinch Stole Christmas.* I was thinking the exact same thing."

"They look like tiny hell bulls rather than hounds, don't they?"

Daniel appeared distraught. "Yes, I'm sorry about that. We didn't think of the spiked collars, either, until it was time to get them dressed, and then there wasn't time to do anything about them. Sally had some bells left over from a Morris dancing class, so we used those instead . . . although we had to wrap them around their middles rather than their necks."

The hellhounds, each wearing a belt of jingle bells, and crowned with what looked remarkably like steers' horns, pranced about as menacingly as they could, but I could see that their hearts weren't in it.

"Er . . ." Stewart said, a comical expression of horror on his face as he looked at them.

"They'll have to do." I dismissed the issue of the jingling hellhounds as we made our way through the crowd.

It was pitch black out, the fires creating little dots of light that flickered eerily over the three hundred or so gathered druids. They milled around the grounds, waiting for the procession to start, some of them tending the bonfires, others passing out food and mead, still others selling a variety of merchandise. I stopped by the main booth to peruse the items available this year, frowning at the lack of choices. "No commemorative glasses this year?"

"No, my lord."

"No Belgian chocolate deer with the marzipan eyes?"

"I'm afraid we didn't get any," the druid handling the stand said with a nervous glance over her shoulder.

"Hmm." I flicked through the T-shirts, thinking Megan would like one to mark this important date. "No ladies' tank tops with lace insets?"

"Erm . . . no."

"What about the plates? You can't tell me Elfwine didn't get any plates. She's had days!"

The druid started to look a little frightened. "I'm afraid not, Lord Cernunnos."

"Bonfire-scented candles?"

"No."

"Commemorative bottles of ale?"

"I wish we did—I could use six or seven. But no, I'm sorry."

"Hug-a-tree banners?"

"None," the druid answered, close to tears now.

I turned to Stewart. "You see? Something is definitely up. When's the last time you can remember there being no hug-a-tree banners at a Beltane celebration?"

He frowned. "You may have something there. But we have little time for speculation, I'm sure it just slipped Elfwine's mind this year. She *is* getting older."

"Hrmph." Perhaps he was right. Perhaps she needed assistance from someone younger.

"The May Queen will be along at any moment, and we need to get the Red Imps and the escort of Blue Men in place before then," Stewart added, shooing me toward the far end of the grounds, where an extra-large bonfire was blazing away like a pagan beacon.

I don't know how other Beltane celebrations are organized, but ours follow a pattern that was handed down for centuries. True, we've made some humane changes over time; sheep and other animals are no longer sacrificed during the ceremony (although the chickens consumed at the après-celebration barbecue would probably not feel any great strides had been made in that area). As I stood at the summit of the ruins and looked over the bonfires laid out in a giant cross shape over the castle grounds, I was much anticipating the procession. Especially the part where Megan formally became my goddess.

Stewart moved to my side and spoke into a walkie-talkie. "We are go for May Queen launch. Repeat, we are go for May Queen launch."

"Good copy," came the reply, and the door to the tower opened. The sound of a horn throbbed into the night, alerting all that the festivities were beginning. Drummers lining the path from the tower to the summit began a slow rhythm.

It was too far away to see individual faces, but I knew what was happening. First, the May Queen's White Women would spill out down the steps. The queen, garbed in traditional white and red, would follow, stopping at the crossroads to greet the quarters and to acknowledge the elemental points: fire, earth, air, and water, each represented by a druid.

Then my guard of Blue Men would join the procession and begin to escort her to me.

"How many Red Imps do we have this year?" I asked, pulling my sword and testing it for balance, just for something to do. It being one of my favorite weapons, I'd honed its blade myself just that morning.

"As to that . . . just three, I'm afraid."

I stared at him in surprise. "*Three*? That's all?"

"I'm sorry, sir, we had a shortage of men this year

for all the parts. We had to either short the imps or lose two of the Blue Men, and you know their number is set as six."

I grunted in dismay. "My one chance to dazzle Megan with my prowess in battle, to astound her with my sword-fighting ability, and I don't have a dozen imps to fight? *Three* druids? It'll be like fighting kittens." I snorted in, and kicked one of the bales of hay that lined the path.

"Actually, it's just two druids—Lord Taranis offered to take the role of a Red Imp when he learned of the shortage."

"What?" My head whipped around to peer into the bonfire-lit darkness. I could make out Megan's form as she walked behind the line of four White Women, within the guard of Blue Men. She was approaching the crossroads, where tradition specified that Red Imps, wakened by the May Queen from their winter's sleep, would spring forth and attack her party in an attempt to bring back winter.

As the Green Man, it was my job to defend the queen. Some Beltane groups had purely ceremonial fights, but I had always insisted on some realism in our festival. Just as the goddess was truly hunted yesterday, so now would I actually fight the Red Imps to save her. And if Taranis was one of the Red Imps . . .

"He's going to try to take Megan!" I shouted, fury filling me and spilling out in the form of the manifestation. I raced down the hill toward the crossroad, the pack of snarling, jingling, horned hell poodles streaming behind me.

The two druids portraying Red Imps were clad in red jumpsuits, each clutching a reproduction long sword. They looked up with surprise as I charged at them, cracking one on the head with the butt of my sword, knocking the other backward over the barrier bales of hay. Both hit the ground hard, neither moving as I turned to the third man. Taranis, clad in black trousers and a red shirt, was just strapping his sword to his waist when he heard the druids yell.

He looked confused for a second as I lunged for him, but godly instincts being what they are, he had his sword in hand by the time I reached him.

"What the hell are you doing?" he snarled as I leaped at him. "The queen isn't here yet! We haven't started our attack! Oh, for God's sake, man, put those horns away. You're going to poke someone's eye out on them one day."

"You treacherous bastard! You thought I didn't know what you were doing, didn't you?" As I slashed at him with my sword, he parried and backed up a step, looking confused and slightly annoyed. "You want me dead so you can put one of your seven hundred sons in my place."

"I only have one hundred and forty-two children, of whom seventy-eight are sons. None of them wants your job!" He parried another lunge, and blocked a backhanded attack. "Well, the youngest does, but he's an idiot and I wouldn't trust him with a toaster. Your job is perfectly safe!"

"Ha! I don't believe you. You've wanted me out of this job forever. It's not going to happen, though.

Megan will be my goddess, despite your best efforts to keep her from me, and we're going to live happily ever after, dammit!" I leaped onto the nearest bale of hay, and threw myself at him in the best Errol Flynn manner.

"I'm not trying to kill you, you daft fool!" he shouted, spinning out of my way and checking my sword thrust.

"Ha!" I repeated, giving him my best scornful look. "Then why are you fighting me now?"

"Because I'm a Red bloody Imp, that's why. And I'm not actually fighting you, I'm just trying to keep you from messing up this shirt! Deidre made it herself, and she'll gut me alive and roast my spleen over an open fire if I ruin it."

I lowered my sword slightly. "Deidre?"

"My wife!" Taranis was panting slightly, a faint sheen of sweat on his forehead. I felt distinct pleasure that I wasn't even breathing hard. "She's a fury, and believe me when I say it's wiser not to make her angry. That's her there, next to the bonfire."

I looked where he had waved. A tall blond woman was gaily throwing small pieces of wood on the fire. "A fury? I thought you only married mortal women?"

"I haven't married a mortal in three centuries," he answered, lowering his sword and mopping at his brow. "They were always getting pregnant. Do you have any idea how expensive it is to feed and house one hundred and forty-two children? Deidre's very good at keeping them all in line; otherwise I'd be stark raving mad by now."

"So you're saying you aren't going to try to steal Megan away from me so that I'll die and you can fill my position?"

"Steal her?" He shot a quick glance toward his wife and shuddered. "The repercussions of such an event are too horrible to contemplate. I don't know where you got this ridiculous idea that I'm trying to get rid of you, but I have no such intentions."

I raised my sword until the tip was against his neck. "Then why did you try to win her at the hunt?"

He actually had the audacity to roll his eyes at me. I thought lovingly of plunging the sword into him, but the fruitlessness of such an act stayed my hand.

"Complacency, man! You were so complacent with Fidencia during previous hunts, I figured it would bring a little life back to you if you thought this new goddess wasn't going to be yours quite so easily."

"Do I look like a man who needs new life?"

He eyed me carefully. "Actually, you look like a man in the throes of intense jealousy. Do you love this mortal woman, then?"

"Of course I love her! She's going to be my goddess!" It took an effort, but I managed to contain the anger that had filled me. "Don't you love your goddess?"

His eyes shot to the blond woman, now heaving large pieces of broken furniture onto the bonfire with great gusto. "I'd be afraid not to. That is, yes, of course I love her."

Behind us, the two druids helped each other to their feet.

"Then perhaps you'd explain why, if you're not trying to replace me, you held off having me summoned until a week before Beltane, thereby making it almost impossible to find a new wife by Beltane?"

He frowned. "What are you talking about? It wasn't I who delayed summoning you. Elfwine told me you had unfinished business in the Underworld, and that she'd summon you when you were ready."

I blinked in surprise. "That doesn't make sense. I had no such business, and certainly didn't request not to be summoned at the appropriate date. Elfwine told me you wouldn't give permission to summon me, and that it took her a full month of nagging before you got around to it. Why would she say that if it wasn't true?"

"You'd have to ask her that, but I assure you it wasn't me who delayed your summons. Ah, here comes the May Queen."

My frown, which had started with a contemplation of just what Elfwine was up to, faded as Megan's party approached. In front were the White Women, four druids dressed in long white robes and wearing white masks. Behind them was Megan, the Blue Men standing guard on either side of her. My breath caught in my throat at the sight of her. She was garbed in a delicate white robe edged in crimson and gold, a matching crimson and gold chain girdle hung around her hips. On her head she bore a garland of white and red roses, white ribbons streaming down her back.

"Hello," she said as the group stopped in front of

us, a twinkle in her eye. "Oooh, you have your horns out. May I touch them?"

"Later, my dearling, you may touch anything you like. You look every inch a goddess," I said, taking her hands, my voice low enough that only she could hear. "I should go down on my knees and thank the sovereign for sending you to me."

I pressed a kiss into her hands, then straightened and spoke in a voice loud enough to be picked up on the digital camcorders filming the festivities. "Most gracious lady, I have slain for thee the Red Imps that have sprung forth to attack. Might I beg a boon as my reward?"

Megan, the Blue Men, and the White Women all turned to look at the three men playing imps.

"Ahem," I said to the Red Imp druids.

"Eh? Oh! Arrrrgh! You've slain me!" The first druid clutched his throat and fell over backward. The second looked at him in surprise for a moment until the first one pulled him down.

"He's slain me as well," the second said, finally remembering his role.

Taranis sighed, sheathed his sword, dusted off the nearest bale of hay, and sank upon it with a languid wave of his hand. "I die."

Megan giggled.

"It's normally more exciting than that," I reassure her. "Things have been a bit bollixed up tonight."

"Gotcha." She consulted a small piece of paper she was holding and raised her hand to me. "My lord Cernunnos, you have saved us from an attack by the

forces of chaos. We will grant you any boon you desire. Name it, and it shall be yours." She took a step
forward and made a somewhat wobbly curtsy.

I bowed over her hand, lifting my gaze to hers. "I
request your hand, beloved lady. Wed me this night,
and I will be content for eternity."

"Nay, it cannot be! The May Queen cannot consort with the Green Man!" said one of the masked
White Women.

The Blue Men, representing my forces, each held
one of the White Women to keep them from encirc-
ling their queen.

I got down on one knee before Megan. "With you
at my side, there is no challenger I cannot best, no
trial impossible to overcome, no pursuit we cannot
achieve. You are my life, my heart, my being. I will
keep you and honor you above all women until the
day I cease to exist."

A soft little sigh escaped her. "Oh, Dane, that's the
most romantic thing anyone has ever said to me."

She leaned forward to kiss me—not in the script,
but I wasn't about to point that out—when a hiss
from one of the White Women recalled her to her
duties. "My lady!"

"Sorry, I was just . . . um, where was I?" She
looked down at me, her face shining in the torchlight.
"I accept you as husband, keeping you and honoring
you above all men until the day I cease to exist."

The warm glow inside me filled me with such joy,
I couldn't keep from standing up and pulling her to
me, kissing the very breath out of her lungs.

"Huzzah for the May Queen! Huzzah for the Green Man! May their union be fruitful!" the outer druids yelled, throwing grains of wheat on us.

"Woe is upon us! Woe is upon us!" cried the White Women.

Megan had been reciprocating my kiss, her tongue just as bossy and demanding as mine was, but she pulled back at the pronouncement of the druids.

"Fruitful?" she whispered, looking worried.

I kissed her lovely forehead. "It's a reference to the harvest."

"The Green Man has taken the May Queen! He must die for that crime!" The nearest White Woman broke free from the Blue Man holding her, and raised a silver dagger over her head as she rushed toward me.

I had only a second to notice that the dagger wasn't the usual wooden one before it was plunged into my heart.

I stared down at my chest in surprise, my hands still holding Megan's.

"You stabbed me," I told the White Woman, not understanding what had happened. "You're not supposed to do that. Didn't Elfwine tell you what to do?"

She pulled the mask from her face, revealing herself to be Elfwine. "I know very well what to do, *my lord*."

The venom in her voice sent me staggering back a pace. Or maybe it was the silver dagger in my heart.

"Dane?" Megan sounded confused. "Is something wrong?"

"She stabbed me," I said, blinking to clear the black spots from my vision. "Not play-stabbing as she should have; she stabbed me in the heart with a silver dagger. You know what that means?"

"No. What does it mean?"

"It means my blood is on the blade—"

"My lord? Is something amiss?" Stewart burst through the crowd. "Merciful sovereign! A silver dagger?"

"What's the holdup?" Taranis's voice rumbled. "I promised Deidre you were having an American-style barbecue, and you do *not* want her getting grumpy because she's hungry."

"Why are you doing this?" I asked Elfwine. "You are the druid elder. You have served me for years."

Elfwine pulled off her white robes to reveal a dark green shirt and matching pants. "I've had enough of serving you. You're not Cernunnos—you're a weak, miserable excuse for a god," Elfwine snarled.

I straightened my shoulders, and the hellhounds leaped up and bayed en masse.

"Seize him!" Elfwine yelled, and the Blue Men surrounded me. One ripped my sword from my waist; two more grabbed Stewart as he leaped forward to help me. The remainder held tight to my arms to keep me from moving.

"What the hell do you think you're doing?" I snapped.

"What I should have done years ago. All those years while Fidencia was out with other men, you just let her walk all over you. And now you're panting after an *American* instead of one of my virgins. The time is long overdue for a new Cernunnos, and *I* intend to fill that role!"

Taranis cast a worried glance at his wife, who had run out of things to throw on the bonfire and was looking around in a displeased manner. "Cernunnos, if you could please hurry this along, I think we'd all appreciate it."

"Yes, maybe we should finish this up," Megan said, shooting me a sultry-eyed look. "I have . . . uh . . . things I'd like to discuss with you. Alone. Bring your antlers. Here, I'll just take this fake dagger out, and we can finish up with this fire thing."

"Leave it, love," I told her, stopping her as she was about to pull it out of my chest.

Her hand was on the hilt, but before I could explain, she gave it a slight tug. "Oh my God! This is really in your chest, isn't it? Good God, Dane! You're really bleeding! But . . . you're immortal! Why . . . what . . ."

"We are here! Did anyone miss us? What am I saying, of course you did. Dion, darling, would you mind fetching me a chair so I might sit and watch the imp fight? It was always my favorite part of the festival. Hullo, yes, I am Lady Fidencia. The first goddess, you know. First and best, as the saying goes." Fidencia marched into the circle of people, nodding her head and blowing little kisses to various people in the crowd. "Hullo! Nice to see you, too. This is my husband. Isn't he delicious? Did we miss the imps?"

"Someone call an aid unit!" Megan demanded, pushing Fidencia out of the way. "Dane is hurt!"

"Well! Noony, darling, I have to say I don't think much of your new woman's manners." Fidencia gave Megan a scathing look before her gaze dropped to my chest. "Oh, we missed the imps? Damnation. I'm sorry, my darling. All that is left is boring ceremony. Let's go into town, shall we? The rest of the fire festival is too tedious for words. There used to be a very nice club that I just bet would play some salsa music for us."

"Bad luck, mate," Dionysus said, looking closely at the dagger in my heart before allowing Fidencia to drag him off toward the car park.

"We won't be back until later," Fidencia called over her shoulder. "Don't wait up for us."

"The time has come for the change!" Elfwine said, striking a dramatic pose in front of me. "In accordance with the laws set down by the Court of Divine Blood, I hereby state my intention to claim the position of Cernunnos."

The hellhounds instantly surrounded her, their deep, threatening voices at odds with their somewhat less than awe-inspiring appearance. The druids looked stunned, most of them clustered together in small groups. The Blue Men tightened their hold on me. Stewart struggled to free himself, but his guards were just as adamant he not move.

"Oh, no," Taranis said, a distinct note of worry evident in his voice as he looked over the heads of the crowd.

"It's all right," I told him. "Just a minor challenge to my position. I'll handle Elfwine."

"You'll do nothing but die!" she swore, pushing forward. Or she tried to—the hellhounds tightened their circle and kept her about twelve feet from me.

Taranis slid a quick, dismissive glance my way. "Don't be daft, man. There are much more important threats to our safety than a power-mad druid. Deidre is looking bored and heading this way!"

"Challenge?" Megan asked, looking confused. "I don't understand."

"Of course you don't, you ignorant American—" Elfwine started to say.

"Leave Megan out of this!" I demanded. "This is between you and me, not her."

"Dane, what's going on?" Megan asked, moving closer to me.

"Elfwine has lost her mind."

"You'll pay for that," Elfwine snarled, and tried to lunge at me. The hellhounds growled and snapped, keeping her out of arm's reach.

"She evidently thinks she can destroy me and take over my position," I told Megan, one wary eye toward the druid.

"But you're immortal," Megan repeated.

"Yes, but if I lose the position, I'll die. However, we seem to be at an impasse. Elfwine might have the means to take over my job—that's the dagger, dearling. It has my blood on it. To claim the position, one must mix one's blood with the current position holder. But Elfwine can't do that if she can't get close to me, and the hellhounds, for all their idiotic appearance, are still beasts of the Underworld. They're not going to let her get near me."

"Husband?"

One side of the druid crowd parted as if Taranis's fury goddess was Moses. She wandered over to us, a slight frown between her brows. "There is no more wood to burn. Are we going to eat at the American barbecue soon?"

"Yes, my sweet, just as soon as a few things are settled here," Taranis answered in a soothing tone.

"Are you people all deaf?" Megan spread a glare around at the druids who were gathered around us. "Someone get the paramedics! And police, to arrest that woman. Dane, you really shouldn't be standing. Perhaps if I remove the dagger—very carefully—we can get you into the house where you can rest until the aid unit arrives."

"It's better in than out," I told her.

"Oh, you poor dear, you're delusional. It's probably shock. Please, everyone, clear some space so Dane can lie down. Come and lie here, love, until the paramedics come."

I blinked at Megan, a surge of joy filling me despite the desperate circumstances in which we found ourselves. "Love? You called me love?"

"Did I? It must have slipped out. Here, lie on this shawl thing I was wearing. Oh, your antlers have gone away." She spread out a gauzy white bit of fabric before turning to the crowd with a black scowl.

"What is wrong with you people? Can't you see he's in shock? Would someone *please* call the aid unit!"

"You said 'love.' You can't deny it. You love me, don't you?" I tried to catch Megan's arm as she was about to go into the crowd and snatch a mobile phone from an unsuspecting druid, but the Blue Men kept me firmly in their grip.

Megan turned to look at me with those beautiful eyes, and my heart melted completely.

"Well . . ."

I tried to let her see the love I had for her. "Nothing matters in this world so long as you love me. You make me whole, Megan. With you filling my life, I need nothing else."

"Oh, Dane!" Megan exclaimed, trying to rush to my side. The Blue Men kept her from me, however.

"Oh, Lord," Elfwine said, rolling her eyes. "When I'm Cernunnos, I'm going to appoint a god consort who isn't prone to such romantic drivel."

"Romance makes the world go around," Megan said, her eyes bright on mine.

I wanted to hold her, to kiss her, to merge ourselves body and soul. I wanted everyone and everything to go away, and just let me worship her as was her due.

"I smell barbecue chicken," the fury Deidre said, sniffing the air. "Shouldn't we be eating now? I think we should be eating. Husband, let us go partake of the offering Lord Cernunnos has made for us."

"Erm . . . we can't just yet, my sweet."

"We can't?" Deidre, who had started moving off to where the barbecue had been set up, turned and shot him a look that would have scared several years off my life had it been directed to me. "Why not?"

"That woman there," Taranis said, nodding to Elfwine, "wants Cernunnos's position. He doesn't want to give it up. If she takes the dagger from his chest and mixes the blood on it with her own, she has the right to become the next Cernunnos."

"I don't know exactly how this happened," Megan said to me in a soft voice, glancing nervously at the men holding me. "It really makes absolutely no sense, and is totally unlike me to do this, but I think . . . I'm afraid . . . oh, man, it's all so wrong, but you're right, you're absolutely right. I have fallen in love with you. And I'll be damned if I'm going to let some crackpot druid do me out of a lifetime of having a sexy Irishman fulfilling every wild fantasy I have."

Megan sprang at Elfwine before the druid had an inkling that she was in trouble. The two women went down in a tangle of flailing legs and arms, Elfwine shouting obscenities that were wholly unsuited to a druid.

I twisted a second later, jerking the four men holding me off balance. Megan and Elfwine rolled around on the ground; one moment Megan was on top trying to subdue Elfwine, and a second later their positions were reversed.

I roared my anger, the manifestation bursting to life again as I dragged the four men to the women, intent on rescuing Megan. I disabled one of the Blue

Men, lashing out with my foot to catch another on the knee, sending him to the ground to roll around in a ball of agony.

"I'm coming, my love!" I yelled to Megan as she heaved Elfwine off her.

"No, stay away! She can't get the dagger!" she panted, twisting to the side when Elfwine balled up her fist and tried to punch her in the face.

"Help my goddess," I yelled, trying to dislodge the two remaining druids from my arms. "I command you to help her!"

One of the women ran forward, but two others snatched her back. They stood in a huddled mass, clearly unwilling to go against their leader to help Megan. That infuriated me even more—they were devoted to worshipping me, not Elfwine!

"Are you just going to stand there?" I snarled to Taranis.

He shrugged, and lifted his hands. "You know the laws as well as I do. I cannot interfere in a power struggle."

"Husband? I distinctly saw one of the cooks looking over here in a meaningful way." Deidre's frown was growing blacker, a dangerous look in her eye as she tugged the cloth of Taranis's shirt. "We should go and eat their lovely food. It would be rude of us to do otherwise, and you know how I abhor rudeness to mortals."

"I'm afraid we can't yet, sweet one. Not until this Cernunnos business is settled," he said, nimbly stepping aside as Megan and Elfwine rolled toward him.

Deidre focused her attention on me. I had fallen to the ground, having stumbled over Stewart, and was trying to crawl out from under the two guards, one of whom pinned my legs, the other of whom was trying to knock me out by braining me with his walkie-talkie.

"Lord Cernunnos! My husband says we may not partake of your lovely chicken barbecue sacrifice until you are free. Will this take much longer?"

"Megan!" I yelled as Elfwine got in a particularly good punch. Megan, who had managed to get to her knees, looked at me with dazed eyes for a moment before they rolled back in her head and she toppled over.

"This will end now!" Elfwine shrieked, lunging at me. She jerked the dagger from my chest and staggered to her feet, clutching her side with one hand. She was bloody, dirty, and hunched over as if she couldn't stand straight. "I have it! It is mine! And now I will join the blood with my own and claim the position that is so rightly mine."

I head-butted the nearest Blue Man. "You can eat everything if you stop her," I shouted to Deidre as I crawled to Megan's inert form. "Oh, my dearling, my love. What have I brought upon you?"

"Everything?" Deidre glanced over to the food garden, looked thoughtful for a moment, then turned to Elfwine and smiled. "Good-bye."

There was a burst of blue light, followed by a crash of thunder that shook the earth. The dagger flashed in the torchlight as it spun helplessly to the ground.

Elfwine was gone.

"Megan? Are you all right, my dearling?" I cradled her head and felt wetness on my cheeks as I gazed at her muddied cheeks. Her lip was cut, and there was a swelling around one of her eyes, but as her eyes opened, I could see no signs of serious injury.

"Dane? You antlered up again. That means you're still Cernunnos. She didn't get the dagger?"

"No, my love, she didn't. And now you are mine, and I can give you that wedding night I promised."

"But that's just one night," she said, wincing slightly as she smiled, one hand going to the manifestation. "What else do you have to offer me?"

"How about an eternity of undying devotion, love, and wholesale worship?"

"Hmm. Good, but not good enough."

For a horrible fraction of a second, I thought I'd lost her. The twinkle in her eyes, coupled with her fingers stroking along the manifestation, restored my faith. "You have to bring these to bed sometime. I can't tell you how unbelievably kinky they are."

"You are a strange woman," I said, kissing gently around her bruised mouth. "And I am the luckiest man in history that you're mine."

Epilogue

So this is the Underworld. It looks more like a mall. Is there supposed to be shopping in hell?"

My eyes popped open at the voice. It was a familiar voice, a cherished voice, a voice I hadn't expected to hear upon my awakening. Not here, anyway. "Megan?"

"Right here. Are you okay?" A shadow fell over my face. My vision, always blurry after a transition, slowly focused on much-beloved features. Megan was smiling, but there was worry in her eyes. "Hello, handsome."

"You're here," I said, dazed. "What are you doing here?"

She bent down and pressed a little kiss on my forehead. I tipped my chin up until she laughed and brushed her mouth against mine. "Silly man. Did you really think I was going to leave you alone half the year?"

I sat up. "Possibly. No, I was sure you would come with me."

"Boy, you really do get disoriented transitioning from one world to the other."

I rubbed my head, trying to get my brain to work

properly again. "It's always been that way. You had no problems?"

"Not a one. I woke up a few minutes ago. That was a heck of a going-away ceremony the druids held. Do they indulge in that much pomp and circumstance every year?"

"No, but it's a new group of druids. They're a bit enthusiastic, although I suspect the fact that the previous druid leader was sent to the Akasha—that's limbo—by a hungry fury has something to do with their determination to please us." I looked around. I was sitting on a long green chaise butted up against black-and-white marble walls. "We're in the black palace."

"This is a palace?" Megan got up from where she had been kneeling next to me, turning in a slow circle as she took in the room. "You have a castle and a palace? What about the mall outside? Wait a sec—*is* it a mall, or is it some sort of illusion meant to torment people?"

I went over to the window and looked down at the brightly lit concourse lined with small shops. People bustled in and out of them, laden with packages and bags of all sizes. "I had it redesigned some years ago, after visiting the Galleria in Dallas. There's an ice rink at the far end, theaters on the west side for movies and live shows, an extensive library on the second floor, bowling, a fitness center with an Olympic-size pool, miniature golf on the lower level, a health spa on the mezzanine, and a petting zoo next to the palace. If you lean out and look to your left, you can see the llama enclosure."

Megan looked and nodded, a bemused expression on her face. "Llamas."

"I'm particularly pleased with the food court, which is located on the east side beyond the butterfly solarium—"

Megan grabbed my arm, looking incredulous. "In *hell*?"

I took her hands and kissed each finger. "The Underworld is not hell, Megan. That would be Abaddon. The Underworld is a way station for people on their way for judgment. I should have explained it better earlier, but we've been so busy the last four months traveling, I didn't remember."

"I vaguely remember your telling me it's a holding area." She blinked a couple of times. "But a holding area with llamas and shopping?"

"Yes, that's it exactly. When some mortals die, their spirits come to the Underworld. There they prepare for the journey to wherever it is they are going. Some go to the Court of Divine Blood or Summerland, others go to Abaddon, still others are sent to the Akasha—it depends on the judgment."

She looked like she was going to ask a question, then shook her head. "I think I'm going to let all that go, since it makes sense in an extremely convoluted way. So you're in charge of all these people who are running around having massages in the day spa, and petting llamas, and shopping until they drop?"

"For six months out of the year, yes. It's not a strenuous job, my love. I will have plenty of time to devote to your happiness."

"So long as we're together, I'll be happy. And this will let me prepare for the next six months of travel, once we get back to reality again."

I slid my arms around her waist, drinking in her warmth and scent and the essence that was Megan. "I command only one of the twelve hours in the Underworld; you may find it interesting to visit the others. Perhaps even write about your visits to them. You know, sort of a Guide to the Underworld?"

Megan laughed and slid out of my arms, peeling off her shirt. "That sounds like great fun. But first . . . it's been a whole day since you made love to me, and I'm feeling sorely neglected."

"We certainly can't have that," I agreed, flashing her a leer as I started toward the door.

"Dane?" In the middle of removing her trousers, she gave me a curious glance. "Where are you going?"

I upped the leer a few notches. "I'm going to have a quick chat with a televangelist."

She glanced from the large bed in the corner to me. "*Now*? Why would you want to talk to a televangelist?"

"Because it will make me angry." I touched my forehead. "*Very* angry."

She gave a delighted squeal and jumped onto the bed, striking a seductive pose. "I'll be ready and waiting for your horny self."

"In spades," I said, my heart alight with love and happiness as I went to find someone to enrage me.

Norse
Truly

One

"Brynna? Är du där?"

Eek! Aunt Agda had found me. I hurriedly stomped out the cigarette I'd just lit and sidled out from behind the woodshed. "Um . . . yeah, I was just . . . looking for gnomes."

"Gnomes? Vättar?"

"Yeah, Rolf told me there were gnomes in the bottom of the garden." My smile was met with a stony look of disbelief. My cousin Rolf—really a second or third cousin some undeterminable number of times removed—was four years old and still sucked his thumb when he got sleepy. "Maybe he's not what you'd call a go-to source for Nordic lore, but I was out admiring the garden and thought what the heck! I might as well look for gnomes."

"The food is now done," Aunt Agda said, narrowing her eyes as she delicately sniffed the air. "You were smoking?"

"Me? Of course not; you know I quit last week. I'm on the patch." A nervous giggled slipped out before I could stop it. I wasn't outright lying—I'd just gotten the cigarette lit and hadn't yet taken a drag on it when Aunt Agda tracked me down. I wondered for a moment if Rolf had turned me in, since he'd seen me sneak the package of ciggies out of my purse, but I dismissed the idea. No doubt it was one of the older, more nosy relatives who'd ratted me out to Aunt Agda.

"Var är sås-sleven, moster? Ah, Brynna, there you are! We were wondering where you'd disappeared to. I was just asking Aunt Agda where the gravy ladle is. 'Sås-sleven' is gravy ladle, and 'moster,' you know, means aunt." Cousin Paul beamed at me. He was a good fifteen years older than me, and his receding hairline was now touched with gray, but his warm brown eyes danced with pleasure. I'd met him only once before, when I was fourteen and my parents brought me to Sweden to spend the summer with their respective families. He'd tried to teach me Swedish then, too.

"She says she was looking for gnomes," Aunt Agda said with a disbelieving look at me before returning to the house.

"Gnomes?" Paul asked, his brow wrinkling slightly. "The word for gnomes is 'vättar.' "

"So I gathered. Can you tell me why you and all the other younger cousins speak absolutely flawless English, when I can't remember more than 'hello' and 'good-bye' in Swedish?"

"It's our superior schooling," he said, trying to look modest at my praise. "I've heard that American schools don't even *offer* to teach Swedish."

"A definite lack in the educational system, I agree. But the least you could do is have an accent."

"I will try to pick up an accent if you try to learn

a few more words of Swedish, Brynna. It is the language of your ancestors."

"I would, but I'm just so rotten at languages.
Even my folks gave up on teaching me." I walked up
the few stairs to the wide, covered veranda that ran
around three sides of the old farmhouse.

Paul delicately sniffed the air.

"Oh, for heaven's sake . . . I didn't smoke! I didn't
do more than light it. I swear, Aunt Agda is part
bloodhound," I grumbled. I pulled my leather jacket
off and reached around to my back to make sure
the nicotine patch was still attached to my skin.
"I think this patch is defective; it's not doing anything to relieve cravings. Maybe I should put another
one on."

"I don't think it would be wise to add another.
Surely the doctors have measured most carefully the
amount needed to quit smoking. To tamper with that
might lead to—ja, Maja?"

Paul's wife, Maja, a petite woman with dimples
that always seemed to be present, flashed a smile at
me and said something through the screen door.

"Oh, they found the gravy ladle. Excellent! This
means we may now proceed in to supper." Paul
opened the screen door and held it for me. "It should
be very good. Roast venison!"

"Er . . ." I stopped in front of the coat rack. Rolf,
who had been sliding around the floor of the entryway on his back making motorboat noises, leaped
up and ran to me, getting both my knees in a choke
hold. "Paul, you know that I'm a vegetarian—"

He laughed. "Yes, I know. My mother prepared a quiche just for you."

"Oh, thank you. I've had enough family lectures about the sins of smoking, the folly of being unmarried at thirty-three, and the crime of not visiting family enough, not to mention the dangers of living in the U.S. The last thing I need is another conversation about my choice of diet. Rolf, no! That's not candy!"

Rolf squealed like a monkey when I tried to grab the package of cigarettes that had fallen out of my jacket pocket. Clutching his prize to his chest, he raced toward the main living room with me in hot pursuit. The room was empty, since the call to dinner had gone out, but it was an obstacle course of furniture and folding chairs. I almost had him when he slowed down to hurdle an ottoman, but the little rat was faster than I was and dashed off to the dining room before I could get a grip on him.

"Oh, hell," I said, skidding to a stop outside the double doors that led to the large dining room. "Now I'm done for."

"Yes, yes you are," Paul said cheerfully, coming up behind me to give me a friendly pat on the shoulder. "You shouldn't have involved Rolf in your subterfuge."

"I didn't, he involved himself! And now all the aunts are going to see the cigarettes, and the smoking lectures will start all over again. I think I'll go to bed."

"Brynna?" My aunt Pia, Paul's mother, emerged from the steamy depths of the kitchen, where a good

95 percent of the females in my family had been cooking up a meal for the twenty-four family members
who had descended upon the house for my great-
grandmother's one-hundredth birthday. "Oh, good,
there you are. Supper is ready, dear. Paul, we have run
out of cream, and we must have it for the dessert."

I strained my ears to listen to the murmur of conversation heard through the dining room doors. I
could have sworn I heard Rolf's high-pitched excited
tone.

"I'll go to the store," Paul answered in a wearied
tone, reaching into his pocket for his car keys. "For
the third time today. I do wish you ladies would
make a list of everything, rather than making me go
out for each item."

A muffled shriek sounded from the dining room.
Damn Rolf and his light fingers.

"We are as organized as is humanly possible, given
the circumstances. Brynna, Moster Agda is calling for
you."

Shouting was more like it. No doubt she'd seen
Rolf's prize. I'd made a point of telling everyone when
I arrived a week before that I was giving up smoking,
and under no circumstances was I to be near cigarettes—something the entire (nonsmoking, drat them
all) family embraced, to the point of watching me suspiciously each time I stepped outdoors.

What I needed was a little time away from everyone, out of the microscope that the farm had
become with so many family members watching
my every move. For the millionth time, I wished I'd

gone with my parents on their trip to Africa rather than spending a month visiting family, but at the time, a lovely Swedish July getting to know my relatives seemed to outweigh the idea of war-torn refugee camps. As doctors, my parents had the ability to help the injured and sick, but I knew from prior experience that the skills garnered in my job as a secretary to an insurance salesman were pretty much worth squat when it came to dysentery, gunshot wounds, and the myriad other afflictions suffered by refugees.

"Brynna?" Pia's gentle voice brought me back. "I believe Agda wants you."

I snatched the keys from Paul's hand and tossed him a quick "I'll go to the store for you, Paul. You go in and have dinner."

"Do you know where it is?" he asked, following me to the door.

"Sure, I was there yesterday with Thor." Paul's younger brother had visited for the weekend, returning home after only two days with the family, the lucky duck. "I know exactly where it is. I'll be back in a flash." I gave a quick wave and dashed out to Paul's car.

As I drove down the narrow path that led from the farm to the road, I didn't wonder why my one-hundred-year-old great-grandmother Hildigunn Dahl continued to live in a house that was older than her, one filled with steps that had to be hard on arthritic hips. Located on the eastern coast of Sweden, halfway between the northern and southern tips, the Medelpad region was absolutely breathtaking. I'd already fallen in love with the Indalsälven River which came out of the north, the wild, rugged coastline, and the gorgeous heavily forested hills. Momo Hildi ("Momo" is Swedish for "Granny") had been born in this farmhouse, where she lived with her daughter, my somewhat scary Aunt Agda, and Agda's son and his family.

The road wound alongside the coast as I drove toward the town, whistling a happy "I've escaped" song.

My favorite area was coming up, a tiny stretch where the road sat twenty or so feet above an isolated, rocky beach. The waves pounded on the shore with ferocity, terns wheeling overhead while little shorebirds with flashing legs ran along the sodden sand and rocks. It was wild and untamed, and my heart rose at each sight of the area. I had begged Paul the day before to stop so that I could explore the bit of beach, but he muttered something about it having a bad reputation, and drove on.

"Bad reputation? What do you mean?" I had asked, craning my head as we drove past the beach.

"No one goes there. Even the fishermen give that stretch a wide berth. There's a prettier area for you to go to a few kilometers to the north. I'll take you there one of these days."

"I don't want to go to a pretty area. I want to see this part of the coast. It's so . . . oh, I don't know, primitive, I guess. You can practically see the Viking longboats setting out to sea."

Paul jerked, sending the car into the opposite lane. An oncoming driver slammed on his brakes. Paul swore to himself and gave an apologetic wave as we returned to our lane, then slipped me an odd look.

"What?" I asked, confused by both his reaction and the questioning look.

The road curved away from the shore and back into the dense woodland, and I sat back with a sigh of disappointment.

"You said Viking longboats."

"Yeah, so?"

He slid me another quick look. "It is said that ghosts haunt that area of the coast."

I nearly laughed at the thought of my stodgy cousin believing in anything so ridiculous. "Viking ghosts in longboats?"

He nodded, his eyes on the road. "So it is said. The area is considered to be bad luck."

That conversation came to my mind as I drove down the stretch of road that afforded such an excellent view of the (supposedly haunted) beach. I was just scanning the shoulders for a place to pull off the road, when a deer suddenly ran in front of me.

"Gah!" I slammed my foot down on the brake, jerking the car to the left, and the car skidded off the pavement, and over the side of the cliff. I screamed and threw my hands up over my head, sure I was about to meet my end. The car rocked and bucked as it hurtled down the slope to the rocky shore, headed straight for the water. The airbag exploded as the car slammed into the surf, spun a full circle, then crashed into a sharp boulder that jutted up out of the sea like a dagger's point.

A dark, spinning nothing sucked me in, until the world I knew was utterly extinguished.

Two

" . . . don't normally like redheads, but this one is pretty. I bet her hair is curly when it's dry. I wonder what color her eyes are?"

The man's voice drifted through the hazy darkness that surrounded me in a soft, warm cocoon that bobbed ever so gently.

"It's her nipples I wonder about. Don't redheads have pink ones?"

"You have nipples on the mind, Torsten," the first man said. I frowned, trying to remember something important, but it skittered away. "There's more to a woman than her breasts."

"Breasts are good," said a third man with a very deep voice. I liked the first speaker's voice the best; it had a rich timbre that made me feel all warm and fuzzy inside.

"I don't dispute the importance of breasts, I simply mention that there is more to enjoy on a woman than just her breasts. All things considered . . . I'll go with pink."

Several male voices murmured their agreement.

The darkness that enveloped me shifted a little, and I frowned as I realized it was rocking slightly.

"Look, she's scowling. I guess she's not dead," said

a softer voice, with a heavy accent that didn't sound quite Swedish.

"Of course she's not dead," said the good voice. Its accent was softer, more sing-song than the other one. "She's a Valkyrie. She just got knocked out when she crashed into the sea."

Crash? Valkyries? Was I dreaming?

"Thank God for . . . what are those called?"

"Airbags."

Airbags? Oh my God, I wasn't dreaming! In a rush, the plunge off the cliff came back to me, filling me with adrenaline.

"What the hell?" I shouted, my eyes popping open. I stared in bewilderment at the four male faces that peered down at me in concern. All of them were bearded except one young man; all had long hair.

"Blue eyes," the nice voice said with satisfaction.

"It's good to see you awake." One of the faces beamed down at me. "Let's hope for no brain damage."

"Brain damage?" I reached up to touch my forehead, and was met by a warm, solid obstacle. I tilted my head back and discovered a fifth face, one that was upside down. It was by far the nicest of all the faces, with a short, reddish-blond beard covering a strong jaw, intriguing hazel eyes that were filled with concern, and a long, thin nose that bore a scar midway down, where an obvious break had sent the bone slightly off center. For some reason, the sight of his crooked nose made my stomach tighten pleasurably. "I don't have brain damage, do I?"

"No," the man told me. I realized then that I was lying in his lap, and it was his stomach my hand had run into while I was trying to feel my head. "You are probably a bit confused, though. Does anything hurt? We looked at your limbs but didn't see any obvious breaks."

I sent out a query to my arms and legs and was pleased with the results—although my head hurt, everything else seemed to be fine. "I think . . . I think I'm okay. I'd like to sit up."

The man helped me up to a sitting position.

"What am I doing in a boat?" I stared around me in stunned surprise. I was sitting on the wooden floor of a boat, surrounded by five men clad in odd garments of leather and wool, with occasional bits of fur poking through, as if they were wearing historical garb. I blinked a couple of times, hoping my vision would clear. "And why were you guys speaking in English instead of Swedish?"

"Your Volvo crashed into the water. You were going to drown, so Alrik rescued you. Your passport was in your pocket, so we knew you were American," the man with the very deep voice said. He had a round face, a dark beard and hair, and even darker eyes.

"I am Alrik Sigurdsson," the man who had been holding me said. He looked even more handsome right-side up, although he, too, was clad in a linen tunic and wool pants with leather leggings.

"Are you guys some sort of reenactors?" Perhaps I'd stumbled across a group of history enthusiasts, or a movie set?

"Reenactors?" The man named Alrik frowned and glanced at the others.

"Yeah, you know, those people who really get into history and reproduce old battles and things, right down to the costumes and weapons."

Alrik's frown cleared. "No. We are the real thing."

I laughed. "Yeah, sure you are." None of the men laughed with me. "You're not . . . er . . . serious, are you?"

"Another unbeliever," one of the men behind me said. I turned to look at him. He had hair almost as red as my own. He shook his head. "We're going to have to show her."

"Aye," Alrik said, getting to his feet and stepping over me to join the other four men. The boat rocked slightly at his movements, causing me to gasp and clutch the side nearest me.

"A landsman, too," the man with the round face said, looking disappointed.

I glanced toward the shore, trying to calculate how far out we were, and whether, if I jumped overboard, I'd be able to make it to solid land before one of these very strange men could reach me.

"You won't make it," Alrik said, correctly reading my thoughts. "We're very fast swimmers."

"Aye, we are," said a blue-eyed man. The others nodded. "We've had centuries to practice."

"Centuries?" I asked, scooching back a couple of feet. It was odd that this boat didn't have any benches on it. I glanced around, noticing even more abnormalities—a stack of oars in the center, alongside a raised platform from which the mast rose, but no oarlocks. Instead, holes had been cut into the sides of the ship. I looked down, gently touching an iron rivet that had been pounded deep into the wood of the ship. I turned to look behind me, my eyes widening at the sight of a prow that rose at least six feet into the air, topped with an intricately carved dragon head. "This is a longboat. A replica Viking longboat?"

"Not a replica at all. We'd best show her, lads," Alrik said, standing at the back of the boat. Despite my initial concern that we'd tip over if people moved around too much, the boat seemed remarkably stable. It was broad at the bottom, what they called a shallow draft, while the ends of the ship rose high fore and aft. Stacked neatly at intervals were wooden barrels, crates, and what looked to be iron-bound sea chests. The men stood as I carefully got to my feet. I noticed with disgust that they looked remarkably at ease, and didn't cling to the side as I did.

"Show me what?"

"That is Bardi," Alrik answered, nodding at the dark-haired, deep-voiced man.

"Hello," I said politely. "I'm Brynna Lund."

He put his hand on his chest, and bowed. "It is a pleasure to meet you."

Before I could do so much as blink, he disappeared. My jaw sagged a little as I looked in confusion to Alrik.

"And that is Bardi's cousin, Grim," he said, gesturing toward another dark-haired man, whose long beard had been split into two and braided.

"Grim?"

"Aye," he said, then he, too, simply disappeared from sight.

I couldn't help myself. I rubbed my eyes, but when I opened them, there were only three men remaining. "So . . . you're a magician? A historical reenacting magician's troupe? Or wait—this isn't the Swedish version of *Candid Camera*, is it?"

"Jon is the redhead," was all Alrik said.

Jon stepped forward, took my hand, and kissed my fingers. Then he blinked out like someone had turned off a switch.

"Okay," I said slowly, backing up a step. "Um. You know, I think I really need to be running along now."

"I'm Torsten," a white-blond man said, grinning at me with such delight that my lips twitched in response. "I am very pleased you have come to save us. The last Valkyrie we had was not nearly so pretty."

"Thank you. I think," I said, watching him closely. *Valkyrie?*

His grin increased; then suddenly it was gone . . . along with the rest of him.

I looked to the last man remaining. Alrik stood with his arms over his chest, his legs braced wide. A sudden wind had the waves moving restlessly, which made the boat shift. I held firm to the side, but Alrik moved with the boat with the ease of one who's spent his life on the water.

"So. As I see it, there are two possibilities—either I've gone insane, or I hit my head during the car crash and I'm being raced to the nearest hospital for immediate brain surgery, while hallucinating this very strange experience. Are you the aid unit person, or the brain surgeon that I've somehow incorporated into my fantasy?"

He walked forward until he stood right in front of me, his eyes an interesting mix of greens, browns, and gray that seemed to shimmer and shift with his expression. "I am Alrik Sigurdsson, as I have told you. I was born midsummer in the year 719 and died in 758."

"You . . . died?" I stopped admiring his eyes and gawked for a moment.

"In a manner of speaking." He grasped my shoulders with both hands, leaning in to me until his breath brushed my face. For one wild moment, I thought he was going to kiss me. What bothered me was how much I wanted him to do just that. "We're cursed men, Brynna Lund. And we need your help."

He was gone before I could so much as scream. One moment he was there, the next he wasn't. I looked wildly around the now empty ship, waving my hands through the spot where just a second before Alrik had stood. I could still feel the warmth of his hands on my shoulders—how could he disappear like that?

"This has to be a trick," I said, making my way down the boat by dint of clutching the side. I waved my free hand through the air, hoping to find . . . I don't know what. "This is ridiculous. One minute I was driving down the road, and the next I'm on a longboat with people who think they're Viking ghosts. This sort of thing simply does not happen!"

"It does, you know," a voice said behind me. I spun around, but there was no one there.

"Over here," another one said. Bardi popped into view.

I picked up a small hatchet that had been lying on top of a chest, and pointed it at him. "Okay, fun and games are over—"

He disappeared before I finished the sentence.

"Alrik was cursed by a witch, you see. She cursed all of us, too. We've been in this boat ever since then," red-headed Jon said as he appeared next to me.

"You're trying to drive me insane, aren't you?" I asked him.

"No. We want you to save us," he answered.

I reached toward him and his form dissolved into a vague, milky shape, as if he was hidden behind several layers of nearly transparent cloth. The ax I held passed effortlessly through him, causing the hairs on my arm to stand on end.

"You're a Valkyrie, Brynna. You can help us. You can take us to Valhöll," Alrik said from behind me.

I whipped around, narrowing my eyes at him. This wasn't happening to me. It just wasn't possible! I marched forward toward the Alrik hallucination, clutching the ax tightly, sure I would walk right through his image.

"Oof!" I said as I bumped into him. He grabbed my arms to keep me from falling, our bodies so close I could feel the heat of him through my thin linen shirt. His head dipped a tiny bit until his mouth was less than an inch from mine, those gorgeous eyes of his going more gray than hazel. "You're *real*?"

"Very much so. Please help us, Brynna. Please take us to Valhöll."

His lips brushed mine as he spoke, starting a burn deep inside me. I had an almost overwhelming desire to tilt my head up just a fraction of an inch, so his mouth would be pressed fully against mine, but a shred of dignity kept me from doing so. I never kissed men I had just met! Especially not ones who had been dead for almost thirteen hundred years. My mind did a double take at the fact that I was so willing to believe Alrik. It had to be an illusion of some sort. Didn't it?

I reached up with both hands and grasped his wrists firmly. He wore gold metal bands on each one, but the flesh beneath them was warm and silky over steel muscles. "Now disappear," I said, tightening my grip slightly.

"As you wish." His lips brushed mine again as he spoke; then he leaned forward in a kiss that damn near burned my mouth, it was so hot.

I opened my mouth to tell him that I wasn't a naïve little girl to be seduced, but before I could draw in a breath to speak, he was gone, simply melting before my astonished eyes . . . and regretful lips.

My hands were in midair, holding nothing where a moment before Alrik's wrists had been. I could still taste him on my lips, a faintly sweet, earthy taste, like that of the mead I'd once had at a Renaissance Faire.

"Oh dear God," I said softly, my hands dropping to my sides as I absorbed the impossible fact that I'd just been kissed by the most incredibly sexy man I'd ever met . . . and he had been dead for more than a thousand years.

Three

Nope. Not buying it. I'm willing to admit that you guys are . . . er . . ."

"Ghosts," Jon said.

"I'm sure the politically correct term is living impaired. I'll concede that you're not alive, because I prefer to go with that reality rather than to assume I've gone so very insane there will be no going back for me. But this bit about my being a Valkyrie? Nuh-uh. I'm a secretary to an insurance salesman. I live with two cats and a deranged parakeet. I drink eight glasses of water a day. I've had only three boyfriends, none of whom lasted more than six months. I've never had a traffic ticket and don't like rap music. I'm probably the most white bread, boring person in the world—in short, I could not be less Valkyrie-like if I tried."

All five ghosts were back now, sitting or standing around where I was perched on top of a barrel. The longboat seemed to drift aimlessly, her sails down, the steering paddle in the back raised out of the water.

"We know a Valkyrie when we see one," Jon said.

"How many have you seen?" I couldn't help but ask.

"Two, including you. The other one refused to help us. You're our only hope now."

"We'll get back to that point, if you don't mind. Right now I'm just trying to get a handle on who you guys are. You said you were cursed by a witch?"

"Alrik was," Torsten answered, sending the handsome Viking a look of pride. "He crossed her in love."

"I didn't cross anyone in love," Alrik answered, leaning against the mast. "I simply didn't pledge her my heart."

"Alrik always had women after him," Torsten told me in a confidential voice. "He is a ladies' man, you see."

"Yes, I can see that," I said, eyeing the tall Viking.

Alrik scowled at his friend. "Don't exaggerate. I was no different from any other man."

"He had many women," Torsten continued with a grin.

"No more than you had."

"He had at least five times as many as we had," Bardi corrected, and I got the distinct feeling the men were enjoying ragging Alrik.

"Aye, he did," Grim agreed. "They used to follow him around town whenever we were ashore, just like puppies."

"Bah!" Alrik snorted, and stomped over to the other side of the ship.

"So, he was a tomcat on the prowl who had a one-night fling with a witch, and she decided to end his immoral ways?"

"No," Alrik answered, crossing his arms over his

chest and glaring at me. "She decided that I needed to be punished for the fact that I wasn't in love with her, and cursed me to an eternity of sailing the shore until the day that I changed my mind. Unfortunately, these four lunatics spoke up against her, and she cursed them, as well."

I looked at all of them. "You guys are cursed to sail around in this ship until Alrik falls in love with a witch?"

They nodded.

"You don't get to ever go ashore?"

"No."

"Ouch." I turned my attention back to the man in question. "But that doesn't make sense. If this was thirteen hundred years ago, how were you supposed to fall in love with her after she cursed you? Surely she was dead forty or so years later?"

"She was immortal too," Alrik said. "I didn't know Hilda was a witch when I met her. She seemed like any other woman, until I tried to leave the next morning."

"Wow," I said, imagining what it would be like to be in their shoes. "With no hope of an end in sight? That's a high price to pay just for a little nooky. Did you ever . . . er . . . think about going along with her, just to break the curse?"

Alrik looked vaguely offended. "That would be wrong! I am not in love with her, nor will I ever be. But that does not matter now."

"It doesn't?"

"No." A smile came to his lips, and I felt my knees

go a bit weak at it. Torsten was pretty darned handsome in a white-blond Scandinavian way, but Alrik, with his red-gold hair, and that manly stubble that made little butterflies pop up in my stomach, was downright breathtaking. And when he smiled . . . well, let's just say the effect was damn near overwhelming.

Until he spoke, that is. "No, it doesn't matter—because now we have you. You offer us the one way to break the curse: You must summon us to Valhöll."

My mind, busy fantasizing about what he looked like without those leather pants and linen shirt, ground to a halt. I sighed. "We're back to that Valkyrie thing again, aren't we? I'm sorry, Alrik, I wish I could help you, I really do, but it's impossible. I'm just not a Valkyrie."

"Yes, you are."

"I think I'd know if I was some warrior chick who runs around raising dead guys! I'm sorry to disillusion you, but you've got the wrong woman. Oh, man, I need a smoke. I don't suppose any of you have any?"

"A smoke?" Bardi frowned. "A smoked what? Fish?"

"No, no, a cigarette."

"Ah, cigarette!" Torsten said, nodding his head at me.

I beamed at him. "Can I bum one off you? I'm trying to quit, but I think this qualifies as an emergency."

"What is this cigarette?" Alrik asked, eyeing me suspiciously. "Is it a weapon?"

"You remember cigarette," Torsten said to his

buddy. "We saw a documentary about lung cancer, and the effect of . . . what was it called?"

Grim cleared his throat. "Passive smoking. Very bad. It is illegal to smoke in public places in Sweden."

The men all nodded, then turned to look at me.

"Smoking kills," Alrik said in that smug tone that nonsmokers have. I would have hackled up at that, but there was something in his lovely, changeable eyes that made me think he was speaking in all sincerity, and that he really did believe what he said.

It occurred to me then that not only did they speak extremely good English for thousand-year-old ghosts, but they had more than a passing familiarity with contemporary society. "How do you guys know about documentaries and passive smoking and all that if you've been on this boat for the last thirteen hundred years?"

"Down the coast near town, an old man lives in a house that sits over the water. He's been there for sixty years—now his son lives there. We met him when we were hunting for food, and he has given us much that we could not get easily—magazines and newspapers—"

". . . toilet paper, and medicines," interrupted Bardi.

"Better arrows, and more sharpening stones," added Grim.

Torsten grinned. "Big Macs and fries!"

They all murmured at that.

"We especially liked the Big Macs," Bardi acknowledged.

"The old man's son, Tomas, has a television that he sets up so we can see. We learned English, French, and Italian from television university courses."

"Wow, I'm impressed. I can't even pick up a few words of Swedish, and you guys have learned three other languages."

"We've had many years to learn," Bardi said kindly.

"True." I glanced at my watch. "Well, this has been fascinating, but my family is waiting and I'd better be getting on my way. Can you pull in to shore so I can get off?"

"Yes, it is best we do this now," Alrik agreed, nodding toward the men.

I have to admit I was a bit surprised by his attitude—for some reason, I thought I might have a little difficulty getting him to release me, what with him believing I was his key to getting to Valhalla. Surprised as I was by that, I was more so by the actions of the Vikings. Rather than put out the oars and send the boat to shore, they all hurried to various chests, whipping out bits of animal skins, and piling them high with assorted belongings.

Before you could say "delusional Viking ghosts," they were gathered around me, each bearing as many of the now bound skins as they could carry.

"We are ready," Alrik said, giving me an expectant look.

"Um . . . ready for what?"

"For you to summon us to Valhöll."

"Look, I already said . . ." I stopped, knowing that

they weren't going to listen to me. "You're not going to let me go, are you?"

"Not before you take us to Valhöll, no," Alrik said, his mouth a thin line. "We have been patient, Brynna. We are worthy of the halls of Odin. We will not shame you."

I opened my mouth to tell them I had no doubt that as warriors they were the pick of the litter, but instead, a self-preservation instinct kicked in, and I threw myself over the side of the boat.

Their shouts were somewhat drowned in the splashing I made as I swam for shore. Another splash followed, and I took a quick glance over my shoulder.

That was a mistake. That, and not believing the Vikings when they said they had centuries to practice swimming. It took Alrik just a few powerful strokes before he caught up with me, grabbing my foot and jerking me backward until he had both arms wrapped around me.

"I thought you said you couldn't leave the ship!" I sputtered, spitting out a mouthful of seawater.

His eyes were now more gray than hazel, matching the color of the water around us. I spent a moment in awe about the ability of his irises to change before I realized that now was not the time to be admiring the eyes of a man who could easily drown me if he so chose. "No, I can leave the boat. I cannot go on land."

"What happens if you do?" I asked, unable to quell my rampant curiosity. Or maybe I just liked to be held by him, even if it was in the middle of the cold North Sea.

"It is impossible. The only way I can touch land is to be summoned by a Valkyrie."

"Ah."

"Why do you not wish to summon us to Valhöll? Do you wish payment of some sort? We have gold; we will pay you." The water glistened on his beard stubble. I wanted badly to lick it off.

"I said I would help you if I could. But I can't!"

"You can. You must."

"Okay, I tell you what. You let me go, and I'll give it a shot, all right?"

His lips narrowed. "You will not trick me again? You will not try to escape?"

I had every intention of doing just that . . . until I saw the utter desperation in his eyes. It touched something inside of me, some unknown need I had to help him. "I'll do everything in my power to break this curse."

"Swear it," he said, his face disturbingly close to mine. I started thinking again about that quick kiss he'd give me before, and how much I wanted to repeat the experience.

"I swear I'll do everything I can to help you. But you need to prepare yourself for the ugly reality that I'm not what you think I am."

His eyes darkened a little before his head dipped, and once again I was the recipient of the hottest kiss I'd ever felt. I knew what sort of picture it made— by now I was clinging to his shoulders, both of us treading water in a sea that was growing increasingly cold with each second I spent in it. I knew that

it was absolutely insane to let him kiss me in such
a manner, his tongue demanding entrance only to
swoop around my mouth like it owned the place.
I knew it was utterly and completely crazy to find
myself becoming more and more aroused by a man
I'd just met—a *ghost* I'd just met. All those thoughts
swirled around my brain, but none of them mattered. I kissed Alrik back, making him groan in the
back of his throat when I suckled his tongue. He still
tasted like mead, sweet and rich. His mouth was so
hot, my toenails were steaming by the time he broke
it off.

"I can see why the women followed you around
like puppies," I said, trying to drag my mind from its
demand that I kiss him again.

"No woman has ever followed me," he said, looking at my lips. "Nor has any of them offered to save
me. You alone have done that."

I pushed against him. Reluctantly—or so it
seemed to me—his arms relaxed and let me slip from
his grip. I swam backward toward the shore, my lips
tingling, my blood burning, and deep, inner parts of
me on full red alert. "Alrik, I really would help you if
I could, but I just don't think this is going to work."

His face bobbed above the gray water. "I have
faith in you, Brynna."

My feet touched land. I was safe, on solid ground
where Alrik couldn't get me. I could simply turn my
back on him and run up the rocky beach to the road.
Someone was bound to come along looking for me.
All I had to do was leave.

I scrambled out of the water and stood on the shore, water pouring off me. "How do you know I won't just leave you?" I yelled.

Even at a distance of sixty or so feet, I could see him raise his eyebrows. "You swore to help us."

I wrung out my shirt as best I could, glancing behind him to the longboat filled with hopeful Vikings. I couldn't turn my back on them, yet I was completely out of my depths with all this Valkyrie talk. Somehow, I'd have to find someone who knew something about Viking history. Perhaps Momo Hildi could help—my mother had urged me for years to talk to my great-grandmother, since Momo Hildi was extremely well versed in Swedish history. "Yes, and I meant it. I think I know someone who might be able to help. She's really old and frail, though, so I won't be able to bring her to see you."

"Summon me," Alrik said.

"I don't even know where Valhalla is supposed to be," I said, slapping my hands on my wet jeans. "How can I summon you there?"

"You must try," he insisted.

"Boy, you really are the most stubborn Viking ghost I've ever met. . . . Fine, you want me to summon you? Alrik Sigurdsson, I summon you."

It was on my lips to explain about my momo when he disappeared from the water . . . and reappeared directly in front of me.

The men on the boat cheered as Alrik looked down at his feet in surprise, then let loose with a whoop of joy that made my ears ring. That was forgotten quickly as he wrapped both arms around me and lifted me, swinging me in a circle. "I knew I couldn't be wrong about you," he said, before planting yet another hot, wet kiss on me.

I was still more than a little bemused by the kiss when he demanded I summon the men. In less than a minute, I was surrounded by dancing, laughing, and singing Viking ghosts.

"I don't understand," I told Alrik as he accepted a couple of furry bundles from Bardi. "I just don't understand. Wouldn't I know if I was a Valkyrie? Wouldn't someone have told me? Don't I need a certificate or something to be one?"

"Now you can take us to Valhöll," Jon said, dancing past me.

"Yes," Alrik said, brushing a strand of wet hair off my cheekbone. The touch of his hand sent a little zing of heat through me. He took a step closer, his lips curving slightly. "You can take us to Valhöll. You will visit me there frequently, I hope. I have much . . . *gratitude* . . . to show you."

It was impossible to miss the innuendo.

"You may be Mr. Sexy Ghost and all that, but what makes you think I'm at all interested in you in that way?"

His thumb brushed against my lower lip. I opened my mouth and bit it.

"Oh, all right, I'll visit you in Valhalla, assuming someone tells me how to get you there. But I refuse to run after you like a puppy. And just so you know—I don't share!"

"Possessive, eh?" He smiled, damn him. "Normally I dislike that, but with you . . ."

The rest of his sentence was cut short by the sound of a car honking, and my name being called down from the road. I turned to see my cousin Paul at the wheel of my aunt's car. I waved back at him and yelled that I'd be right there.

"There's a town a few miles away," I started to say, but Alrik interrupted.

"We will go with you."

"I'm staying with my family here," I explained. "There's not a whole lot of room. I'm sleeping on the porch in a sleeping bag, so although I'd like to bring you home with me—God knows what I'd say to the family—it's not going to be possible."

Alrik shook his head, and took my hand in a firm grip. "You summoned us. We are now bound to you, until you take us to Valhöll. We will come with you."

"But—"

"Where you go, so do we. That is all there is to it."

"But—"

In the end, all my explaining did no good. Every last man of them insisted that since I had summoned them to me, they were bound to me. Good or bad, I was stuck with five extremely virile Vikings.

There were women who would pay good money to be in my shoes, I thought as I marched my little gang of ghosts up the rocky cliffside to the road where Paul waited. And as I slid a little glance to

Alrik, still holding my hand, I had to admit that there were worse things to be bound to.

The ride back to Momo Hildi's took five times as long as normal because of the explanations Paul demanded. At first he threatened to call the police and have them haul off what he perceived as ruffians. Once the men convinced him that they were who they were, and he absorbed the fact that I wasn't what I appeared to be, he shook his head and said he always knew nothing good would come of my parents' leaving the homeland.

Telling him his car was fifteen feet underwater was another subject, one that was extremely painful for several minutes. Eventually Paul got the worst of the swearing out of his system.

"You're going to have to tell my insurance company what happened," he muttered, giving the water a forlorn look before taking the wheel of Aunt Agda's car.

I was still trying to work out how on earth I was going to explain the deer and five dead Vikings to an insurance company when we arrived back at the farmhouse.

"You're going to have to explain this to Moster Agda, as well," Paul warned in an undertone as I climbed off Alrik's lap, where I'd been forced to sit due to shortage of space in the car (and if you think I was going to complain about that, you're crazy).

"You're older, you should do it," I answered in a craven attempt to get out of what was sure to be an unpleasant task.

He shook his head, and said cryptically, "No, you must do it. You're female."

"But— Aw, hell."

"That is your family, I assume?" Alrik asked, looking with interest toward the crowd of people milling around the wrap-around veranda. In the center, Aunt Agda was helping a tiny, doubled-up form to a chair. Everyone froze when they saw all the Vikings get out of the car.

"Yeah. Looks like it's Momo Hildi's daily half hour to sit outside. Oy vey. Well, I just hope she knows something about Valhalla."

Alrik smiled at me, which made me stumble. He grabbed my hand and squeezed it, his thumb stroking the palm of my hand in a way that made my blood sizzle. I thought seriously of jumping his bones, but reminded myself that even if he was the sexiest Viking in the history of the world, it didn't mean I could just fling myself into bed with him. I wasn't cheap, and no amount of knee-melting smiles would change that fact.

"I have faith in you," he repeated as we marched up the front steps of the porch. The look in his eyes arrested me for a moment. Confidence was there, as well as desire. I was floored by the knowledge that he really did believe I could end his curse. Floored, and aroused as hell. "I have faith that you will fulfill my every need."

"I have no doubt you're pretty good at fulfillment, as well," I answered.

Paul was standing with his mother, his hands

moving as he clearly tried to explain who the Vikings were.

I tugged Alrik toward where my great-grandmother sat, looking like a small child in an oversize rocking chair. "I'm going to have you talk to my momo. She's—"

"Hilda!" Alrik came to a dead stop, his hand tightening painfully around mine.

I glanced back at him. His face was a mask of disbelief. "No, it's Hildi. It's short for Hildigunn."

He marched forward to the rocking chair, pulling me the last few steps. "She has changed her name then, since it was Hilda when I met her."

"You met my momo?" I stared with open-mouthed surprise at Alrik. "You're not saying that my great-grandmother is—"

"Hilda the witch. The one who cursed us!"

Four

The small bundle in the chair stirred and Momo Hildi's head rose from where her chin had been resting on her chest. Her eyes, once a startling blue, had faded to a milky color that held only a hint of their former hue. A horrible crackling noise started up, and I realized that it was Momo laughing.

"Alrik, son of Sigurd," she said in an equally crackly voice. She lifted a palsied hand and pointed her finger to him. "You have returned. I always knew you would. You are weak, just as your father was. Kneel down and pledge your eternal love for me."

"You have got to be kidding me," I told Alrik. "You slept with my *momo*?"

"It was a millennium ago," he said, his lips thinning.

I jerked his hand and moved to block his view. "You *slept* with her?"

"Thirteen hundred years ago! I barely remember it." He still held my hand. I tried to pull it away. His fingers tightened around mine.

"Barely?"

Alrik straightened up a smidgen and looked down his crooked nose at me. "Brynna, please, there are more important issues here than the fact that I had sex with your great-grandmother."

"You know, there are some sentences that are on my Never Want To Hear Anyone Utter List—and 'I had sex with your great-grandmother' is right at the top."

"There are extenuating circumstances, which you very well know." He gently pulled me to his side, continuing to hold my hand despite the fact that I was prepared to cast him from my smutty fantasies. "So you have survived all these centuries, eh, Hilda? Your evil plans have come to naught. I will never kneel before you! Brynna has sworn to release us from your curse and take us to Valhöll."

"Brynna?" Momo Hildi turned her milky eyes on me. Although I'd seen her in the last few days, she'd not spoken more than a handful of words to me. I honestly hadn't known she could do much more than eat and doze, since that had been all I'd ever seen her do. As she pinned me with a look that would scald a frozen turkey, I realized there was much more to her than your average one-hundred-year-old great-grandma. "Ah. My namesake," she said.

"Namesake?" My voice came out as a squeak. I cleared my throat and tried again. "I don't see how Brynna is related to Hildigunn."

Momo Hildi's clawlike hands scrabbled on the arms of her chair. Evidently Aunt Agda recognized the signal, for she leaped to her feet and heaved Momo out of the chair. The old lady stood there for a moment, her tiny body stooped so far over I wondered that she'd ever had a straight back.

"Hildigunn is not my true name." Momo Hildi seemed to shimmer for a moment, her image flickering before my eyes, slowly dissolving into that of a stunning young woman. Her hair was long, as red as my own, bound into two braids hanging down to her knees. She had a wicked jaw, flashing blue eyes, and wore a white linen robe girdled with gold cord that glittered in the early evening sun. "You were named for me, Brynnhilde, just as each of my true daughters has been."

Beside me, Alrik sucked in his breath.

"Brynnhilde?" I asked the red-headed vision. She faded back into the little gray old lady. "Not . . . *the* Brynnhilde? The one in the Wagner opera? Siegfried, and Thor helmets, and fleshy women in metal breastplates? *That* Brynnhilde?"

"It's Sigurd, not Siegfried," Alrik said, his fingers so tight on mine, they were beginning to cut off my circulation.

"You're hurting my hand," I said quietly.

"I'm sorry." He loosened his grip but didn't let go. "This has come as a shock to me. I had no idea she was Brynnhilde. But it all makes sense now."

"You inherited your lack of brains from your father," Momo cackled. Around us, the family stood silent, undoubtedly stunned. I was having trouble putting thoughts together, myself.

"I don't understand. What does your father have to do with any of this?" I asked.

Paul took a step toward me, his gaze flickering between Alrik and Momo. "Er . . . it's the legend of Sigurd and Brynnhilde. I'm sure you've heard of it."

I looked at Alrik. "Yes, I know it. Brynnhilde was in love with Sigurd, and he with her. Something happened to mess things up, though, and he ended up marrying someone else—"

"Gudrun," Alrik and Momo said at the same time. They glared at each other.

"—and Brynnhilde got pissed off and killed Sigurd, then . . . er . . . I'm a bit hazy about what happened after that."

"She swore to have revenge for the ills she claimed he did to her," Alrik said. "That's why you seduced me, isn't it? So you would have an excuse to curse me?"

Momo's crackling voice cut across Alrik's. "Did you think it was fate that sent you across my path? You are more foolish than I thought. I swore upon your father's bier that I would have my revenge for all he did to me, and this is but the beginning."

"What exactly did Alrik's dad do?" I asked.

Momo waved a gnarled hand at Alrik. "He took my ring! He loved me, took my innocence, and returned it with treachery when he married that whore's daughter, Gudrun."

"Alrik did?" I asked, more confused than ever.

"Sigurd!" Momo answered.

"My grandmother was not a whore," Alrik snarled. I could feel how tense his muscles were, as if he was keeping himself in check, and gave his hand a little squeeze to remind him not to lose that control. Momo might be just as old as him—or more likely, older—but she hadn't stood the length of time as well as he had.

"She made Sigurd lose his memory because she wanted him for her own daughter!" Momo yelled in a surprisingly strong voice. "He gave her my ring! Then he disguised that idiot Gunnar as himself, and sent him to my bed! Odin himself swore I would have the finest warrior in the land, and what did I end up with? A half-wit, a fool, brother to the one who stole my true love. Me, Brynnhilde, the most beautiful of all the Valkyrie! I will be revenged! The crimes against me must be redressed!"

"Oh my God. Your *dad* slept with Momo Hildi, too?" I gawked at Alrik. "What is *with* your family?"

"That was before my time," he answered quickly, his eyes narrowed on Momo. "You speak of justice, but you have not told everything, have you?"

Momo spat at him. She literally spat, but Alrik easily sidestepped the spittle. "Skitstövel! Liten skitstövel!"

I leaned toward Paul. "What does that—"

"You don't want to know," he whispered. "It's not at all proper."

"So Momo has a bit of a potty mouth on her?"

Paul shot me a look. I decided to keep my levity to myself.

"You don't wish to tell everyone what happened after you murdered my father in his sleep?" Alrik turned to face the rest of the family, huddled together in a stunned silence. "When Odin heard of what she had done, how she had deprived Valhöll of my father's presence by murdering him in his bed, he put a curse on her."

"Okay, I'm totally confused," I said, tugging on Alrik's hand until he looked at me. "Why would Odin—oh, man, I can't believe that it seems almost normal to talk about Nordic gods as if they were real—where was I? Oh, why would Odin be so ticked off that your dad couldn't go to Valhalla?"

"Ragnorök," he said succinctly, returning his gaze to Momo. "The battle at the end of the world. Sigurd was the best warrior there had ever been, and ever would be. Odin needed him at his side for the battle between heaven and hell, and Brynnhilde deprived him of that."

Momo snorted and did what I'd call a head toss on a younger woman. "No great loss."

"Odin declared that she would never know peace until she had paid for her crimes against Sigurd," Alrik told me. "My mother told me that Brynnhilde killed herself on my father's bier. Evidently she was wrong."

"He took my heart," Momo howled, slumping back into her rocker. "I died that night, when that she-witch took his memory of me from him, and wed him to her daughter."

"I'm a bit confused about the players," I said in a whisper to Alrik. "Who's the woman she keeps talking about?"

Alrik's jaw tightened again. "My grandmother.

Evidently my father was wounded, and my grandfather found him and brought him home to be healed. He fell in love with my mother, and married her a few days later."

"He loved me! I was the one he was pledged to. He gave me his ring! That she-witch stole it all from me! She made a potion that took his memory of me from him!"

Alrik's fingers twitched. "My uncle married Brynnhilde after I was born."

"Disguised as Sigurd!" Momo struggled to her feet unassisted, hobbling the few steps over to Alrik to poke him in the chest with a bent finger. "Sigurd disguised that idiot as himself, and sent him to my bed! It was trickery that wed me to him, nothing but trickery!"

"So in revenge, you killed Sigurd, then hunted down Alrik several years later and seduced him, then cursed him?" I asked, frowning at my great-grandmother. "Even though he's totally innocent of everything but dubious taste in women? That's not fair, Momo, not fair at all. Alrik isn't responsible for what his family did to you."

"He carries his father's blood," she replied with an injured sniff, limping back to her chair. "He must redress the offenses committed against me so long ago."

I glanced at Alrik. "I don't suppose you'd consider apologizing—" His outraged glare was all the answer I needed. "Right. I suppose I don't blame you, considering what you've suffered."

"It is only a fraction of what is due me," Momo insisted.

"I understand that you've been through a lot," I said with as much diplomacy as I could rally, "but honestly, I think Alrik and his men have suffered enough. So why don't you show them that you can be magnanimous, and lift the curse so they can go off to drink beer and ogle beer maids in Valhalla?"

"Never!" Momo swore with a glare at me.

"Fine," I said, shrugging. "Since I inherited the Valkyrie abilities from you, I'll just take them all to Valhalla myself."

Momo's thin, wrinkled lips split into a smile. "Daughter of my blood you may be, but you are not a Valkyrie yet."

I glanced at the four Vikings behind me. "But I summoned them all to me from the ship."

"You have powers, but you are not yet a true Valkyrie. Until you are recognized as such by me, you cannot take them to Valhöll. Only I can grant that by lifting the curse, and I will not do so until I have been revenged."

"I will not give you the satisfaction of that!" Alrik all but snarled.

I rubbed my forehead, where a headache was beginning to blossom. "We just seem to be going around in circles. Momo, couldn't you just—"

"No!"

"Fine. Alrik, could you—"

"Never!"

I sighed. Paul had been standing next to me with

an absorbed look on his face. I knew that he had a firm grasp of Nordic history and lore, owing in part to his position as the curator of an antiquities museum in Stockholm, but mostly because he had a deep love of all things Swedish.

"There may be something . . ." Paul started to say, as if he was thinking out loud.

"What?"

He looked from Momo to me, his eyes doubtful. "I'm not sure, but according to ancient Nordic law, if Momo Hildi can hold Sigurd's issue responsible for his actions, then likewise, so her issue can accept any repayment due her.

"Okay. What does that do for us? Repayment isn't the issue here. Alrik just said he won't do it, and I don't really blame him. He and his men have gotten the short stick."

"He said he wouldn't repay Momo," Paul answered, looking over my head to where Alrik stood. "Do you have an objection to repaying the debt itself, or offering repayment to Momo Hildi?"

Alrik's eyes narrowed on Momo. "She killed my father, destroyed my mother's life, was responsible for the death of my uncle, and cursed my crew to an eternity of hell. I owe her nothing."

"Just as I thought." Paul nodded. "The solution is simple, then: Alrik can repay the debt owed by his father to one of Momo's issue."

"What, like blood money or something?" I turned to Alrik. "You said you had gold, right?"

"No, Brynna, not that sort of repayment," Paul

interrupted. "If I understand the situation correctly, Momo Hildi is asking for recompense for the fact that Sigurd promised to marry her, and then married someone else."

"Yeah? So how do you repay that?"

Alrik's eyebrows rose. His hazel eyes—now more brown than anything else—lightened a few degrees as they considered me, scanning me from head to foot.

"It's easy," Paul said, smiling. "Since Sigurd can't marry Momo Hildi, Sigurd's issue will have to marry *her* issue."

A horrible idea began to form in my head. I stared at Alrik with increasing astonishment.

He winked at me.

"And since you're the only marriageable female in the family under fifty . . ." Paul clapped a hand on Alrik's shoulder. "Welcome to the family, cousin."

Five

"You're insane!"

"On the contrary, I think it's quite an elegant solution." Paul turned to the old lady crumpled up in the chair. "Momo, would you accept that as repayment of the debt owed to you by Sigurd?"

I whacked Paul on the arm. Hard. "You're downright cracked! Seriously nutso!"

Momo Hildi was silent for a moment, her scrunched-up face even more inscrutable than ever. She said something in Swedish before her head dropped back down to her chest.

"What did she say?" I asked Paul.

"She's thinking about it."

I spun around to where Alrik was huddled up with his men, evidently having some sort of a conference. "Surely you can't think this is a reasonable solution!"

Bardi lifted his head from where he was whispering to Jon. "You don't want Alrik? I don't understand; all the ladies want him. They follow him around like—"

"Like puppies, yes, I know, but when I get married, I want a man, not a hound master."

The Vikings broke their circle so that Alrik stood in the middle, flanked on either side by his men. I tried to keep from looking straight at him. He had the most unnerving ability to make me lose my train of thought with just a glance of his eyes, a tightening of his jaw, or a flash of that wickedly sexy smile.

"He isn't as decrepit as he looks," Bardi said, waving a hand toward Alrik, as if he was trying to sell a side of beef. "He has good health, a strong back, and all of his teeth. Well, most of them. A couple were knocked out by a bear."

Alrik had been smiling at me, a noticeable gap visible on the far left side of his teeth. He quickly changed his smile to a closed-lip one.

"And he has his own longboat," Jon added. "He can fish . . . somewhat. And no stag has ever gotten away from him, no matter how old and feeble it is. He's especially good with the old and feeble ones. He will be able to provide for your children."

I couldn't help but roll my eyes. Alrik shot Jon a dirty look.

"He can handle a sword tolerably well without injuring himself," Grim said. "Well, except for the time he accidentally embedded the sword in his foot, but we got that out without too much trouble."

Alrik shook his fist at Grim, who just grinned.

"He has a very large bed, as well," Torsten said with lascivious meaning. "And land to go with the house. It's up north in Lapland where no one else wants to live, true, but long cold nights just mean more time to spend in the bed keeping warm."

Alrik waggled his eyebrows at me. I had to clamp my lips together to keep from laughing.

"Mind you, he hogs the blankets, and sprawls all over a bed, taking up all the room, so you'll probably end up sleeping on the cold floor, but eh. No one is perfect."

Alrik shot Torsten a look that should have dropped the ghost dead on the spot.

Bardi clapped his friend on the back. "He can skin—sort of. And he knows the seasons for planting . . . just not how to plant. He is good at swindling and pillaging, though! He's relieved many a priest and monk of their money pouches without their being any the wiser."

Alrik tried to punch Bardi in the gut, but the latter caught his fist, laughing openly.

"I've heard the ladies say he has a fine manroot, straight and without—" Torsten started to say, but I raised my hand to stop any more of the sales pitch.

"That's all well and good, but there are two major stumbling blocks that no amount of fast talking is going to get past: One, he's a ghost, and two, he's a ghost."

Bardi frowned. "That's just one point."

"Yeah, but it's a whopper—"

"I have decided!" Momo's crackly voice shot out, causing everyone to turn to her. Aunt Agda helped her to her feet again. She raised her cane and pointed it to Alrik. "Son of Sigurd, come forward."

Alrik marched over to stand in front of Momo. He towered above her—he had to be at least three or four inches over six feet since he was a foot taller than me, which meant he was at least two feet taller than little old Momo Hildi.

"Yes?" His hands were on his hips, an angry light in his eyes.

"I will lift the curse if you pay for the three injuries done to me."

I moved over to stand next to Alrik, partly to make sure she didn't try to wallop him with her cane (I wouldn't have put it past her—I'd always known she was a tough old lady, but now her history made her downright scary), but mostly because I felt better when I was near him, a fact I didn't want to examine too closely.

"What is the form the repayment is to take?" Alrik asked suspiciously.

"First, the son of Sigurd will wed the daughter of Brynnhilde, to fulfill the promise made to me and broken. You will wed Brynna."

"I agree," he answered quickly.

"Hey! I'm standing right here!" I said, spreading a glare between Alrik and Momo Hildi. "And I don't appreciate people thinking they can marry me off without my having any say in it."

"Be quiet," Momo snapped, and shot me such a venomous look, it stunned me into momentary silence. "This matter is beyond your feeble understanding! Second, you will return to me the ring that Sigurd gave Gudrun."

Alrik pursed his lips for a moment, then nodded. "If it still exists, I will find it and return it."

"Why don't we just do the ring, and leave out this whole marriage business?" I suggested.

Paul shushed me as Momo lifted her chin to look

from me to Alrik. "For the last payment, you must secure my pardon from Odin himself."

"Odin!" I stared at Paul in surprise. "Odin is still around?"

He shrugged, his glance flickering over to Alrik. "You're standing in the presence of the son of Sigurd and Brynnhilde herself. It wouldn't surprise me at all to find all of Asgard in downtown Stockholm."

"Not Stockholm," Momo said. "Astrid Lindgrens Värld."

"Astrid . . . the Pippi Longstocking amusement park?" I asked, astounded. What on earth was the father of all Nordic gods doing in an amusement park devoted to a children's author?

Momo made an abbreviated movement that I assumed was a shrug, and addressed Alrik. "If you repay those three debts, I will remove the curse. Do you agree?"

Alrik's gaze slid to me for a moment before he nodded to Momo Hildi. "Yes, I agree."

"Yeah? Well, I don't," I said, giving my great-grandmother (or however many generations back she really was) a firm look. "I refuse to be held responsible for the fact that some man thirteen hundred years ago dumped you at the altar. It seems to me that you've had your revenge, and you need to just move on. All that hostility is bound to be doing a serious number on your psyche."

"Do you honor your oaths?" Alrik asked quietly. "You swore to help us. Do you now refuse to do so when a solution is offered?"

I turned to tell him that this situation was not covered by the promise I made earlier. I even got so far as opening my mouth to say the words, but the pain in his eyes, the tightness in his face, and his closed, wary body language drowned out the sane part of my mind.

What was the worst thing that could happen if I agreed to go through a sham marriage with him? It wasn't as if it would be a real marriage, after all. He was a ghost—as soon as we found Momo her ring, and got Odin's pardon, he'd be toddling off to Valhalla to hang out with all the other ghosts, and I'd be on my own again, just as I was before I met him.

So then why did my heart plummet at that thought?

The other Vikings stood mute behind Alrik, their expressions just as easy to read. They were tired of their undeserved punishment. They wanted to move on, to receive their reward for the centuries of friendship and devotion to Alrik. They deserved it. So what if ensuring they made it to Valhalla demanded a little sacrifice on my part? I couldn't abandon them now, when they needed me most.

"Brynna?" Alrik said, taking my hand. His thumb rubbed over the top of my knuckles. "Will you have me as husband?"

I bit my lip for a moment, then dragged my eyes up to his. "I said I'd do everything I could to help you, and I meant it. Yes, I'll marry you."

"The wedding will be in the morning," Momo Hildi said, pushing between us as she hobbled toward the rickety screen door. "Agda will see to the preparations. My daughter will have the wedding that was stolen from me."

"I am *not* your daughter," I yelled after her as Aunt Agda, a couple of other elders, and a whole slew of cousins followed Momo into the house. "You've got probably thirty or so generations on me . . . Damn. She's not even listening."

"I think she's speaking more metaphorically than literally," Paul said, giving me a sympathetic pat on the arm before he, too, went into the house.

I was left alone on the porch, just me and four inanely grinning ghosts, and one so-sexy-it-hurt Viking stroking my fingers, giving me the most intense look I'd ever received from a man.

"I will make you a good husband," he said in all seriousness.

I thought about telling him it didn't matter, but all I did was shake my head and go into the house to try to bribe that little rat Rolf into handing over my cigs.

Six hours later, I was ready for the madhouse.

"Look, I told you guys space was at a premium. I told you there was no room in the house, and that I was sleeping out on the porch." I shook out the sleeping bag I'd been using at night on a rickety wicker divan at one end of the porch. "So I don't want to hear one word of complaint about the fact that you have to sleep in the gazebo. You've got blankets and pillows; that's the best I can do."

"I am not complaining about sleeping out of doors," Alrik said, picking up the sleeping bag I had just spread out. "I object to the fact that you wish to sleep elsewhere. We are betrothed. You will sleep next to me."

"Setting aside the fact that being engaged doesn't mean I can't sleep by myself, I don't want to sleep in the gazebo. There are rodents out there."

Alrik puffed out his chest. "I will protect you. You will sleep next to me."

"Look, I—"

"You will sleep next to me!" He bent and scooped me up and over his shoulder.

"Hey! This is the twenty-first century, in case you were dozing the last few hundred years. You can't just pick women up and haul them off like you're a caveman or something. Set me down."

Alrik walked down the steps to the lawn, pausing to ask, "You will sleep with me?"

I muttered a few choice words to myself. Not because I found myself hanging upside down on his back (I had to admit I didn't really mind that, what with the wonderful view of his behind in the tight-fitting wool pants), but because deep down, I was more than a little interested in him physically, and figured a marriage—even a brief one—might give me the opportunity to taste a little forbidden fruit in a way that not even the stodgiest of family members could find questionable.

But admitting to myself that I had the hots for a Viking ghost, even one who felt as warm and real as Alrik, was no easy thing.

"How come I can feel you?" I asked, temporarily

sidetracked by a thought. "Ghosts are supposed to be wispy and insubstantial, and untouchable. Aren't they?"

He set me down. I weaved a moment at the loss of all the blood to my head, grateful when Alrik steadied me with his hands on my hips. "We are not that sort of ghosts. We were cursed to this state, so we are just as substantial as you are. Are you worried I cannot do my duty by you?"

"You ought to bottle that roguish twinkle," I said, pointing at him. "You could make a fortune on it, Mr. Innuendo. And no, I wasn't impugning your manhood. I just wondered why you could disappear at will, and yet seem just as tangible as a living, breathing person."

"I breathe," he said, placing my hand to his chest. His heart beat a strong, steady rhythm beneath my palm. "I live. In a fashion."

"So you do," I said, getting a little breathless at the combination of a moonlit night, Alrik's closeness, and the warmth of his body beneath my hand. "Look, I know you're going along with this whole bizarre marriage thing just so the curse will be lifted, but—"

"That is not the only reason," he interrupted, his hands sliding around to my butt.

My breath caught even tighter in my throat as I was pulled up against his body, all the hard lines of it making me very aware of the basic, fundamental differences between the male and female bodies.

"It's . . . uh . . . it's not?" Somehow my arms ended up around him, my hips wiggling against his in a shameless plea that left me simultaneously shocked and thrilled.

"No. I want to possess you."

It's funny how something like that sounds incredibly corny when spoken by someone who isn't a virile, earthy Viking. But coupled with the burning desire in Alrik's eyes, it didn't sound the least bit hokey. Quite the contrary, in fact.

"We just met," I said, grabbing his head and kissing the breath right out of his mouth. He was just as hot and sweet as I remembered, with that intriguing masculine taste that made me wild for more of him.

"Does that matter?" he asked a few minutes later, having allowed me to thoroughly explore his mouth.

"Yes. I have a rule—no jumping into bed the first day I meet someone.

"I desire you. You desire me. What is the problem?"

"It's just that you don't really want *me*, you just want a body. I mean, I'm a girl, and you haven't had girls for centuries," I moaned when one of his hands slid around my front, under my shirt, the heat of his palm warming the breast he cupped. "I don't blame you. If I was in the same position, I'd probably be just as . . . er . . . anxious as you are. I mean, shoot, all that time without a little lovin' . . . whew!"

"What makes you think that?"

I shoved his tongue out of my mouth and leaned back so I could focus on his face. "Are you saying you have had intimate relationships with women since you were cursed?"

A little line appeared between his brows. "Yes. Many women like to sail, you know."

"Oh. I didn't think about that. Have all of you . . . er . . ."

"Yes. Except Bardi. He is married, and much in love with his wife."

"But she's dead by now," I said slowly, trying to sort through my hopelessly tangled emotions. I sensed a rising feeling of jealousy about the idea of Alrik and other women, but told myself firmly that what happened before I met him was not important. Still, the thought that once he was in Valhalla he'd be free to play the field, bothered me. Immensely.

"We don't bring that up," he answered, searching my eyes. "You are jealous?"

"No. Well, I am actually prone to that with men in my life, but not about your getting it on before we met. I mean, I don't want to see pictures or hear who did what to whom, but I'm not going to throw a hissy about the fact that you've evidently spent the last thousand plus years sailing around looking for nooky."

One side of his mouth quirked. "I must remember to watch more American television. Some of the words you use are not familiar to me."

"I'm not jealous about your past. It's just that . . . oh, never mind. It's not worth talking about."

He watched me closely for a moment, then nodded and pulled me back into another mind-stopping, burning kiss that came close to singeing my clothes right off my body. "You are wrong. It is not just a female body I crave—I want *you*."

"You don't know me," I protested, deftly ignoring the hypocrisy of my statement.

"I know that you're courageous, honorable, and adapt well to difficult circumstances. I know that you are not intimidated easily, use reason, but are not so stubborn that you won't entertain new ideas, and that your curiosity is great about things which you do not understand. I know that you will never bore me."

My eyes widened as I read the truth in his face. He truly meant what he said. He wanted me. But . . . why?

"If you're going to swive the lady Brynna, you could at least take her to a sheltered area," Bardi said as he strolled past with a couple of six packs of beer.

"We're not swiving, assuming that means what I think it means," I called after him. Grim emerged from the bushes, doing up the laces to the front of his wool pants, giving us a curious look as he followed his cousin.

"We're not?" Alrik asked, frowning.

"No. At least . . . no, we're not. Remember the rule about no sex on the first day? That means no."

"I would find a sheltered area for us, if you wished," he offered.

"Thanks, but no thanks. I'm willing to sleep in the gazebo if you promise to de-rat it first, because that divan on the veranda is awfully uncomfortable. But there will be no sex."

He bit my lower lip and pulled my hips against his body, grinding me against him. "Your body does not say no."

"Of course it doesn't. I'm a normal, healthy woman, and you're a normal, healthy man. Well . . . minus the normal part. Just standing near you makes me go all girly inside, but that doesn't mean I'm going to give in to the almost overwhelming urge to jump your bones. I have to have some standards."

His lips pursed slightly. I gave in to temptation, and licked them. "You are so different from the other women I've had. They were quick out of their clothing. But you—you speak of desire, but deny yourself. I do not understand these standards. My bones wish for your jumping. We are betrothed, so it is fitting that we enjoy each other."

Reluctantly, I pried myself off him and with shaking knees, retrieved my sleeping bag, pillow, and a canvas book bag containing snacks, paperback books, my MP3 player, and assorted other things I might want during the night.

"Are you the kind of man who doesn't understand how to take no for an answer?" I asked as I walked past him, heading to the gazebo at the far end of the lawn.

He fell into step beside me, taking the sleeping bag and pillow from me, his face thoughtful. "Women have said no to me before. Not very often, but it has happened. Once, for certain. Possibly twice."

I sighed, wondering what on earth I was getting myself into. I recognized the signs—I had a tendency to fall in love at first sight, and it was pretty evident that Alrik really revved my engine. That could only mean trouble, given the fact that he emitted some sort of superattraction hormones that evidently every living female for the last thirteen centuries had enjoyed. "Great. Just what I need in my life: a studmuffin extraordinaire."

"Studmuffin?" He looked like he didn't know whether to be offended or pleased by the word.

"It's an American term. It means . . . well, it means someone like you."

"Ah. Virile. You do not think I will honor my oath to you?" he asked, whipping around in front of me.

I sighed as I moved around him, following a bend in the yard to the lower section, where a small apple orchard was situated next to the gazebo. "No, I didn't mean that at all . . . what on earth are they doing?"

Ahead of us, a fire burned bright orange and yellow, the figures of Alrik's men moving around it visible even from where we stood.

"Cooking supper, I suppose."

I peered into the night, my eyes widening as a large shape—it could only be Bardi—arranged a spitted animal across the bulk of the fire. "Oh dear God, no! If they've killed any of my Aunt Agda's pets . . . argh!"

"It's only a pair of rabbits Grim caught in the woods," Alrik said.

"Ew. Poor bunnies."

"Better they should be killed quickly by Grim than taken by a fox," he answered as we continued to walk toward the gazebo.

"True, but I could have gotten you some food

from the house. I didn't . . . uh . . . I wasn't quite sure
if you guys actually ate or not."

"Of course we eat! We eat fish when we cannot
barter for meat, but fresh rabbit is a treat."

I made Alrik go into the gazebo first, to make sure
there were no rats.

"I told you I'd protect you," he said with a manly
roll of his eyes.

I set my bag down next to his small trunk, eyeing
the shadows suspiciously. "Yeah, well, let's just make
sure the rats know that. Stay here—I have to go back
to the house. I'll be right back."

I ran back to the house before he could question
me. It took ten minutes to sweet-talk my Aunt Agda,
but by the time I returned, my arms laden with po-
tato salad, bean salad, cold fried chicken, a sweet
form of cornbread Aunt Pia made, a hunk of ham,
and a huge container of green salad, Alrik was pacing
before the fire.

"Your family betrothed you to me. I do not like
for them to now keep you from me," he said as I arrived, panting slightly from my burden. "You are my
betrothed. If you go somewhere, I must be allowed
to do so as well."

I blinked at him in surprise, realizing what he
must have thought. "Oh, no, Alrik—it's not that the
family wouldn't allow you in the house. I just figured
I'd get you guys something a little more nutritious
than charred dead bunny. Can you, uh . . . thanks,
Grim."

The men, who had been sitting around the fire

guzzling beer, were happy to unload me. Jon made little cooing sounds of happiness as he uncovered the leftovers and showed them off. The oohs and ahs that followed the revelation of each dish were most gratifying.

"And last but not least . . ." I pulled out a wad of paper towels, a handful of plastic forks, and a small stack of paper plates from where I'd stuffed them under my shirt. "Bon appétit, guys."

Alrik stood beside me as the men dived into the food without waiting for their dead rabbits to finish cooking. I gave him a little shove, smiling as I said, "Go on, I'm sure you're just as hungry as they are."

"You are not hungry?" he asked, his eyes on the plate of fried chicken. His Adam's apple bobbed up and down a couple of times.

"No, I'm more tired than anything else. I'm just going to get some sleep. Er . . . I don't need to remind you that I said no, right?"

He gave me a thin-lipped look. "I remember your ridiculous rules."

"Okay. Just wanted to make sure we're on the same wavelength. I don't mind sharing the gazebo with you, but I'll sleep on this side, and you can have the other."

I fell asleep watching his silhouette as he sat with the men around the fire, my eyelids growing heavy as I pondered the odd twist my life had taken.

Six

I dreamed. Alrik, naked, stood all golden and gloriously male in the warm summer sun, beckoning
me forward to a longboat filled with cigarettes. The
cigarettes turned into little white birds that swirled
around us in a tightening spiral, forcing the two of us
closer and closer together until the soft little touches
of their wings generated almost as much heat as that
which came from Alrik.

I woke up shivering with arousal, and craving a
smoke.

"You are a heavy sleeper." A male voice came from
out of the darkness. "But you are awake now. Good."

"What . . . Alrik? What . . . hey!"

I was still dreaming. That's the only explanation
for the fact that Alrik had, with one deft move, extricated me from my sleeping bag, hoisted me up into
his arms, and, stepping over the still forms on the
floor, carried out of the gazebo to the crescent of
apple trees that made up the tiny orchard.

The warm, naked shoulder next to my cheek felt
real. So did Alrik's bare chest, rubbing against my
arm. For one wild moment, I debated sliding my
hand down along his belly to regions south, just on
the offhand chance he had stripped off all his clothes,

but I decided that I wasn't that shameless, even in a dream.

"This is a pretty darned good dream," I told Alrik. "It would be better if I could have a smoke, though."

Dream Alrik frowned down at me as he stopped before a strange little structure. "You said you have quit smoking."

"Yeah, well, that's in real life. In my dreams, I can do whatever I want."

"You must forget about cigarettes."

My feet touched the cold ground, where something sharp stabbed into my foot.

"Ow! Damned sticks . . . Holy *cow*." I hopped around on one foot, as I took in Alrik's stark naked glory. Even in the moonlight, shadowed by trees, he was a sight to make any woman's jaw drop. "Wow. You really stayed fit on that ship."

"We swam a lot. I made this tent for you since Bardi said you would enjoy privacy."

It took willpower, but I managed to wrestle my gaze off his seductive self and onto the odd little structure that lurched somewhat drunkenly next to me. It appeared to be made up of several long branches, bent into a dome and covered in animal skins. Inside, a couple more skins had been tossed on the ground.

"Huh. Pretty slick, although I don't want to think about where you got the skins. Um, that's my T-shirt you're grabbing."

"Yes." Alrik tossed the shirt he'd pulled off me onto the low branch of a nearby tree.

As he proceeded to strip me as naked as himself, it occurred to me that perhaps I'd been wrong.

"This . . . uh . . . this isn't a dream, is it?" I asked as he frowned at my undies. I'd gone along with this because I figured what the heck, a girl was entitled to an erotic dream now and again, and Alrik was certainly a worthy subject. But as I stood there, naked except for my underwear, the night air sending just as many goose bumps up and down my flesh as the touch of Alrik's hands, it suddenly dawned on me that this felt far too real to be a dream.

Besides which, there was a distressing lack of ciggies.

"No. Lie down."

I stopped him as he was about to yank off my undies. "Okay, enough fun and games. Do you remember what I said before I went to bed? That whole conversation about not sleeping with guys I just met?"

His eyes glittered in the darkness, their gaze moving between my breasts (now covered by my hands) and my face. "You said you do not swive men the first day you meet them."

"Exactly."

"It is past midnight. Technically, it is the second day."

I opened my mouth to protest that, but couldn't think of a good argument. Not when I was so close to him I could feel his body heat, and all my girl parts were clamoring to visit his boy parts. As I saw it, there were three options available to me. I could gather up my clothes and march back to the house, sleeping on the floor of the living room—a highly uncomfortable solution, especially since three cousins were stretched out on the available couches and chairs, all of whom had a tendency to frequent nighttime bathroom trips, as my sole night sleeping on the floor inside had taught me. I'd been stepped on so often that first night, I'd sworn then and there I wouldn't sleep in the house again, so out went option number one. Number two involved an explanation to Alrik that I wasn't interested in him that way . . . but that wasn't true, and we both knew it. If there was one thing I'd always prided myself on, it was my honesty, even to myself. Bye-bye option number two. Which left number three, the most dubious of all my options, but the one my body most wanted: Damn common sense, and give in to the attraction I felt for him.

The only problem was, we had no future together. Once the situation with Momo was resolved, Alrik and his men would be marching off to Valhalla, and I'd be alone again. Hmm. So what would it hurt if I had a little fun with him? I looked at Alrik, really looked at him, and decided to throw common sense out the window and go along with my heart. It might be foolish to get involved with a man with whom I had no future, but a little inner voice told me I'd regret letting the opportunity slip away.

"When I was alive, it was common for betrothed couples to be bedded," Alrik said as he picked me up and deposited me onto the nest of skins. "It ensured compatibility and fertility."

"Well, I'm not . . . Oh, wow. Fur on bare skin is . . . hoo! Hey!" Just as I was squirming around on the furs, feeling as if I was one giant erogenous zone, Alrik pulled off my underwear, flung himself on me, shoved my legs apart, and without so much as a "Hi, how ya doin'?" thrust into my body. I pushed him back, trying to dislodge him. "What the hell do you think you're doing! Get off me, you big oaf!"

"It is the second day. You did not say you had a rule about the second day!"

It was dark in the little fur tent, but moonlight slid in through the opening. Confusion was rampant on his face as I shoved him off me.

"No, I don't have a rule about a second day, but I really am not into wham, bam, thank you, ma'am! Can we take this a little slower, please?"

"Slower?" He looked down at me. "You want me to fondle you?"

"Oh, Lord, don't tell me you're one of those men who thinks foreplay is a couple of wet kisses and a pinch on the nipples? Because if you are, we can just call this whole thing off—"

"Foreplay? That is fondling?"

I sat up, all my tingly parts de-tingling with the horrible realization that he truly had no idea what constituted foreplay. "You can't make me believe that they didn't have foreplay in your time!"

"I have heard that some women liked to be fondled, but I had never met one."

"You're kidding. You mean you just . . . jump on a woman?"

He rubbed his chin, still looking confused. "No, I do not jump on women. That would hurt them. I simply take my pleasure of them."

"But what about *their* pleasure?"

"They get that the same time I do," he answered, squinting at me. "Are you a virgin? Do you not know how this is done?"

"No, I'm not, and yes, I know how it's done. But I have my doubts about you!"

He sighed. "Where do I fondle you? And for how long must I do it before I can bed you?"

My jaw dropped a smidgen. "How long . . . Okay, let's back up a bit, and start this whole thing over again. We'll start with foreplay, which is much more than just you fondling a woman."

"What is it, then?"

I put my hand on the arm he was leaning on, and stroked it up over the muscles. He sat up straighter, looking very attentive. All of him.

"It's a form of play, really. It's a way for me to find out what you like, what drives you wild with desire, and what gives you immense pleasure."

"You will do that if you lie down and open your legs," he said, his breath sucking in as I slid my hand down over his chest.

"That's the entrée. We're still on the appetizers. Lie down."

He squinted at me. "Are you going to ride me?"

"Possibly. But right now, I want to feel you. All of

you. Every last inch of that glorious Viking body of yours."

He was flat on his back in less than a second, an expectant but slightly befuddled look on his face. "I begin to think this foreplay is worth investigating."

"You have no idea," I purred, kneeling beside him. I traced a little pattern down the muscles of his chest, drawing lazy circles through the golden chest hair. "Oooh, nipples! I love nipples."

He sucked in his breath a second time as I bent over him, giving first one nipple, then the other a quick swirl with my tongue, followed by the gentlest of nips.

"Gods! I had no idea . . . do that again!"

I did.

He moaned.

"I must tell the others about foreplay," he said on an outright groan as I kissed a path down to his belly button, nibbling on his ribs and sides along the way. "They will want to know about it."

"No kissing and telling," I said, straddling his knees. His penis was bobbing around in front of me, clearly trying to get my attention. "I don't play that game, and I expect you not to, as well."

His lips pursed for a moment, his eyes the color of mossy granite. "Will you foreplay me again if I do not?"

"Oh, yes."

He grinned. "Then they will simply have to learn about it on their own. Are you biting me?"

"Yeah." I swirled my tongue over the spot on his hip I'd gently bitten. "Do you like it?"

"Yes. I like everything you have done. Continue with the foreplay."

"Mmmhmm. Let's see, what do we have here?" I touched the tip of his penis, already crowned with moisture. He wasn't circumcised, but that didn't faze me, having had a boyfriend who was similarly equipped.

"My cock. Are you sure you've done this?"

"It was a rhetorical question. I know exactly what a penis is. Let's see how you like this—"

I was about to see just what a Viking tasted like when he stopped me, holding me back as I leaned over him. "You are going to take me in your mouth?" he asked, a frown pulling his eyebrows together.

"That's the idea, yes. You can't possibly object to that. I thought men lived for oral sex."

He looked troubled for a moment. "I would like it, but . . ."

"But what?" I put my hand on his cheek, my fingers teasing his short beard. "I don't mind, if that's what you're worried about. I've always enjoyed doing it, to be honest. Besides, your chest tasted wonderful. I can't imagine the rest of you will disappoint me."

"It is not that. It's just that in my time . . ."

I waited for him to continue. He toyed with a strand of my hair, looking extremely uncomfortable.

"What? Did you guys do it differently? I don't quite see how, but if you tell me what you like—"

"Only paid women take a man into their mouth," he said quickly, his eyes searching mine.

"Paid women? Prostitutes, you mean?" I asked.

"Yes. Wives—proper women do not do it."

I was stung for a moment by the knowledge that he'd think I was loose, but decided it was a societal thing rather than an insult directed at me.

"Alrik, most women in this time enjoy giving and receiving oral sex. It's nothing shocking, or immoral, or sinful. It's a way to give your partner pleasure, that's all. I won't do it if you're uncomfortable with the whole idea, but before you go making a decision, I think you should just relax and let me see what I can do about changing your mind."

His eyes rolled back as I wrapped my hand around the base of his penis, bending over to curl my tongue around the underside of the sensitive head. I used both hands to explore him, allowing my tongue to dance along the hot, velvety hard length of him, working up a rhythm that soon had his hips moving with me. I waited until his breath got extremely ragged before lifting my head and smiling at the dumbstruck expression on his face.

"Still think that only prostitutes know how to do this?"

"Gods, no!" His hands were clutching huge wads of the skins, his chest heaving as he struggled to breathe. "You've convinced me I was wrong. Are you stopping now?"

"Do you want me to stop?" I asked, slathering my tongue around the top of his penis.

* He groaned, his hips thrusting upward. "No."

"Okay." I wrapped both hands around him and watched as he exploded into orgasm, amazed when he yelled out my name. None of my boyfriends had ever done that.

It took him a few minutes to get his wits together. I used a corner of one of the rugs to clean off his belly, filled with feminine knowledge and power as he pulled me down onto him for another of his brain-meltingly hot kisses.

"Foreplay is good," he said in a rough voice. "Thank you for teaching it to me."

"You've only seen half of it," I said, biting his chin. "You have very soft whiskers. I like that. My first boyfriend had a mustache, but it hurt when I kissed him. It was like kissing a hairbrush, all prickly. But your beard isn't like that at all. It's soft and silky."

"I'm glad you like it. What is the other half?" he asked against my lips.

"It is traditional that both people be involved in the process."

He stiffened beneath me. "Ah. Yes, of course. I was being selfish. You must have your turn at foreplay. Um . . . you will lie on your back."

There were so many things I wanted to say to him, but I bit my lip and kept quiet, preferring to know if he was going to be one of those men who was considerate of a partner. I was willing to cut him a little slack due to the situation, but I wasn't going to be a martyr. I rolled onto my back, my legs relaxed, but closed.

He knelt beside me, looking me over as if I was a

deer he was about to gut, his brows pulled together. "I will now fondle your breasts."

"That sounds like a good start."

He clamped both hands on my boobs, giving them a rough squeeze.

"Ow! Alrik, not so hard! They're not udders to be milked!" I put my hands on his to stop his manhandling.

"I'm sorry. I didn't mean to hurt you." He jerked his hands back. "I won't touch them again."

"No!" I gave a little laugh at the frustrated look on his face. "My breasts like being touched. They especially want *you* to touch them. See? They're all tight for you. But they like gentle touches."

He looked worriedly at my breasts. "I do not know how to do this. I will just hurt you again."

"No, you won't. You liked the way I touched your chest, didn't you?"

He grinned.

"I thought so. Just take the things you liked me doing to you, and do them to me."

The words weren't even out of my mouth before his head dipped down and he had one of my nipples in his mouth, suckling with an intensity that just about had me coming off the ground. "Holy shit!"

He lifted his head. "Did I hurt you again?"

"No, but . . . hoo! You took me a little by surprise there. Maybe you could approach my nipple with just a little warning next time?"

He frowned at my chest for a moment, then brushed his jaw against the underside of my breast.

I shivered in response, my hands hard on his shoulders. "Oh, yes."

I'll give him this—he may have spent a thousand years ignorant of the pleasures of foreplay, but he was a fast learner. By the time he was finished with one breast and had turned to the other, I was squirming on the skins, thinking I wouldn't last until we'd gotten down to serious business.

I knew I wasn't going to make it when he laved my belly button, nibbling my belly as he slid his hands under my behind, curling his fingers around to nudge apart feminine parts. And when his breath steamed on those parts, his beard rubbing on my sensitive inner thighs, I knew I was a goner.

"Do you wish me to oral-sex you as well?" he asked, his fingers doing an intricate little dance up my legs that had my muscles tightening in anticipation.

"Normally I'd say yes, but I think we're ready to move on to the entrée," I said, pulling him forward until he was propped up above me. I slid my legs around his, feeling his once-again-happy penis nudge those parts of me that were now in serious danger of spontaneous combustion. "Oh, shoot. I don't suppose you have any condoms, do you?"

"Condoms? Sheaths?"

"Yeah. Never mind, I have a couple. My aunt gave me some earlier."

His eyes were wild as I gently pushed him from me. "Your aunt gave you sheaths?"

"Yeah. She knew I wasn't likely to have them, and she figured I'd need them after the wedding."

I felt him sigh. "This is important to you?"

"Yeah. They're in my purse, next to my sleeping bag. I'll just go get them—"

"Stay here," he growled, standing up outside of the tent. "My men are there. It is not fitting for them to see you."

I smiled as he marched off into the night, thoroughly aroused. He was just as aroused when he returned, the night air having done nothing to quell his ardor. It took me a minute to show him the ins and outs (so to speak) of a condom before he was suited up and ready to get down to business.

"You were right about foreplay," he said a moment later as I pulled him down onto me again, his eyes glittering wickedly as he pushed just a smidgen into me. My hips bucked upward, trying to take in more of him. "It has enhanced the bedding. I enjoy hearing you groan and watching you squirm when I touch you here."

His thumb brushed sensitive flesh.

"Alrik!" I grabbed his butt with both hands and jerked him forward onto me, pulling my knees up higher on his hips, but he had both arms braced, and refused my body's demand that he fulfill my raging need. "Now you're just tormenting me!"

"Yes, as you tormented me earlier. I am enjoying it. Are you enjoying it, as well?"

"Argh!" I yelled as he gave a short little thrust forward. "Please, if you have any mercy, stop playing with me and just do it!"

"But I thought you wanted to play," he said, teasing me with yet another short thrust.

I reached down and found his balls, raking my nails along them. He stiffened above me for a second, his eyes wide, then he thrust forward until he was fully enveloped.

"A gentleman always makes sure his partner finishes before him," I groaned in gasps as he pounded into me, my body moving with his to make the most amazing sensations I'd ever felt. "Oh dear God, do that thing to the left again . . . holy moly! Oh, yes!"

He started groaning in Swedish, murmuring what I assumed were sweet nothings into my neck as his hips pistoned, driving me higher and higher.

"Käresta, I cannot last much longer," he said, his voice hoarse.

"You don't have to—" My world shattered into a billion little pieces of rapture, his shout of completion harsh in my ear.

A little bit later, I said, "Normally I'd kill for a smoke after making love, but you've actually worn me out to the point where I don't care." I was curled up next to Alrik, his arm heavy around me.

His hand spread across my butt, pulling me tighter against him as he threw a leg over mine. "You will not smoke anymore. Whenever you get the urge to do so, I will simply bed you until you forget."

I smiled into his neck, and pressed a little kiss against his pulse point. I had a feeling I was going to be craving a cigarette at every possible moment.

Seven

S o. Here we are. Naked. All of us." I tried to rally
a bright smile at the women inside the small
wooden room that sat off the kitchen.

Aunt Agda jerked my towel off and shook a bundle
of birch twigs at me. "No towel. It is not healthy."

I pointed to where Momo Hildi was huddled on
a wooden bench, half-hidden by the steam pouring
into the sauna. "She gets one!"

"Be quiet. This is a ritual."

"Uh-huh. Okay, here's another question—why
did all of you guys accept the fact that Momo Hildi is
Brynnhilde, and Alrik and his guys are Viking ghosts,
and I'm a Valkyrie with training wheels, without
even batting an eyelash?"

Aunt Agda tied up another bundle of sticks. "No
one batted an eyelash, as you so colloquially put it,
because no one was surprised."

Well, I sure as hell was. "You weren't taken aback
by the appearance of five authentic Viking ghosts?"

All of the women shook their heads.

I turned to Aunt Pia. "What's going on here?"

She sighed. "Your mother was supposed to have
told you this when the time was appropriate, but
she's so busy with the clinic and her charity work—

all the women in the family know of Momo Hildi, Brynna. Every generation has done its best to take care of her, and every few hundred years, one of her female descendants is born a Valkyrie. Moster Agda was the last one until you."

I snapped shut my mouth, which I'm embarrassed to say was hanging open. "You're a Valkyrie, too?" I asked Aunt Agda.

"I was born one. But Valkyries do not come into their power unless they're recognized by one of the Aesir, such as Hildi. I have not yet been graced by such recognition, but I have faith that my selfless actions will be rewarded."

"Aesir is . . . uh . . ."

"The gods and goddesses who reside in Asgard. Your ignorance shames the family."

Agda suddenly whacked me on the butt with the birch twigs. I yelped in surprise and tried to get away.

"Yeah, well, it would be nice if someone had told me all this before." I turned to Aunt Pia. "You said the women all know—what about the men? Paul didn't seem to be as surprised as I thought he would be when he met Alrik and the other Vikings."

She sighed. "We've found they're generally happier if they are ignorant of such things. However, Paul has done significant research on our family history, and he ran across pictures of Momo from a hundred years before, so we had to tell him the truth."

That explained why Paul thought nothing of my

marrying a Viking I hardly knew. "He could have clued me in."

"Stop being so foolish, and sit still! You are being purified for the ceremony." Agda applied the birch twigs across my back a few more times. It didn't hurt, but made me feel very itchy.

"Right. Um . . . does someone want to fill me in on why we're doing this the old-fashioned way, rather than zipping down to the local love chapel and having a quickie ceremony?"

"My daughter will be married in proper style," Momo Hildi croaked, pinning me back with those uncanny eyes. "We hold to the old ways here."

Aunt Agda poured another beaker of water on the rocks, picking up her bundle of twigs with a threatening look. I hurriedly sat down between Aunt Pia and Maja, Paul's wife. Two older female cousins whose English wasn't the best sat across from me. They smiled my way sympathetically before going back to a whispered conversation.

"Old ways. So, what exactly does this entail?"

"You should be ashamed to know so little of your own people," Aunt Agda said, sitting down with a huff.

"History was never my best subject, I'm afraid."

"It is not mine, either, but I have learned some things from Paul," Maja told me with a little touch on my arm. "The ritual cleaning you know about. The bride is washed clean of her status as a maiden. The groom will do the same. At the ceremony, the bride price is paid to her family, and her dowry is likewise exchanged before witnesses. A sacrifice is made, then swords are exchanged, and finally rings. After that is the feast."

"Sacrifice?" I asked, horrified. "I am a vegetarian! I'm not going to stand for any animal to be sacrificed!"

"Paul said he will take care of that," Aunt Pia said with a complacency I couldn't even begin to muster. In a way, it was wildly romantic that I was having a historic version of a wedding, but I had an unpleasant feeling that it was going to be a whole lot more trouble than a simple civil ceremony.

"There's another problem," I said an hour later, as Pia and the cousins were helping me get dressed. Momo Hildi sat overseeing everything, her milky eyes seemingly able to see all. I held my arms up for my best dress, a long copper colored gown that almost identically matched my hair. "You said there is a sword exchange. I don't have one."

"You will be given one," Aunt Agda said as she bustled around the room. From a closet, she pulled out a small metal lockbox, which she opened from a key that hung on a chain around her neck. From the box she took a small green bundle, handing it reverently to Momo Hildi. "The crown."

I craned to see the item Momo was slowly uncovering. "A crown? Jewelry? I get to wear cool jewelry?"

Momo Hildi held up a gold circlet. It had evidently just been polished, because it glittered brightly, its points alternating in flowers and clover. Along the bottom of it, precious gems had been set.

"Holy cow! That's gorgeous! It has to be worth a fortune!"

"The value is in its age," Aunt Agda replied with an acid look.

"I wore this crown to my wedding to that fool Gunnar," Momo Hildi said, turning the crown around in her hands. She didn't look too happy to see it. "So shall my daughter wear it to wed Sigurd's son."

"It'll go wonderfully with your dress," Maja said as Aunt Pia pushed me down into a chair, wielding a hairbrush and several flowers. "Now, let's see what we can do . . ."

I have to admit, as I emerged from the room, clad in my best dress, and an ancient gold crown on my head, I felt pretty darned special, almost tingling with excitement.

"What's going on with Alrik? I haven't seen him all morning," I asked Paul as he came whipping into the house.

He paused to eye me. "You look very nice. Although that crown looks uncomfortable."

"It is. Alrik?"

"We just got back from shopping," he answered, donning an extremely martyred expression. "Four hours of running around after five deranged Vikings intent on purchasing everything that catches their eye . . . and me footing the bills. I had to threaten to leave them behind to get them to finally leave. Maja! We're back." His wife nodded and hurried after Pia on some errand or other.

"Shopping? What did they need to shop for?"

"Proper clothing, although what they ended up with . . . you can't hold it against me, Brynna. I tried to get them into a men's shop, but . . . well, you'll see. Then Alrik decided he must have a morning gift for you. I think you'll find it . . . interesting."

"We're supposed to give gifts?" I wrung my hands, careful not to move lest I disturb the crown and flower-bedecked elaborate upswept hairdo my aunts had managed to create from my normally tangled mop of curls. "I don't have a morning gift!"

He patted my hands. "Don't worry, you don't give the groom anything but a sword and a ring. Oh Lord, the rings—I managed to rein Alrik in, but it wasn't easy. I hope you don't mind a simple band. Damn. I'd better go see if Njal has them safe . . ."

He was off and running, assumedly to hunt down yet another cousin, this one a lanky teen who spent most of his time hunched over his Game Boy.

People were running all over the house, calling to one another as they got ready for the wedding ceremony, speaking so quickly in Swedish I didn't stand a chance of understanding what was being said.

"Is everything good with you?" Aunt Pia asked at one point, a distracted glint to her eye.

"With me? Absolutely."

"Good." She hesitated a moment, then added quietly, "I have been concerned that perhaps we rushed you into this marriage without giving you a chance to think it through."

"I'll admit it wasn't my first choice, but after thinking about it . . . meh. It's not like it's a real mar—"

Little Rolf ran up and said something in a rushed voice to Aunt Pia. She moaned and hurried after him, calling over her shoulder, "I'm glad everything is all right. Excuse me for running, but Uncle Tobias has taken off all his clothes again and is wandering around the neighborhood. I must find him before the neighbors call the police. Rolf, dear, would you please tell Moster Agda that it looks like her dogs are into the wedding cake . . ."

She hustled off, yelling for another cousin to remove the dogs from the house. I slumped back in my chair, smiling politely fifteen minutes later when crazy old Uncle Tobias tottered into the room wearing nothing but a tablecloth wrapped around his waist, quickly falling asleep on the couch.

I was just wondering if I could slip away and zip down to the local store and buy some smokes when Paul stuck his head in the door and yelled something. Everyone in the room turned to look.

He smiled at me. "We're ready."

"Oh. Uh, okay." I stood up carefully, suddenly filled with a nervous energy that made me feel twitchy all over. Paul held out his arm for me. I gathered he was designated to walk me down the aisle . . . or out to the orchard, where the actual ceremony was taking place, Vikings being big on outdoor celebrations. I took his arm and followed at the end of a train of my relatives, Momo Hildi in the lead. "What's this business about a sacrifice?"

"Hmm? Oh, don't worry about that. Alrik wanted to sacrifice a goat or a sheep, but I convinced him mead would do instead. Of course, now his men are all drunk since they insisted on testing the mead for quality control purposes, but I figured you'd prefer drunken Vikings to an animal sacrifice."

"You got that right. Now, about these swords . . ."

As the family in front of me parted to make way, Alrik stepped into view. The words dried in my mouth as I stared in astonishment at the man who was waiting to marry me. Alrik in wool pants and a linen shirt, with long, wild hair and a scruffy beard, was sexy. The blond man in black pants, a flowing amethyst silk shirt unbuttoned enough to make any red-blooded woman drool, with a sword strapped to his hip, was absolutely devastating.

"Holy cow," I breathed, stumbling to a stop as I clutched Paul's arm. "I never imagined . . . *holy cow*! Did he get a haircut?"

"No, just tied it back. I did persuade him to get a beard trimmer, which he seemed to like. So did the others, but I don't expect you have eyes for them. I would like to say once again that I am not responsible for their choice of garments. I tried to get them into decent clothing, but . . . well, you can see for yourself."

I blinked a couple of times just to make sure the vision of hunky Alrikness wasn't going to go away, then managed to drag my eyes to the rest of the Vikings, standing in a line behind him. They all had been spruced up, some having cut their hair and beards, but that wasn't what caught and held my attention.

Baldi, a giant of a man, had evidently fallen victim to a sporting equipment shop. He was clad in garish electric blue, lime green, and white spandex biking shorts that left little—if anything—to the imagination. A salmon-colored tank top, swimming goggles, and a bilious yellow headband finished him off.

"Good God."

Grim was at least relatively subdued, wearing khaki cargo shorts, a mossy green mesh shirt, and bright blue sunglasses. Jon had opted for a pair of blue and red satin sleeping pants, and a T-shirt of a topless woman.

"I see Torsten stopped by the Davy Crocket shop. Where on earth did he find fringed buckskin in Sweden?"

"You don't want to know. You truly don't want to know."

I moved forward when Paul gently pulled me, still too dazzled by the Vikings to do much but blink. "At least you kept Alrik from running amok. Although, hoo boy, I'd like to run amok on him. You get bonus points for getting him into that shirt and those tight pants."

Paul laughed and gave my hand a squeeze. "I can't take any credit for him; he picked the things out himself. Brynna—these last few days have been so strange, what with the Vikings and Momo Hildi, and now you becoming involved. But I want you to know that Maja and I truly wish you a lifetime of happiness."

That reminder of my nonexistent future with

Alrik sobered me. The realization that my time with him was limited made it too painful to look at him, so I stared at my hands instead. "Thank you. Things don't look very bright for a lifetime of happiness, but I've decided to live in the here and now. Worrying about something beyond my control won't make anyone happy, least of all me."

Paul slowed down. "But it *is* in your control. You don't have to take the Vikings to Valhalla, you know. You could . . . well, to be blunt, you could just fail at that."

"I thought of that, but I couldn't do that to Alrik and the others. They've earned their reward, and I'm not going to be the one who withholds it from them."

"You're a better woman than I am," Paul muttered.

I giggled at that, the smile on my lips freezing as Alrik hove into view. Most of the actual ceremony was a blur, my attention being solely focused on the gorgeous man at my side. He grinned when I stopped before him, giving me a thorough once-over that had a light of desire burning in his changeable eyes. They were a golden gray now, bright with emotion.

"You look very beautiful," he said, his hand on his chest as he bowed formally.

"You're not so bad yourself," I said, trying hard not to drool. I turned my smile on the Vikings standing behind him. "All of you look . . . very colorful."

"We wanted something special for the wedding," Baldi answered, beaming at me.

"Well, you've certainly outdone yourselves," I said politely.

"We will be the best-dressed warriors in all of Valhöll," Torsten boasted, twirling the fringe on the arm of his buckskin jacket. "There will be no one to rival us in our fine clothes."

"My wife will not recognize me," Bardi added, a wistful look to his face. "It has been so long, I couldn't blame her if she didn't."

"She loved you as much as you loved her," Grim said, punching his cousin in the shoulder. "She will recognize you. She will sing the praises of Brynna for returning you to her arms."

My eyes went to Alrik. It was clear that he was looking forward to his reward as much as the rest of the Vikings. I was just a diversion, a pleasant interlude . . . a means to an end.

I suddenly wanted to cry.

"We will start now." Momo Hildi interrupted my pity party, settling into a chair placed before Alrik and myself. She waved a gnarled hand at him. "First, the business. You have the bride price?"

"I do." Alrik accepted a small leather pouch from Bardi, handing it to Momo. She opened it eagerly, gold coins spilling out over her lap. "Five hundred marks."

"Good Lord!" I said, staring at what must be a fortune in authentic gold coins. Momo swept them back into the bag, and handed it to Agda. I turned to Alrik. "You didn't have to give Momo money for me!"

"It is the bride price," he answered.

"But—"

"It is fitting," Momo interrupted, then gestured to Agda, who gave her a file folder. Momo handed it to Alrik. I peeked over his shoulder to look inside it. There appeared to be some sort of legal documents, stamped with old-fashioned sealing wax and bits of red ribbon. "The dowry. Five hides of land in Jutland."

I wondered what the heck a hide was, and why Momo was willing to dower me with some of her land. I leaned to Paul and whispered, "Is that like five acres?"

"More like five hundred," he answered, looking surprised. "I knew she had some land in Norrland, but I had no idea it was that much."

I was stunned, uncomfortable with the thought that Momo was giving up a huge chunk of land—albeit in a very remote area of Sweden. But then, Alrik had handed over a fortune in gold coins, so perhaps it was an even trade.

Momo started talking, her voice creaky as she went through a formal summary of the terms of the marriage, then reiterated what we must do to lift the curse. She called upon the gods to witness this marriage, and splashed everyone with a bundle of fir twigs dipped in mead—part of the sacrifice, according to Paul.

"I just hope there's a good dry cleaner in town," I muttered as I brushed splattered mead off my bodice. "I'm going to be really pissed if this dress is ruined."

"Just be thankful it wasn't the blood of a freshly

sacrificed animal," Alrik whispered as I worriedly eyed his silk shirt. Luckily, it escaped the baptism.

"Oh, man, that's heavy. Thank you, Alrik. Er . . ." Alrik suddenly thrust a sword into my hands. What was I supposed to do with it?

"It is the sword of my ancestors," he told me earnestly. "My father's sword, and his father's before him. You will give it to our son."

I raised my eyebrows. "We're having a son?"

"Many," he said in all seriousness.

"Uh-huh. Well, we'll just leave that subject for further discussion, shall we? I think I have a sword for you, too—ah, thanks," I said as Njal handed me the sword he carried. It wasn't as ornate as Alrik's, having no gemstones set into the hilt as the other, but it was twice as heavy, and had an odd line of runes on the blade. "This is for you. It belonged to . . ." I glanced at Momo.

"It is the sword of Sigurd, given to me as his pledge of marriage," she answered, her eyes narrow on Alrik. "It returns to you now, son of Sigurd."

Alrik took the sword easily in one hand, tracing the runes along the blade, outright amazement and delight on his face. "Can it be? This is Gram," he said in a reverential tone. "It has been reforged?"

"Aye, it is Gram, the blade that killed the dragon Fafnir. With this wedding, I forgive the debt of marriage which Sigurd owed me."

Alrik strapped the leather sheath to his belt, carefully handing the sword to Baldi. Paul stepped forward and placed a ring on the sword hilt, which

Alrik took. "I will honor and respect you as my wife until the end of my days," he said as he slid the plain silver ring on my middle finger.

Njal held out the sword Alrik had given me. On its hilt was another silver ring. I took it and repeated Alrik's words, feeling an indefinable bonding, a sense of rightness as I slipped the ring onto his finger.

"Now you are wed," Momo said with a sharp nod at Agda, who helped her to her feet. "We feast."

"That's it?" I asked as the family broke up and headed to the main yard, where tables had been set up with enough food to feed a small army.

Pia and Maja gave me a hug and congratulated me.

"That's it?" I asked again as Paul kissed my cheek. "Don't we have to sign a wedding license or something?"

"You would if you had a civil ceremony," he answered, giving Alrik a hearty whack on the back. "This is more akin to a hand fasting. Less formal, but just as legally binding. Congratulations, cousin. Oooh, the roast pig is done!" He hurried off.

I turned to Alrik, who stood patiently beside me.

"What—"

That was all I got out before he wrapped his arms around me, and kissed the very thoughts right out of my head. It was a doozy of a kiss, a real epic-quality one, and oddly fitting with the bizarre ceremony in which we'd just participated. Alrik's tongue was everywhere at once, tasting me, teasing me, driving me wild until all I could think about was kissing him back just as thoroughly.

Just when I thought I was going to pass out from lack of oxygen, he set me back on the ground, holding on to me as I swayed.

"Wife," he said, with a distinct note of possession in his voice.

"Two can play at that game. Husband!" I answered, and lunged at him, twining my hands through his hair as I took my turn kissing him.

Behind us, his men cheered and called out several suggestions that I thought it best to ignore. By the time I was through kissing Alrik, his eyes were a molten dark gray.

I'm not sure how we made it through the feast without my wrestling Alrik to the ground and having my way with him, but I held on to my libido, promising it a wedding night to end all wedding nights. The feast itself took several hours, the light starting to fail by the time it was over. I had long since changed out of my dress and Momo's wedding crown, and was just wondering if I was going to have to spend another night in Alrik's makeshift tent when Paul sidled up to me and handed me a set of keys.

"Moster Agda's keys," he said softly, his eyes on the wide veranda where Momo and company had moved. The Vikings were out in the orchard with some of the younger family members, laughing as they set out a target and tried to use a couple of ancient-looking archery bows. "She won't be going anywhere for the next few days."

"Thanks. I guess we'll be leaving tomorrow to go

find this ring that Momo insists on being returned. Alrik said he talked to you about it?"

Paul frowned and was about to say something when Alrik emerged from the bathroom, his eyes searching me out immediately. He'd been next to me almost all day, and I had to admit I didn't mind the attention at all.

"Yes, I did talk to him about it. Alrik, haven't you told Brynna about the ring?"

"Andvari's ring? No, there has been no time."

"Told me what?" I asked, wanting nothing more than to be alone with him. I might only have him as a husband for a few days, but I fully intended to enjoy every minute of it.

Paul answered, "Alrik asked me to do a little research on the history of the Andvari ring. It's out of the range of my specialty at the antiquities museum, but I thought I'd be able to find out something about it. There is much mythos about the ring before Sigurd died, but nothing after."

"It was given to my mother," Alrik said, stroking my back. Little frissons of fire triggered by the touch made me shiver. "She cherished it. It must be buried with her."

"You don't mean we're going to dig up your mom's grave and rob her corpse, do you?" I asked, appalled.

"Of course not," Alrik said, stepping forward as he cupped his hands around his mouth and let out a yell. "I would never do anything so outrageous."

"Good. So, how are we going to find it, then?"

The Vikings answered his call, charging up en masse from the orchard.

Alrik picked up his iron-bound chest, heaved it onto his shoulder, and started around the side of the house to the area where the cars were parked. Paul and I followed, the rest of the Vikings close on our heels. "We're going to ask my mother for it. Bardi, did you get Brynna's things?"

"Right here," he answered, tossing Alrik a leather satchel. Paul opened up the back of Aunt Agda's station wagon, helping the Vikings put their chests and fur bundles into the back.

I tugged on Alrik's sleeve, confused. "What do you mean, we're going to ask your mother for it? Isn't she . . . you know . . . dead?"

"Yes. You will drive."

He marched around to the passenger side of the front seat, the others piling into the back.

I looked at Paul.

He shrugged.

"How are we going to talk to her if she's dead?" I asked, bending down to peer into the car.

Alrik sighed, got out of the car, and escorted me around to the other side, pausing at the door to point at the sky. "You see the moon?"

"Yeah. What about it?"

"It is the last night of the full moon."

I nodded. I thought it was romantic.

Evidently Alrik thought otherwise. He glanced at Paul. "I can't believe you people are so technologically advanced, yet so clueless about everything else. Everyone knows that the only time you can summon and speak to the shades of your ancestors is during the full moon. You will have to drive quickly if we are to reach my mother's grave before the moon sets. It will be a month before we have another opportunity to talk with her again." He pushed me gently into the driver's seat.

I looked in confusion through the open window to where Paul stood. "We're going to *talk* to a ghost?"

"Lucky, lucky you," my cousin answered, giving me a rueful smile. "Drive safely."

"We can talk to ghosts? Real ghosts, not like you guys, but *ghost* ghosts?"

"Yes, if you know how. And I do—my aunt was a ghost talker. She taught me when I was young."

Hey, I was the descendant of a Valkyrie, married to a Viking ghost—I really had no right to question anything at this point. Besides, there was something more important at stake.

"Yes, but . . . now?" I asked Alrik. "Tonight? What about our wedding night?"

Behind us, the Vikings burst into song. I had a feeling it was a risqué song because there was lots of elbowing going on, as well as many grins directed toward me.

Alrik patted my knee. "I'm sorry, Brynna. This must come first. I will do the best I can to satisfy your lustful desires later, after we have spoken to the shade of my mother and located the ring."

I felt like a great big sleazeball, putting my own desire ahead of the happiness and welfare of Alrik and his men.

"We're going to talk to a ghost," I repeated to myself as I started the car. Sometimes, it was just better not to question life too closely.

"Don't worry," Alrik said, giving my knee a little squeeze. "My mother will be furious when she finds out I married you, but I won't let her hurt you. I'm sure she'll be reasonable after she gets used to the idea."

Eight

I think we're going around in circles. Doesn't this bit of trees look familiar?" I whapped back a sticker bush and glared at the rocky hillside.

Alrik helped me over a fallen log and looked where I was pointing. "No, it only seems familiar because of the darkness."

Jon sprang out from the dense shrubbery. "There's nothing up there, Alrik. Bardi thinks we're too far north. He says the house used to be near a stream."

"The house, yes, but we're looking for the spot where my mother wanted to be buried. She loved these woods. I distinctly remember her grave being on the hillside so she could look over the valley. You check down there. I'll go over here. Ah. Is that a stone? Brynna?"

I clicked on my lighter, holding it high as I followed Alrik past a clump of willow trees. "It's almost out of fuel, so I hope we find it soon. Man, I could use a smoke."

Alrik turned back from where he'd been scouring the ground, pulling me into an embrace with such strength it startled an "Oomph!" from me.

"I am the worst of husbands, and you are the most

patient of wives. I promise you that I will reward you handsomely this evening."

His kiss was hot and sweet, driving out all thoughts but how much the man in my arms was coming to mean to me.

"Wow, are you going to do that every time I have a nicotine craving?" I asked when I managed to retrieve my tongue.

He wiggled his hips against mine. "I told you that I would make you forget your desire for cigarettes."

I touched his lower lip, my stomach turning upside down as I followed the delicious curve of his mouth. "You are so much better than a nicotine patch. We're going to have to get you some industrial strength lip balm, because I anticipate having non-stop cravings."

He laughed, gave me a quick kiss that left me breathless and nearly mindless, and returned to his search of the area.

I wasn't sure what a thousand-year-old-plus grave would look like, but I did my best to look around for something that looked out of the ordinary.

"There is nothing but nettles down there." Jon re-emerged from the undergrowth. "I'll try to the south."

"This is it," Alrik said, triumph in his voice as he squatted down next to a crumbled bit of stone. I knelt next to him, not seeing anything about the stone to indicate a grave.

"Are you sure?" I asked. "There's no writing on it or anything."

Jon yelled for the others. They came from where

they'd scattered to search the countryside. Although Alrik had said a grand manor house had once stood on the top of the hill, there were no signs of it. Everything was overgrown and wooded.

"My mother has been dead for many centuries. The writing will have long since weathered away. I am sure this is her grave; I feel it," Alrik said, standing. From his boot he pulled out a small dagger, using it to nick the tip of one of his fingers. He held out his hand for me.

"You're not going to use that on me?" I asked, shoving my free hand behind my back. Around us, the Vikings formed a circle.

"I need blood to summon the shade of my mother. She has been sleeping for more than a thousand years—if I use my blood only, she may not wake up. But with the blood of Brynnhilde's descendant defiling her grave, she will be sure to answer the summons."

"Oh, lovely. I get to meet my mother-in-law, and she's going to hate me right from the start." Reluctantly, I held my hand out to Alrik. "Ow!"

He grinned as he tucked the dagger away, squeezing the tiny cut on my finger until a bead of blood welled up. "My mother can be formidable when she wishes, but I will put my gold on you."

"Thanks. I think." Despite my general grumpiness, I had to admit I was looking forward to seeing a real ghost summoned. I watched with interest as Alrik drew a circle on the ground, etching odd runic symbols into the dirt before squeezing out a few drops of blood from first my hand, then his own.

"Now what happens?" I asked as he pulled me back a step, his hand warm on mine.

"Now we wait for her to wake up. I'm hoping that it won't take too—"

A huge blast of air burst upward from the ground like a tornado spawning directly in front of us. Alrik and the men were knocked backward by it, but I stood rooted to the ground, almost as if something held me there. Horror crawled along my skin as the air in front of me thickened, twisting into the form of a middle-aged woman with a long nose, high cheekbones, short blond hair . . . and an extremely pissed expression.

The woman pointed at me and shrieked something.

"Uh . . . hello," I said. I knew the meeting with Alrik's mother was bound to be awkward at best, but I was determined to remain calm. I would not let a ghost rattle me, no matter how scary she looked.

"Holy cripes!" I yelled a second later, as the woman seemed to grow a good twenty feet as she loomed over me. "Alrik! Help!"

"Do not fear, wife. She is just expressing her unhappiness at having her sleep disturbed," Alrik said, rushing to my side. He said something to the twenty-five-foot-tall woman, and she shrank back down to normal size.

"Wife?" the now-normal woman shouted. "WIFE? You have married this . . . this . . . this spawn of Brynnhilde?"

Alrik's eyebrows rose in surprise. "You speak English? Where did you learn to speak English?"

His mom turned a scornful look upon him. "Do you think I've done nothing but sleep away the centuries? I am not as slothful as your father! I learned English from the same place I learned Pilates and Chinese cooking—Niflheim."

Alrik gawked at his mother. I was long past the point where I could feel astonishment. Niflheim, I remembered from the fairy tales my mother had read to me, was the place where people who didn't get into Valhalla went after they died—it had several levels, ranging from an area where sinners were punished, to a heavenly realm where evidently people exercised while learning how to make Kung Pao chicken.

"Well. That's good, then," Alrik said slowly, continuing to look befuddled. I slid my hand into his and tried out a friendly smile on his mother. "How is Father?"

"He is asleep. He went into a rage when he was denied Valhöll, and refused to enter Niflheim. I have not seen him since then." Her eyes narrowed on me. "What is this creature doing on my grave? And why have you wed her, spawn of the one who murdered your father?"

"It's a long story," he answered with a grin at me, his fingers tightening around mine. "But let me do this properly. Brynna, this is my mother, Gudrun, daughter of Grimhild, wife of Sigurd."

"I do not have the time to listen to such foolishness," Gudrun interrupted. "You bring shame on your father's name by wedding this creature. Clearly she has bewitched you. I will have her head cut off, burned, and the ashes scattered to the four winds. Then you will be free again."

My eyes just about popped out of my head. "*Hello!* I'm standing right here!"

If looks could have killed, the winds would have been scattering ashy bits of me all over Sweden.

"She is my wife," Alrik said calmly, his thumb stroking the back of my hand. "I am not bewitched. Brynna is a Valkyrie and is helping us get to Valhöll. But to do so, we must have your ring."

"My ring?" she asked suspiciously.

Alrik ran through a brief explanation of the last few days. Gudrun chuckled at his description of Momo Hildi, and made some rude comments about women who didn't age well, but I figured she was entitled to do a little venting, since Momo had murdered her husband.

When Alrik finished, I said, "I'm sure you can think of just about anything else you'd rather do than give Momo Hildi your ring, but it comes down to Alrik—either you give us the ring so he and the others can toddle off to Valhalla, or they will stay cursed for forever."

"The ring of Andvari . . ." She looked thoughtful for a moment, then marched over to me. I didn't want Alrik to think I was a coward, so I lifted my chin and stood my ground.

"You are of Brynnhilde's blood," she said, taking

my chin in chilly fingers, turning my face first one way, then the other. "You have nothing of her looks."

"Does that matter?"

Her eyes, a watery green, seemed to sear right through to my soul, leaving me feeling as if she could see every mistake, every regret, every good intention that I'd failed to fulfill. Suddenly, she smiled and patted my cheek. "This must infuriate Brynnhilde, seeing you with Alrik." She turned back to Alrik and nodded. "Very well, I will give you my blessing. I will not kill your bride to break this enchantment that she must surely have cast in order to catch you, a warrior second only to my beloved Sigurd in valor."

"Gee, thanks," I said.

"Are you with child yet?" she asked me, studying my midsection. "You don't look like you are, but I cannot believe that my Alrik, beloved of maids all over the eastern coast, would not have you with child. Are you barren?"

"Mother," Alrik said, shooting me an embarrassed glance. "We were just married today."

"You weren't married to that maidservant with the hair the color of raven, and she gave you two daughters."

I gaped at Alrik. "You have children?"

Now he looked really embarrassed. "I was very young."

"That doesn't matter! You didn't tell me you had children!"

"It's just the two, Brynna."

"That you know of," his mother said, buffing a nail on her sleeve.

"*What*?"

She waved away my exclamation. "Alrik's daughters are not of concern here. They were well cared for after he was taken from us, but they, too, were doomed. One died in childbirth, the other perished with her husband when they were caught sailing in a storm."

Alrik looked sad. "I'm sorry," I murmured to him, leaning into his side.

"I never really knew them," he said, wrapping an arm around me and pulling me closer. "If I'd known what was going to happen to them, I would have done things differently."

"It is no good cursing once the egg is broken," his mother said primly. "They are in Niflheim, and happy now."

Alrik bowed to his mother, kissing her hand, and thanked her. "Your blessing gives me great joy. But we still need your ring."

"I do not have it."

"You don't?" Alrik's forehead furrowed as he glanced at me. "But . . . it was the ring my father gave you. You were not buried with it?"

"Of course not!" she said, walking back over to her grave, tucking her hands into the long sleeves of her gown. "It was cursed! You don't think I'm going to have something like that with me for all time, do you? I left it to your sister. You'll have to find her to get it back. Now I must leave, or I'll be late for my fitting. It's Hel's birthday, and we're having a surprise party for her. I'm going as a holly shrub. Farewell, my son. I bid thee well, daughter, and hope to find you with child the next time Alrik summons me."

I slapped a smile on my face and wished like hell I had a cigarette. She said something to the men standing behind us, all of whom bowed to her.

Then she tilted her head and smiled at me. "Be sure to tell Brynnhilde that I have given my blessing to your union." Her laughter echoed around us as her form dissolved into nothing, her words carried on the remnants of the wind. "It will infuriate her no end. May all her hair fall out, and her breasts shrivel up to naught . . ."

I eyed Alrik as one last puff of wind stirred the leaves and twigs at our feet. "You know, I was going to warn you that my parents are a bit eccentric, but I don't think there's any way they can top your family."

Alrik sighed. "They've always been that way. I was the only normal one in the family."

I giggled, wanting to point out that a thirteen-hundred-year-old Viking ghost in an Armani silk shirt wasn't quite the traditional definition of the word "normal," but there were more important issues at stake.

"Right, so now we find your sister. Where's she buried?"

"I have no idea. It was after we were cursed." Alrik's shoulders sagged a little. He looked weary, worn down by the cares of the world. My heart warred with my body, but eventually, the better part won out.

"I know tonight is the last night of the full moon, but you're tired, and so am I. Why don't we just find a hotel and get some rest? We can tackle the problem of the ring in the morning."

"Lady Brynna speaks wisely," Baldi said, rubbing his face.

"Aye, but we must speak to Katla, and tonight is the only night we can do it. I just don't know how we're going to find her . . ." Alrik pinched his lip. My gaze fastened on it, and it was only by dint of immense willpower that I kept from lunging at the man.

But if I wanted to enjoy the attentions of Alrik, I'd have to come up with a way to locate the ring.

"I've got it!" I said after a few moments of furious thinking, and rustled through my purse for the cell phone Paul had lent me. "Paul isn't just a historian, he's also an amateur genealogist. He traced our family back eight hundred years, so I bet he can access all sorts of genealogical records. He's bound to know where your sister was bur—Paul? It's Brynna. Yeah, sorry, I know it's late, and you had a long drive home from Momo's, but this is an emergency. Hmm? Yes and no. We found her, but she didn't have the ring. We need to find—no, he's not naked, and we're not in a honeymoon suite in a fancy hotel, although I sure as shooting wish I was, and with any sort of luck at all, I will be soon, assuming you stop interrupting me so I can ask you a question!"

Bardi snickered. Alrik held out his hand, which I took, talking to Paul while he helped me up the hill, and through the woods to the small clearing where we'd left the car.

"You must get your temper from your father's side of the family," Paul answered in a grumpy voice. I couldn't blame him, since I'd clearly woken him up, but we didn't have the time to wait until morning.

I ran through a quick explanation of why we needed to trace what happened to Alrik's sister. "So if you could fire up your genealogy database, or whatever you use to look up people's records, I'd appreciate it. Alrik's sister's name was . . ." I looked at him.

"Katla," he answered, holding open the car door for me.

I slid into the driver's seat while the Vikings piled in behind me, passing along the information to Paul. "Alrik says they didn't have surnames then, so I don't know how you're going to pick her out from other Katlas of the time, but—"

"That's not necessary," Paul interrupted, yawning loudly in my ear. "I don't need to look his sister up to tell you what happened to her. In fable she was killed by Regin, a dragon who was bent on regaining the hoard Sigurd stole from his brother Fafnir. He didn't get anything but the ring Katla bore."

I repeated the information to Alrik, who snarled, "Regin! He tried to kill my father, but failed. Now he will pay for the murder of my sister! Drive to him, Brynna. I will cut out his heart and cook it before his eyes."

"First of all—ew. Second, a dragon? Maybe when you were alive, but I can guarantee you that there are no dragons lurking around in the twenty-first century."

The Vikings behind me burst into laughter.

Alrik patted my leg. "Dragons are shape shifters, Brynna. Even in my day, they preferred to appear in human form."

"Oh. Um . . . Paul?"

"So glad you remembered I was here," my cousin answered dryly. "And since I wish to get back to my warm bed and warmer wife, I'll answer your next question: Stockholm."

"Huh?"

"Regin is in Stockholm. Legend says he retreated to the Birger Jarls tower on Riddarholmen, the knight's isle. That's in Stockholm, the oldest part of the city. If he's still around, then he might be there."

"Birger Jarls tower," I said, digging through my memory of the brief visit I'd had in Stockholm. "Birger Jarl was a king?"

"No. He was the founder of Stockholm," Paul answered, yawning again. "Is that all you need?"

I thanked him for his help and hung up, chewing on my lip as I started the car and headed down a bumpy dirt track for the main road. "We're going to Stockholm."

"Excellent," Alrik, said, his voice rife with satisfaction. I caught him caressing the sword that he still wore strapped to his belt.

I had a feeling that was not a good sign.

Nine

We were a few hours outside of Stockholm. I was perilously close to falling asleep at the wheel, which led to Alrik's demanding a quickie driving lesson. I agreed, figuring it was a toss-up whether I fell asleep at the wheel and killed us or Alrik did from lack of experience.

To my great surprise, Alrik took to driving like he had been doing it his whole life, so I ended up sound asleep while he drove the couple of hundred miles to Stockholm.

After stopping at a gas station to get a map, I curled up with one of Alrik's skins in the back of the Volvo, waking when he gently shook my shoulder.

"Brynna, you must wake up now. We are here."

"Huh? Wha?" Groggy, I blinked at the vision that appeared before me. A streetlight behind Alrik's head gave him a bit of a corona, his eyes hidden in the shadows. I didn't need to see his features clearly to want him, however. I grabbed his head with both hands and kissed him with every ounce of passion I felt.

He groaned and pulled me from beneath the skin, completely out of the car, backing me up against the cold metal, his body hard and aggressive as he took over the kiss, his tongue pushing mine around, making my knees go weak with the intensity of his heat.

My mind was a whirl of need and desire and something so wonderful it made tears prick behind my eyes. Dammit, I'd gone and fallen in love with a man with whom I had no future.

"Käresta, I want you. I need you," Alrik murmured against my skin as his lips burned a path along the side of my neck. I slid my hands along his back, feeling an answering need deep within me. Simple physical attraction I understood . . . but how could I feel so many other emotions about a man I just met?

A polite cough sounded behind him.

Alrik's breath steamed against me in a sigh I felt down to my toes. With an effort, he pushed himself back. His eyes glittered with passion. "Later, käresta. I promise you that later I will repay you for your patience and generosity."

"I don't want repayment," I answered, clearing my throat at the husky sound of my voice. "I just want you."

"You do not know how that gladdens my heart. But before I can worship you as you are due, we must get the ring from Regin."

I glanced over his shoulder. The other Vikings were very politely ignoring us, standing with their hands clasped behind their backs as they gazed at the sixteenth-century round whitewashed tower butted up against two adjacent buildings. Behind me, water lapped at the concrete barriers, traffic thankfully nonexistent at this early hour.

"Alrik . . . I don't want to sound like a naysayer, but this is a very historic area. That's Wrangelska Palace over there. Is it likely that an ancient dragon—even one in human form—is going to be living in a popular tourist attraction like this tower?"

He stepped back, his hand going to the hilt of his sword, the slow smile curving his lips filled with so much menace, a little shiver rippled down my back. "Dragons have ways of not being seen if they so desire . . . but Regin will not escape me."

I made a mental note to never piss off a Viking, and followed Alrik and the others as they slipped across the darkened road, keeping to the shadows as they hurried to the door.

In my mind dragons were giant fearsome creatures, known for their ability to breathe fire, consume virgins, and hoard treasure. The man Alrik eventually tracked down, a gray-haired, gray-skinned Asian man, slumped in a beat-up chair, clad in stained pants and tattered blue bathrobe, appeared to be anything but a dragon.

"Aha! A dragon! Regin, son of Hreidmar!" Alrik yelled dramatically as he threw open the door, his sword raised high. "Prepare to meet your doom! It is I, Alrik Sigurdsson, come to avenge the death of my sister, Katla!"

Regin slowly lifted his head and looked at us crowded in the doorway. One of his hands lifted in a limp gesture. "Well, you made it here at last. What took you so bloody long?"

Alrik blinked a couple of times, then lowered his

sword. "I was cursed for the last thirteen hundred years. Er . . . you aren't surprised to see me?"

Regin shook his head. I scooted around the Vikings—who had formed a wall of brawn in front of me—and stood next to Alrik.

"Good Lord, no. I've been expecting you these last thousand years, praying for salvation. Would you mind not goring me as you probably wish to do? I can heal a gore mark, so a decapitation would be nice."

Alrik looked at me, then his men. They all appeared as confused as we were.

"Um . . . pardon me for butting in, but we're all a bit . . . well, confused," I said, smiling politely at the despondent dragon. "You are Regin the dragon, are you not?"

"Oh, yes." The man sighed heavily, then slowly got to his feet, spreading his hands to show he was unarmed. Alrik tried to pull me behind him, but I moved back around to offer my hand to the dragon.

His hand was damp and clammy and I surreptitiously wiped my palm on my pants. "I'm Brynna, and this is Alrik. He's a Viking. That's Bardi there with the long sword, his cousin Grim has the crossbow, Jon is next to him with the daggers, and Torsten is the one waving the battleax."

"A pleasure to meet you all," Regin answered, looking back at Alrik and me. "Would you prefer I kneel down for the beheading? Or should I stand? Do you have enough room to swing that sword in here? We can go outside, if not."

Alrik frowned. "Why do you not beg for your life? Do you have no honor? No dignity?"

Regin gave a tired, despondent laugh that made me depressed just hearing it. "Do I have any honor, he asks. Any dignity. Oh, my, that is funny." He made an attempt to straighten up, his very presence so dismal, so hopeless, it seemed to leach all the life out of everything. "My good Viking, I had dignity and honor once. Then I made the mistake of my life, the biggest mistake of the century. I killed your sister for my brother's silly ring. And I have spent the last thirteen hundred years paying for my misguided sense of honor."

"Right. Now I'm totally confused," I said, taking Alrik's free hand to feel his warmth. The room was unheated and as gray and lifeless as its owner. "You *want* Alrik to kill you because you killed his sister?"

Dull, hopeless eyes turned on me. "I seek death to escape my eternal torment, yes. You look like a nice female, sympathetic and kind. I don't suppose you'd like to kill me?"

"Um . . ."

"You repent the killing of my sister, then?" Alrik asked, his eyes narrowed on the dragon.

"Repentance has been denied me. You see before you a broken man, one living an existence of hell on earth, a perpetual torment so hideous I cannot even begin to describe it to you."

Alrik's arm went around me, pulling me close. I leaned into him, filled with despair that seemed to soak into my bones from the air around us. "Were you cursed as well?" Alrik asked.

"A curse is nothing compared to the hell I've suffered," Regin answered. "Each night, I am tormented by the most heinous spirit—"

In the distance, a horrible screech rent the air. Regin twitched, his hands over his ears. "Run! Save yourselves! It is upon us!"

Alrik shoved me behind him again, holding his sword out in front of him. The others moved to stand in a protective circle around me. I stood on my tiptoes and peered over Baldi's shoulder as a light started to form in the center of the room; my breath stuck in my throat as the thing so awful it could drive a dragon to this end appeared before us.

"There you are, you disgusting excuse of a dragon! What a mess you are. Pew! You didn't bother to wash again, did you? Look at you, just look at you! What a slob! You haven't even changed your clothing! Odin save us, you reek! You could bathe once in a while, you know! It wouldn't kill you! Oh my gods, look at the state of this room! I've seen pigsties with less filth!"

The light formed into the shape of a person, solidifying into a young woman with light brown hair, wearing a bright pink exercise halter top and matching skin-tight pants. She stood over Regin, who had collapsed into a ball of misery, her hands on her hips, a disgusted expression twisting her features.

Alrik took a step forward, squinting at her. "*Katla?*"

The woman spun around, astonishment written in her face. "Alrik?"

"Aye, 'tis me!"

The woman squealed with pleasure, throwing herself on Alrik in a bear hug. "After all these centuries! How nice to see you again. You look very well. I thought you were cursed."

"I was." He turned for me, holding out his hand, presenting me to his sister. "Brynna saved us. She is my wife now."

Katla clapped her hands then grabbed me in a fierce hug that came close to breaking my ribs. "You're married! It's about time. Are you with child yet? Oh, I so want to be an aunt! Have you seen Mother? She will be so excited."

"Excited isn't quite the word for it," I said, giving her a wry smile.

Alrik explained the situation to her quickly. "We came to get the ring and avenge your death."

Katla smiled. "As if I couldn't avenge my own death! Silly Alrik. I've been tormenting Regin since the day he killed me. But thank you for thinking of me."

The dragon lifted his head. "You see now the full extent of my hell. Please, if you have any mercy in your soul, kill me now! I can't take another millennium of her!"

"You disgusting little worm!" Katla turned on the man with much pleasure. "Stop groveling on the floor and stand up like a man. Dear God, are those urine stains on your pants? You are worse than the belly scum of a dung beetle! Go put on some decent clothes for a change!"

"Please!" Regin begged. "I'll give you the ring! I'll do anything, just kill me now!"

"Of course you're going to give him the ring," Katla answered, marching over to a small dingy cabinet. She pulled out a wooden box, making disgusted sounds as she poked through the contents, finally extracting a small, tarnished ring of what looked to be gold. "I cannot believe you are happy to live in such a state of dirt! It's clear I've been too lax with you these last hundred years, but that will change starting tonight! You're going to clean up this tower, and you can start right here with those windows. They're almost as dirty as you are. Go get some cleaning products and rags."

Regin whimpered and collapsed on the floor, sobbing. "Save me! Save me!"

"You don't deserve saving, you pestilential boil on the buttocks of the world. Here you go, brother. Take it with my blessing."

"Kill me! Kill me!"

Alrik accepted the ring, his lips pursing as he looked at the writhing man on the floor. "Thank you. Will you be all right with the dragon?"

"Please, any of you! Have mercy on me! Cut off my head!"

"Pfft," she answered, waving the subject away. "As if I can't handle someone as pathetic as him."

"If that's too much, rip my heart from my chest!"

"Go in good health, brother. And Brynna, I do hope you'll make me an aunt soon!" Katla hugged me again, gave Alrik a kiss, then hugged all the other Vikings as well. "Now, as for you, you entrail slime . . ."

"No! No! Please don't leave me with her! Help meeeeeeee . . ."

The night air was incredibly refreshing, washing away the horribleness of Regin.

I glanced up at the windows, the faint sound of Katla's voice drifting down to us. "I can't help but feel a little sorry for him."

"He killed my sister. He tried to kill my father," Alrik said in a rough voice, then his shoulders twitched, and he gave me a rueful grin. "I feel sorry for him, too. Katla was never an easy woman to live with. But she seems happy now."

"We have the ring, that is what matters," Bardi said as we all trooped back to the car. "What is next?"

Alrik slid a glance my way. "We rest. Later in the morning we will return the ring to Brynnhilde and find Odin to ask for his pardon."

My body fired up in response to Alrik's glance, even as my heart dropped down to my shoes. I had only one more day with him. I knew I should be content with that. I knew when I decided to sleep with him that we had no real future, despite the faux marriage. And I knew that my heart would be broken when it was time for him to go Valhalla, and I would be left behind.

But I wanted more than just this short time with Alrik. I wanted him for a lifetime.

Ten

"Alrik, I think I'm falling in love with you. Would you mind not going to Valhalla after all?" No, men go weird at the L-word. "Um . . . Alrik, I think we've got something good going here. I like you, you like me. The whole wild, steamy lovemaking thing isn't bad, either. And there's a lot we could do together, with you being immortal, and Momo Hildi saying I'd be immortal once I'm made a Valkyrie— assuming I am, but Paul says I'm a shoe-in . . . Oh God, now I'm rambling." I swore as shampoo bubbles stung my eyes, and concentrated on rinsing the shampoo out of my hair.

Five minutes later I used a hotel towel to rub clear a patch on the mirror, and stared myself down. "I can't tell him how I feel; that'll scare him off. Men like to know they're desirable sexually, but they get a bit squidgy when other emotions are concerned. Think, Brynna, think! There has to be something you can say to convince him that life with me will be infinitely better than fighting, drinking, and carousing in Valhalla."

My eyes looked back at me in the mirror, worry evident in them.

"Well, hell," I told my reflection. "I'll just tell

him . . . I'll just tell him I need him. He'd like that. And God knows it's true. Damn, I need a smoke! I wonder if they sell them in the lobby."

I shoved down the annoying feeling of guilt that arose whenever I thought of trying to talk Alrik out of going to Valhalla, telling my conscience that I'd make him just as happy as life in the Viking's idea of heaven would.

By the time I finished dressing, Alrik and his men had returned from what he termed a pillaging party.

"We bring you much food!" Torsten cried happily, waving a fistful of McDonald's bags. "Big Macs! Cheeseburgers!"

"Pommes frites and chicken nuggets!" Jon said, stuffing a handful of fries into his mouth. "With four different dipping sauces!"

"So I see. You . . . ah . . . you used the money I gave you to pillage, right?"

Grim rolled his eyes. "It's not pillaging if you have to pay for it."

"But—" I was about to remind them of the lecture I'd given them about modern views of pillage when Bardi nudged me with his elbow.

"We used your money. Alrik grumbled, but he didn't want you mad."

I sat on the edge of the bed, watching with increasing dismay as the Vikings trooped into one of the three hotel rooms we'd rented upon leaving Regin. As the pile of fast-food packages mounded up on the table, I had a moment's qualm about whether my credit card would stand up to the cost of supporting five hungry Vikings. I'd just about maxed it out paying for the rooms and pulling some cash for meals and incidentals.

Alrik entered last, presenting me with a bag. "For you, a couscous salad. It has chicken on it, but I thought you could pick it off."

"Thank you," I said, accepting the salad. He beamed down at me. I glanced from him to the four others as they pulled up chairs, hoping that he'd read the message in my eyes that I really wanted to be alone with him.

Unfortunately, being thirteen hundred years old doesn't go hand in hand with insight into women's unspoken cues.

Alrik grabbed a handful of food and plunked down next to me on the bed, nodding toward the unopened salad. "Are you not hungry, "käresta"?"

"What exactly does käresta mean?" I asked, sidetracked by my curiosity.

He grinned. "Sweetheart."

"Oh." For some insane reason, I blushed. The avid light in his eyes confused me—how could he feel such an attraction for me and not be the least bit disconcerted by the fact that we were a few short hours away from being parted forever?

I popped open my salad to equally gloomy thoughts, half-listening to the men as they chatted about all the things they'd seen on their foraging trip to McDonald's.

"What will you do first when we get to Valhöll?" Grim asked Torsten. "Mead, fighting, or women?"

Torsten laughed. "Do you have to ask?"

Grim nodded. "Fighting first. Then mead. Then women."

"That is the natural order of things," Torsten agreed.

"There's fighting in Valhalla?" I asked Alrik. "I thought it was some sort of Viking heaven?"

"It is," he answered. I took a napkin and dabbed at a bit of ketchup on his lip. He waggled his eyebrows at me.

"You do not know about Valhöll?" Bardi asked, astonished. "But you are a Valkyrie!"

"I think I'm Valkyrie Lite. Aunt Agda said something about my not being a real one until Momo grants me the status. Anyway, all I know about Valhalla is that warriors who are slain go there and wait for Ragnorök."

"Waiting around with nothing to kill and no mead to drink and no women to bed would be hell, not heaven," Torsten answered. "Valhöll is a glorious place, made of spears, shields, and breastplates."

"There are five hundred and forty doors, so wide eight hundred warriors could walk through them at the same time," Jon added.

"Aye, and every morn, the warriors there arm themselves and ride out onto the plains of Asgard to battle each other," Torsten said. "When they return at night, they are served with mead and roast boar. Much bed sporting goes on afterward." He gave a salacious wink.

"In the morning, all who died or were wounded

in battle are made whole again, and it starts over
again," Alrik said, offering me fries.

I shook my head. "And this is your guys' idea of
heaven?"

All five of them grinned at me. Torsten said,
"Fighting, mead, and women . . . there can be nothing more a man could want."

"What about your families?" I asked, sliding a
glance to Alrik. "If only warriors are allowed in, that
means you'll never see your families."

"They are in Asgard, too, in another of Odin's
halls," Bardi answered, a look of yearning filling his
dark eyes. "We can visit them as often as we like. I
do not plan to leave my wife for some time once you
take us to Valhöll."

"Do not look so sad," Alrik said in a low tone,
nudging my shoulder. "Our families are all in Asgard,
and we will see them again. Joyous will be our re-
union with them—and it will all be because of you."

I blinked away tears. If I'd had any question about
whether Alrik was looking forward to going to Valhalla, it had just been answered. I couldn't ask him
to stay when it meant sacrificing everything he'd
hoped for during the last thirteen hundred years.

Just as I was about to sob into my salad, it occurred to me that perhaps Odin wasn't going to be
talked into giving Momo Hildi a pardon as easily as
we'd anticipated. If that happened, Alrik and the
others would continue to be cursed, but I could keep
them from being bound to their ship. It wasn't the
reward they wanted, but was it really such a bad life?

I selfishly brightened at that thought. Maybe there would be a future for us, after all.

"Is it the chicken that offends you? They did not have any plain salads available for pillage." Alrik frowned at my uneaten salad.

"No, it's fine," I said, setting the salad on the nightstand. "I'm just not hungry."

"That is not good. You have not eaten since the wedding feast. Milkshake?" Alrik offered me a sip.

I eyed him, wondering what it would take to get rid of the four other Vikings. "I wouldn't mind a little milkshake," I answered.

He handed me the cup.

I leaned into him and whispered in his ear, "But I'd prefer to lick it off you."

"You must leave now!" Alrik said quickly, cramming the last of his burger into his mouth. "Brynna wishes to lick milkshake off me."

Bardi choked. Grim froze, a McNugget halfway to his mouth. Jon looked confused. Torsten grinned and winked.

I wanted to kill my husband. "Alrik!" I whapped him on the arm.

"What?"

"You weren't supposed to tell anyone that!"

"Milkshake, hmm?" Bardi asked, a thoughtful look on his face. "My wife and I never tried that."

Alrik leaned close and whispered, "Is milkshake licking another form of foreplay?"

"It *was* going to be. Now I'm thinking of ways to use it as punishment."

"Ah. I'm very sorry, then. I did not know." He kissed my fingers, his tongue being sure to caress my knuckles. "There is a change of plans. Brynna is not going to lick milkshake off me, despite it being foreplay."

"Foreplay?" Grim asked, frowning. "I do not know this word. What does it mean?"

I groaned and marched into the bathroom. "Let me know when you're done explaining it to them. I'll be in here pretending I have a normal life until then."

The temptation to put my ear up against the door was so overwhelming, I had to turn the water on to keep myself from eavesdropping. Then I searched my pants pockets for the nine-hundredth time for a cigarette I might have overlooked, finally sitting on the counter.

I didn't have long to work up a pout, though. Evidently Alrik made his explanations quick, because in no time he was in the doorway. "They have gone. Do you wish to come out to the bed, or would you like to not lick milkshake off me in the bathroom?"

I went into the bedroom. "Why don't we give the milkshake a pass and just wing it," I said with a smile, rubbing against him and kissing the tip of his nose.

His eyes brightened as I slid my hands up his silk-covered chest and began to unbutton his shirt. "I have talked with the men without mentioning anything that you and I have done, since I knew you would not like that."

"Thank you. Arms, please."

He held out his arms so I could slide his shirt off.

I tossed it onto the luggage rack, moving around him, admiring the muscled planes of his back. "I've never thought of a back as being sexy before, but I just want to lick yours."

"You do?" He tried to turn around to face me, but I held on to his shoulders and danced my tongue along his spine. He stiffened up, sucking in his breath as I reached around his waist to undo his belt buckle.

"You taste delicious. Could you take the sword? Thanks."

He removed the scabbard from the belt before I tossed it onto his shirt, setting the sword next to the bed before returning to me. I reached for his pants but he stopped me, holding both my wrists. "You are distracting me, Brynna."

For one horrible second I thought he was going to reject my advances, but then I saw the fire in his eyes and knew he was just as aroused as I was.

A little frown furrowed his brow. "Bardi knew of foreplay. He recommended it highly, but he said it was very important that I pay sufficient foreplay attention to you, lest you remain unsatisfied."

He was so serious, I couldn't help but smile. "Sweetness, did I look unsatisfied last night?"

He thought for a moment, then shook his head. "You moaned loudly, many times. You grabbed my hair and demanded more. And you liked it when I did this."

He grabbed one of my breasts, immediately gentling his touch so that it was a caress rather than a grope.

It was my turn to suck in my breath. "Oh, yes. I do like that."

"Bardi also said that there is something he and his wife enjoyed. She would pretend to be a shy milkmaid, and he would be a lusty woodsman who saved her from a wolf. I think the suggestion has merit. You take off all your clothes and stand over there, by the window. Pretend the chair is a wolf that has you trapped. I will emerge from the bathroom and save you."

He pulled off his pants while he was speaking, taking up his sword (the metal one), and marching to the bathroom.

I couldn't help it, I laughed.

He popped out of the bathroom looking indignant.

"Alrik, that's a very interesting suggestion, but I think things are still new enough with us that we don't have to go to such elaborate lengths to get our jollies. To be totally honest, I doubt if we ever will. You make me drool just looking at you." I allowed my eyes to roam over all of him. "While I appreciate your attempt to spice things up, I think we'll be okay without role-playing."

He set his sword down again, his hands on his hips, his penis waving at me. "I do not understand. You don't wish to foreplay now?"

"It's not that I don't want to, it's . . ." I looked into his eyes, and burst into laughter again, wrapping my

arms around him before he could step back in out-
rage. "You're so damned adorable. Go get the milkshake. I'll let you eat it off me, okay?"

He was a bit skeptical that a milkshake could be
more fun than the milkmaid and lusty woodsman,
but by the time he undressed me, nibbling and kissing the flesh exposed by every removed garment, he
was happily drizzling a now room temperature milkshake on various and sundry parts of me.

"I'm getting sticky," I protested when he went
back for seconds on my breasts.

"Then I am not licking you off well enough. I
must apply myself more diligently." He sucked one
rock-hard nipple into his mouth, causing me to
thrash around on the bed.

"Good Lord, you pick things up quickly," I gasped
in between moans of pleasure.

He smiled down at my wet nipple, blowing gently
on it.

I recalled the discussion that had taken place
when I was half-conscious in the boat.

"They're brown. Disappointed?"

"You heard? No, I'm not disappointed. They match
the milkshake." He smeared a little more melted
shake on my breast, laving his tongue over it before
drizzling a chocolatey line down my breastbone, cir-
cling my belly button, and heading to regions south.
His mouth followed, cleaning up the path, until he
was face-to-genitals.

He frowned at my crotch. I frowned at his frowning at my crotch.

"Is something the matter down there? I don't wax, because if there is a torture worse than yanking pubic hair out by the roots, I don't know what it is, but everything is in working order. Why are you frowning at my girly parts?"

"Girly parts? Is that what you call it?" He shifted until he was between my legs, propped up on his elbows, still frowning at my groin. He prodded gently.

"You're making me very nervous. What's wrong?"

He prodded again. "I don't know how to give you the pleasure you gave me. You took me into your mouth, but there is nothing here to take into my mouth."

I giggled. I couldn't help it.

"You laugh at me?" He rose up high enough to glare at me over my pelvic bone.

That just made me laugh out loud. "I'm not laughing at you, sweetness. It's just that I've never had to walk anyone through oral sex before, and it's making me a bit silly. We'll just take this a step at a time."

The next ten minutes were anything but arousing. I felt more like a specimen for budding ob-gyns than a woman awaiting pleasure from her husband. I went over the basic working system, told him what I found pleasurable, and let him go to work while I lay back stifling the urge to giggle again.

"So if I touch you here"—the tip of his tongue dabbed at me—"this is not arousing?"

"Not by itself, no."

"Ah. And here?"

"Nope, sorry."

"Hmm." He readjusted himself. "Now?"

"You're getting warmer. You know, maybe we should just skip this for another time."

"No, you must give me the opportunity to learn. This looks like it has potential. What about—"

His mouth descended upon very sensitive flesh, causing me to buck upward, clutching his head to me as starbursts burst into glorious being behind my eyes. "Holy Mary, mother of God!"

He smiled at my crotch. "Now we are getting somewhere. Let us see if I can find this G-spot you mentioned."

"No, no, I don't think I could take it. Just do what you did a second ago!"

His fingers curved into me at the same time as his tongue did a dance of pure ecstasy around my now highly aroused flesh. By the time he worked out a rhythm that had me gibbering in ecstasy, I was mind-less of all my concerns. The future could worry about itself—right now, all that mattered was the man who had somehow stolen my heart.

"I love you," I told him as he slid up my body, pulling my hips up to meet his. "Don't leave me; please don't leave me."

A rapturous groan was the only answer as my inner muscles tightened around him in an orgasm that just about lifted me off the bed. His voice was hoarse as he shouted my name into my neck, his hips bucking wildly against me, the burning brand of his penis all but searing my intimate flesh as he poured himself into me.

It didn't occur to me until later, when Alrik was snoring softly against my head, his arm and one leg thrown carelessly across me, that he had not answered my plea to stay with me.

I cried myself to sleep.

Eleven

So after we give Momo the ring back, we'll go find Odin, right?" I tucked my travel toothbrush back into its holder and emerged from the bathroom. "How far—what on earth is *that*?"

Alrik stood in the middle of the room, positively oozing handsomeness in his rust-colored shirt and black pants. I couldn't understand the writing on the box he held, but the picture was pretty self-explanatory.

"The girl at the shop called it a Pleasure Pachyderm. It is worshipped by women the country over, and she said it would bring to you much pleasure when I was not with you." He eyed the package for a moment before shrugging. "I do not see how a purple elephant mounted on a plastic shaft can instill reverence in so many women, but if this is an important icon to modern women, you must have one. It is my morning gift to you."

My heart dropped to the floor, crawled under the bed, and shriveled up into nothing. After last night, how could he still want to leave me? I accepted the box, turning my back as I put it into my bag so he wouldn't see the tears burning my eyes.

"Do you like it?" There was concern in his voice.

Concern wasn't going to cut it.

"Yes, it's lovely. Thank you. Shall we go see Momo?"

It almost killed me to force a smile to my lips, but I made a game effort. It didn't seem to fool Alrik, however; he kept sliding me odd glances as I drove to Momo Hildi's.

By the time we had delivered the ring to her and were headed out to find Odin, I had managed to get past the worst of the pain. I had gone into this relationship with open eyes—I had to see it through no matter how much it hurt.

That was, assuming we found Odin.

"This can't be right." I shook my head in disbelief. "Momo Hildi is obviously not all there. Why on earth would Odin, the father of all gods, the supreme being of Norse mythology, live in an amusement park devoted to Pippi Longstocking?"

Alrik eyed a signpost bearing several pointers, one labeled VILLA VILLEKULA. I recognized it from my childhood days as the name of the house Pippi Longstocking lived in. "That is something we will have to ask him. Are you sure she gave you no clue to where in the park he lived?"

"Sorry, no. She got all tight-lipped when I tried to ask." I sighed, and looked around at all the tourists bearing ice-cream cones, cameras, and many shopping bags. Children romped around us, screaming with delight as their favorite characters were brought to life by park employees. "How on earth are we going to find him?"

"I have a map. Perhaps it will tell us something,"

Bardi said, pulling out one of the brochures that were given to us when we paid our entrance fee. He opened it up, squinting first at the map, then at the guidepost.

The other Vikings gathered around him. They were still a pretty colorful-looking bunch, but at least Bardi had exchanged his bike pants for a pair of jeans. Alrik, I was thrilled to notice earlier, was wearing another gorgeous silk shirt. His eyes lit up as he caught me ogling him.

"Käresta, if you continue to look at me in that fashion, I will have to take you back to the hotel room and become a lusty woodsman," he murmured in a low voice filled with innuendo.

I thought about it for a few seconds. Part of me wanted to make the most of every second, but that was procrastination pure and simple—procrastination that would lead me only to more heartbreak. With every passing minute I was falling more and more in love with Alrik, which meant I needed to finish this quest and get him to Valhalla before the thought of losing him forever utterly destroyed me.

Too late, my inner voice said with nauseating cheerfulness.

"We need to find Odin," I told Alrik firmly, ignoring the tiny spark of hope that Odin would refuse to help. I turned to the other Vikings. "Did you find anything on the map?"

"I see Pippi's house," Bardi answered, pointing north. "In the center there is some castle. I wonder if the Allfather could be there."

I noticed a small box on the back of the map, listing the directors and officers of the amusement park.

One of them had an extremely familiar name.

"Does the map show where the administrative buildings are?" I asked.

"Yes. On the north side, beyond the restaurant."

"Did you find him?" Alrik asked, peering over my shoulder. He read the same little box I did. "Ahhh. Very clever. O. Sigtyr, executive director. 'Sigtyr' means god of victory."

"Yes, and it's also on the list of Odin names Paul gave me. Off we go," I said grimly, wanting it to be over with.

Many things went through my mind as we trekked through the crowded amusement park, ranging from the sick knowledge that I was about to have my heart ripped from my chest, to the stunned disbelief that Asgard, the home of the gods, was contained in a location that featured a house made of oversize furniture and a dancing horse. Somehow, it just seemed wrong.

"Here goes nothing," I said a short while later as we arrived at a small block of buildings that were used to house the park staff and administrative offices. No one was present in the outer office, it being lunchtime.

Alrik glanced around, nodding to a door with a small brass plate that read O. SIGTYR. He was about to open it when he thought better of it, knocking instead.

We waited with our breath held.

No one answered.

Alrik knocked again. After another couple of seconds of silence, he opened the door and slipped inside. I followed behind, the Vikings on my heels.

I have no idea what sort of strange vortex Odin had set up in his office, but whatever he'd done, it was a dilly of a mind trip. One moment we were standing in the office, the next we were walking up a grassy slope, heading for a tall stone structure.

"Asgard!" Bardi said, looking around him with huge eyes.

I made a slow circle, taking in the sights. Below, a huge grassy plain stretched out to the horizon. Around us, in a horseshoe shape, several large stone towers perched. A pond was set in the center, upon which swans paddled with languid elegance. "It's just hard to believe that all this is contained in a room in an amusement park. It's a little difficult to wrap my brain around."

"I find it best if you don't try to figure things out," Alrik said with a little squeeze of my arm. "You'll have fewer headaches that way."

"Sounds like an idea. Well, let's find someone to ask about Odin."

"He will be over there," Bardi said, consulting his amusement park map and pointing.

"How do you know that?" Alrik asked.

Bardi grinned at us all. "The map changed. See?"

We all looked. He was right—whereas before the legend read ASTRID LUNDGRENS VAÄRLD, now it said simply ASGARD.

"There is Valaskialf. It is from there that he watches the world," Baldi said, pointing to one of the buildings.

"Valaskialf?" I asked, trying to say the word without tying my tongue in knots. The building was gorgeous, made out of stone with streaks of mica, so the entire place glittered silver.

"That is where Hlidskialf is," Alrik answered as he strode toward the building.

"Man, you guys and your tongue-twisting names. I'll bite: What's a Hlidskialf?"

"Odin's golden throne," Baldi said. "It's where he watches what happens in the—"

He froze, his eyes big as he looked to the left. Slowly, one of his hands lifted, and he pointed. "Val-höll."

Alrik stopped, and the Vikings all gawked. Valhalla was one of Odin's buildings, sitting right there, just a stone's throw away. I glanced at Alrik. His face mirrored the surprise and delight seen on the other Vikings.

"How do you know it's Valhalla?" I couldn't help but ask Bardi.

He gestured toward a sign affixed to one of the double doors. Sure enough, it read VALHOÖLL.

"Great," I muttered to myself, wanting to simultaneously cry and yell and beg Alrik not to leave me.

"What?" Bardi asked, not taking his eyes off Valhalla.

"Nothing. So . . . that's it, eh?" I bit my lip. I wasn't going to shame myself now that the moment was at hand. They wanted to go to Valhalla, and there it was.

I wished the ground would open up and swallow me whole.

"Can it be this easy?" Torsten asked, looking at the others.

They were mute for a moment, staring at the simple stone and wood structure.

"I certainly don't see five hundred doors," I heard my voice say in an extremely grumpy tone. I cleared my throat, and tried again. "There's only one way to find out. Let's pop in and see what's going on, shall we?"

No one moved. I slid another glance at Alrik, then straightened my shoulders and marched forward, throwing open the door to warrior heaven. I stepped forward to enter.

I couldn't. It was as if an invisible net were stretched across the doorway, prohibiting me from entering it.

I pushed forward, trying to break the barrier. "I'm not sure what's going on here, but I don't seem to be able to enter."

"You're not a warrior," Jon said with a smug little smile.

"No, but she is a Valkyrie," Alrik mused, stroking his chin.

He stepped forward to enter, and I threw myself at him, holding him back. "No!"

"What is it, käresta?" he asked as I pushed him backward.

"Uh . . . I just thought . . ." What a lie—I wasn't thinking at all. I desperately dug around for a plausible explanation of my actions. "You want the curse lifted, don't you? If you get into Valhalla now, you won't get the curse lifted."

Alrik looked vaguely insulted. "Do you really think I would not fulfill my word? I agreed to Brynnhilde's terms. I will do as I swore to do. But this is Valhöll! I must at least look inside it."

I bit the inside of my cheek as he gently set me aside, striding toward the door. My heart sang a dirge. Tears formed in my eyes. Once Alrik and the others entered Valhalla, I would never see them again.

"What in Odin's name . . . bah! I cannot pass!" Alrik snarled, apparently fighting the same invisible net I had encountered.

The dirge changed into a Disneyesque song filled with love, light, and dancing mice. If he couldn't go in . . . my entire being was filled with hope.

"Baldi? Grim?"

The Vikings clustered around the doorway, each grunting as they tried to push themselves past the barrier.

Silent and unseen by the five men, I did a little jig of happiness, and spun around, my arms opened wide to the glorious joy of the world. They couldn't get in! I wouldn't have to say good-bye to him . . . at least, not just yet.

A voice cleared behind me, a woman I hadn't seen before stopping next to me. She was about my mother's age, with short, glossy dark hair cut in what I instinctively knew was a very expensive style, wearing an equally expensive-looking taupe linen pantsuit, and holding a bunch of colorful brochures. "Hello. Can I help you?"

"Hi," I said weakly, wondering if the woman had seen me dancing. Alrik and the others stopped trying to heave themselves through the doorway. "You're probably wondering what we're doing here."

"Not really," the woman said with a polite but disinterested smile. "You're a Valkyrie. They're warriors. I see nothing to question about your presence, although it did strike me that you might need some assistance. Is there a problem with Valhöll?"

"No problem," I said quickly. "We were actually looking for Odin. You wouldn't happen to know where he is, would you?"

She sighed, nodding toward the silver building. "Where he usually is—watching TV."

"Oh. Er . . , if he's busy, maybe we shouldn't disturb him right now," I said, seizing on a possible out.

The woman eyed Alrik, fluttering her eyelashes at him. "You're a handsome devil. You look familiar—have we met?"

"I have not had that pleasure," Alrik said, bowing formally.

I gritted my teeth and sauntered casually over to his side, trying to imply possession without beating the woman over the head with it.

"I am Alrik Sigurdsson. This is Brynna, my wife. That is Baldi, Grim, Jon, and Torsten."

"Sigmund's grandson!" the woman said, ignoring the rest of us to smile at him. "How delightful. I always did like your grandfather. He's one of the few mortals who gave Odin sleepless nights."

"You are . . ." Alrik paused.

"Frigga. Oh, yes, you do have the look of your grandsire," she purred as the other Vikings all knelt down and bowed their heads.

I was distracted a moment by that, but when Frigga moved so close to Alrik I could count the wrinkles around her eyes, laying a long-nailed hand on his chest and stroking the shirt, my hackles rose.

"You're Odin's wife," I said, perhaps rather more loudly than I needed to. "Queen of the Aesir."

"Goddess of the sky, marriage, motherhood, love . . . and fertility," she said, looking deep into Alrik's eyes as her hand slid lower, down his belly.

I ground off a few layers of tooth enamel, my hands fisted as I forced myself to just stand there. If Alrik wanted to be fondled right out in the open by strange goddesses, well then, so be it. It was better I learn the truth now, before it was too late.

"We will gladly accept your blessing," Alrik said, moving aside slightly, putting his arm around me. "We have just been wed."

Yay, Alrik! I was about to beam him a smile of approval when Frigga's hand slid even lower, to his fly.

"Hello! I'm standing right here!" I said, pushing her hand off his zipper. "In case you didn't understand, he's taken. By me. And I don't share."

Alrik's eyes widened.

Frigga's eyebrows rose for a moment as she looked down at my hand still on hers. Around us, the sounds of people doing whatever it is they did in Asgard stopped. The wind brushing past us, the birds singing in the trees, even the buzz of bees vanished. I wouldn't have been surprised to find out that the world itself had stopped turning.

It struck me that I had just lipped off to a goddess, the *prime* goddess, one who probably had immense power—certainly enough to squash one little Valkyrie-in-training and the Viking she loved.

"I meant that with all due respect, naturally," I said lamely, waiting for a lightning bolt to kill me on the spot.

Frigga leaned forward, her dark eyes glittering with a light that made me want to squirm. "Do you know that I have the power to see the fate of all people?"

I swallowed. Hard. "Er . . . no. I didn't know that, actually."

A slow smile curved her lips. "Yours is . . . *interesting.*"

The way she said the word "interesting" just about made me curl up and weep.

Frigga stepped back, returning her attention to Alrik. She stood for a moment, watching him, then gave a little sigh. "Sigmund was the same—in love with his wife. Such a waste. Well!" She was back to her brisk self, spreading a distracted smile among the remaining men, her gaze touching briefly on me for a moment.

I was still goggling over the "love" word. I slid a glance to Alrik, trying to see any signs that he was love-struck. He just looked mildly annoyed, and I had an uncomfortable feeling the annoyance was directed at me.

"I'm just off to make reservations for the Bahamas," Frigga said.

"Bahamas?" I couldn't help but ask. "You're going on vacation?"

"No. I've told Odin we're moving. It's been my fondest wish this last century to swim with the dolphins, and snorkel and sail, and if he thinks he's going to keep me trapped in this hellish amusement park, he had just better think again." She shot a dark look at the silver building. "I'm sick to death of Pippi Longstocking. I want sun. I want beautiful balmy ocean waves sweeping sun-kissed beaches. I want half-naked, well-oiled cabana boys attending to my every need."

"Well, so do I, but I'd think a vacation would satisfy that particular need."

Alrik shot me an outraged look.

I patted him on the arm. "That was a purely rhetorical 'So do I,' punkin. You're more than enough man for me."

"I do not understand how it is you can move Asgard out of Sweden," he said to Frigga after giving me one last look. "It would not be Asgard then!"

"Don't be ridiculous. Asgard is wherever Odin decrees, and by the moon and the stars, he will move it to the Bahamas, or there will be hell to pay. *Hell*!"

My Momo Hildi had nothing on Frigga as far as scary went. I swear I felt the earth tremble when she spoke.

Still . . . the farther away Asgard was from Alrik, the happier I'd be.

"Sounds lovely," I said with a bright smile. "But if Odin is busy arranging the move, then he won't want us interrupting him. We can come back tomorrow—"

Frigga laughed. "By all means, go and interrupt him. All he does is rot his brain on TV, anyway," she said, giving Alrik one last sultry look before heading off in the opposite direction.

The Vikings all rose, eyeing me carefully.

"What?" I asked.

"You touched the goddess Frigga," Grim said, awe in his voice.

"You interrupted her," Jon said, the same amazed look on his face. "You touched her and interrupted her."

"You are the bravest woman I have ever met," Bardi said in a reverential tone. "Not even my wife would accost Frigga with such boldness."

All of which made me more uncomfortable. I glanced over my shoulder to make sure that Frigga hadn't decided to strike me down for my impertinence. "Yeah, well . . . it's no big deal. Shall we go find Odin?"

"She is braver than all the Valkyries put together," Torsten said, kneeling before me. The other Vikings followed suit. "You are a fitting wife to Alrik."

"Oh, for heaven's sake—get up before someone sees you!" I looked around me nervously. "Guys, it wasn't that big of a deal! She had her hand on his crotch, and I just told her to knock it off."

"The goddess Frigga!" Bardi said. "Wife of the All-father!"

Alrik pursed his lips as he looked me over.

"Not you too," I said.

To my surprise, he grinned. "I was wondering what I'd done to deserve such jealousy on my behalf, but I decided I didn't care. It was enjoyable, although I would warn you that it isn't wise to cross Aesir. Their memories are long, and their retribution can sometimes take centuries to be exacted."

"Lovely." My shoulders slumped a little, but Alrik took my hand and pulled me along to the silver building, distracting me from the pity party I was about to launch.

Odin waited . . . and with him, all my hopes of life with Alrik.

Twelve

For those of you who hope to someday visit Asgard, I have a tip: The doorman who guards Valaskialf can be bribed to allow you entrance. He likes gold, but practically wets his pants with happiness when given Gargoyles sunglasses.

"That was easier than I thought," I said as we entered the main hall.

I came to an abrupt stop, blinking, as stunned as Alrik and the others by the sight before us.

"Good Lord, it's like some sort of disco palace! The place is wallpapered with mirrors!"

"I like it," Torsten said, striking a pose in front of one of the walls. He admired himself from all angles while the rest of us wandered around the room. It was empty of all furniture, not a huge place, certainly no bigger than the local grange back home, but at least three stories tall, with tiny palm-size mirrors covering the walls. The light reflected upward gave the feeling of vast, never-ending spaciousness.

"Where's Odin?" I asked in a hushed voice. There was a vaguely cathedral feeling about the place.

"There is a door," Alrik answered, pointing. We proceeded over to it en masse, although Bardi had to go back and forcibly pull Torsten away from his reflection.

The noise hit us first when Alrik opened the door. After the brilliantly lit mirror hall, the dark room before us gaped like some horrible maw. The blast of noise slowly resolved itself into sounds from several sources. Light flickering from one side of the room served as the only source of illumination, but it was enough to make out the giant gold-colored recliner centered in the room, and the figure of a man seated upon it, legs crossed.

"Have you ever watched Chinese opera?" the man—who could only be Odin—asked without turning his head. He pointed to the wall opposite and pressed a button on a remote. One of the approximately twenty plasma TVs changed from a scene of Hong Kong to Chinese opera. "It's fascinating. I particularly like the ones where they fight. The Chinese have always put on a good show. Or perhaps football is more to your taste? Brazil is playing Spain today."

The noise from one of the TVs grew in volume as one of the two teams playing soccer made a goal, sending the crowd and announcer into a screaming frenzy.

"You must be Odin. We're sorry to disturb you, but we've come on a mission," I said, one eye on the wall of televisions. Each showed a different channel from a number of different countries, from Martha Stewart to an X-rated channel that featured two women in French maid costumes whipping a man with bunches of celery.

"Are you on a mission from God?" Odin asked, turning his head to look us.

The supreme god of the Norse appeared to be in his sixties, with short, spiky gray hair. One eyelid was closed and slack, indicating the loss of an eye.

I shook my head, confused.

"Don't watch the *Blues Brothers*?" Odin asked, and sighed before returning his attention to the televisions. "A shame."

"You know about the *Blues Brothers*?" I asked, more surprised than ever.

"Old and new. I have all the movie channels here," he answered proudly. "I liked the Belushi-Aykroyd version the best. Can't go wrong with the classics, I've always said."

"Yeah, but TV . . ." I stopped, not wanting to get into a discussion of what I felt an ancient, powerful god should be doing with his time.

A short, harsh laugh burst from him. "Don't look so surprised. This is Hlidskialf, my golden throne. From it I watch the happenings in Midgard."

Midgard, I assumed, meant the rest of the world.

Alrik stepped forward, kneeling before Odin. The other Vikings followed suit. "Almighty Odin, we come before you to seek your assistance in a matter of great importance."

"If you've come about Frigga's idiotic demand that I move Asgard, you're wasting your time. I like it here. Every day, I go out and watch Pippi play. There are other people around, but that doesn't bother me. Pippi enjoys them. She has such pretty red hair."

Alrik peered at me from the corner of his eye. I shrugged. It was apparent that Odin was several bananas short of a bunch. "We do not come from Lady Frigga," Alrik said. "It is for my own sake that we appear before you. I am Alrik Sigurdsson."

Odin glanced down at him for a moment. "Sigurd's son, eh? Now there was a fool. Got himself murdered over a woman." He shook his head. "I told him not to look upon that hussy Brynnhilde, but he wouldn't listen. Had a lust for her, he did, but I knew how it would end. She was a bad one. So you're his boy, eh? And you've got a woman, too. Take a word of advice—don't wed her. Once you're wed, they spend eternity nagging you to do things you'd rather not do."

Alrik stood and held out his hand for me. I thought lovingly of smacking Odin upside his head as I took it, but kept myself in control.

"Brynna is my wife, Lord Odin. She has done much to free me from the curse the witch Brynnhilde laid upon me. It is because of that curse that we have come to Asgard."

Odin examined me with his one pale gray eye. "Valkyrie, eh? I don't remember seeing you."

"I'm not a Valkyrie yet. At least Momo Hildi says so, but she didn't explain how I'm supposed to be officially recognized. We were hoping you—"

Torsten and Jon hooted, and we all turned to look at them, surprised by the noise.

"Sorry," Torsten said with an embarrassed glance

as he waved toward one of the TVs. "Italy just scored against Germany. They're tied now."

"Really? I have money on Italy." Odin leaned to the side to look around Alrik. "I like the German team this year, but they don't hold a candle to the Italians. Oh, well played!"

"We'd like you to pardon Momo Hildi," I said loudly, to get Odin's attention again. "I'm sorry to disturb your TV time, but this is very important, and it shouldn't take long. If you could just—"

"No," Odin said, then prodded Alrik. "Move to the left, boy. I can't see the shopping channel, and it's almost time for *Southwestern Silver Earring Hour*."

Alrik drew out his sword, holding it upright as he moved directly in front of Odin.

"My lord Odin, I come before you bearing Gram, the sword you gave to my grandfather. I have sworn upon this sword to obtain your pardon for the witch Brynnhilde, and I will not leave your presence without it!"

Odin eyed the sword for a moment. "Gram, eh? Reforged a few times, I see. So Brynnhilde is making your life a misery. I told Sigurd what would happen if he gave in to his lust for her, but would he listen? They never listen, mortal men. What a waste that was. She killed him, you know. Brynnhilde. Always knew it would end that way. Women, *tch*. So she cursed you?"

"And my men," Alrik said, waving to the others, who were all now engrossed in the televisions.

"Brynnhilde has agreed to lift the curse so we might serve you in Valhöll, but to do that, you must pardon her."

Odin pursed his lips. My fingernails dug into my palms as I held my breath. What would I do if he said yes? Alrik and the others would march off to Valhalla, and I'd be left with a shattered heart.

To my intense relief, Odin shook his head. "Can't do it. I had to punish Brynnhilde. She deprived Valhöll of Sigurd. I told her I'd find her another warrior, but you know how women are. Because of her, I lost the best warrior. Can't pardon her for that. Wouldn't be right. Besides, she refused to do her duties."

I squeezed Alrik's hand, leaning into him to offer my support. I felt horrible at rejoicing in the fact that the curse wouldn't be lifted, riddled with guilt over the fact that I'd put my own needs before his happiness. What sort of person was I that I could do that? Guilt prompted me to speak when my heart begged me to be silent.

"Is there some way you can get around the curse so Alrik and the others can go to Valhalla?"

"Can't go against someone's curse," he said, and my heart lightened. He eyed me again, a speculative look dawning. "You've got the look of an intelligent woman. You're her issue, eh?"

"Yes. I thought she was my great-grandmother, but obviously there are a few more generations in there."

"You're a Valkyrie, then. If you want Sigurd's son to go to Valhöll, you can take them."

"We tried. We couldn't enter," Alrik said.

"Was that another goal?" Odin asked, trying to peer around Alrik.

"Penalty kick for charging Italy. They missed," Bardi answered.

"Odin, please—" Tears spilled down my cheeks. My heart was breaking, but Alrik's happiness was more important. "Can't you do something to allow them into Valhalla? They've suffered for so long, and Momo Hildi isn't going to lift the curse unless you pardon her. You're our last hope."

Odin sighed dramatically, waving a hand toward me. "Never could resist a woman's tears. Very well, I will pardon Brynnhilde."

"Thank you," I said, more miserable than I thought humanly possible.

"On the condition that you take her place as a Valkyrie."

I looked up, startled. "Um . . . all right. I'm not quite hip to all that the job entails, but I'll do my best."

"Good. You can start with him." Odin nodded at Alrik. "Since Brynnhilde deprived me of the greatest mortal warrior, I will take his son instead. Brynnhilde!"

The air beside Alrik shimmered for a moment; then a woman appeared. It was Momo Hildi as she had been in her prime, standing tall and proud, her long braids shining brightly in the glow of the TVs.

"Odin Allfather," she said, bowing to him.

"Your issue and Sigurd's son have pleaded your

case before me. I have graciously decided to grant them the request."

She inclined her head, a smug smile visible. "I am ready to serve you again."

For the first time, Odin smiled. It wasn't a very pleasant smile at all, and I was aware that although he might appear to be an ordinary man, he possessed hidden depths of power. "I'm sending you to Niflheim. Brynna will be taking your place."

Momo's head snapped up, her eyes furious. "You what? I will never allow—"

Odin raised his hand, and in a voice as loud as thunder declared, "Receive my pardon, Brynnhilde, formerly of the Valkyries. Go in peace to Niflheim."

"Noooooooo!" Momo's wild screech echoed off the walls long after Odin waved a hand and sent her away.

Alrik's men gathered around him, cheering as they congratulated one another.

"Come forward, issue of Brynnhilde," Odin commanded.

I took a step forward, unable to look at the man who stood beside me.

"I recognize you as a Valkyrie. Your first duty will be to escort Sigurd's son and his men to Valhöll. Return to me after, and I will bestow upon you the full power of the Valkyries."

"Thank you," I said, my head bowed. I couldn't stand to see the joy on Alrik's face as he finally received what he most wanted. I hurried out of the room, the sound of happy chatter following me.

Tears blinded me as I stumbled out of the mirror room, retracing the path to Valhalla.

Alrik called my name, but I ignored it. I had done what I had sworn to do—I would take Alrik to Valhalla; then I would crumple up into a tiny ball and die of a broken heart.

I stopped in front of the double doors, taking a deep, shuddering breath. "I am Brynna, recognized by Odin as a Valkyrie. I bring to Valhalla brave warriors who deserve a place in your halls."

The doors opened. Torsten shouted with happiness and ran through the doorway, Jon and Grim following right behind him. They disappeared, and I knew they had finally found their reward.

Bardi smiled at me before he, too, entered the building.

Tears burned my eyes as Alrik hesitated. He was looking at Valhalla with an expression of longing that destroyed that last little shred of hope that he might choose me over heaven.

"Go on," I said, my voice choked and thick. "They're waiting for you."

He flashed a grin at me and walked through the doorway, disappearing from my life forever.

I stared out at the soft, balmy night, listening gloomily to the sounds of night animals as they hurried about their business. A bird called out suddenly, and stopped. A cat yowled in the distance. Even the cigarettes I'd bought on the way back home didn't appeal to me. Nothing did.

Inside the farmhouse, Aunt Agda's voice was audible as she ranted about Odin's choosing me to take Momo Hildi's place over her.

"It's my right! I should have been next, not her!"

Paul's mother, Pia, was in with her, soothing her as best she could.

"Now she will be immortal! I will wither and die, and she will go on! This is not fair! This is not just!" A door slammed, shaking the veranda beam I was leaning against.

A few moments later, the screen door opened softly behind me. Pia touched my shoulder. "You are a very brave woman, Brynna. I am pleased that Odin recognized this, and rewarded you for it."

A hot tear welled and burned its way down my cheek. Aunt Pia didn't see it in the darkness.

"Oh, yes, I've been rewarded," I said, my heart contracting painfully.

"It is so. You are immortal now. You will never know disease, or old age, or death," she said, her voice soft in the night air.

And I will never know love, or happiness, or a moment's peace without Alrik. Another tear burned its way into existence. I was surprised that I had any tears left, after having spent the time since I'd returned from Odin sobbing into a pillow. I felt raw inside, as if someone had taken a knife and cut out all the important parts of me, leaving nothing but a bleeding, hollow shell.

I will spend eternity without Alrik. I'd been keeping that thought at bay as best I could, but at last it pierced me with a pain so intense, I crumpled to the floor.

"Brynna? Brynna, are you all right? She just collapsed! Poor thing, she must be exhausted after all the excitement. Put her over there, on the sofa. I'll get some water . . ."

Hands lifted me. I curled into a ball, sobbing silently, feeling like I would shatter into a million pieces from the pain.

"What is wrong? Are you ill? Have you hurt yourself?" a voice asked as I was placed on the sofa at the far end of the veranda. "Käresta? Can you hear me?"

Käresta?

My heart gave a lurch as I uncurled myself, spinning around to look at the man who loomed over me, a worried expression on his face.

"Alrik? What are you doing here?"

The worried look changed to one of mild irritation. "I am trying to find my wife. Why did you leave me? Why did you run away?"

I blinked at him, absolutely confused. "I didn't leave you. You left me. What are you . . ." Hope flooded me, pushing out the pain that threatened to destroy me. "You thought I left you?"

"I *know* you left me. When I came out of Valhöll, you were gone. I went back to the hotel room, but you weren't there, either. I did not know where you had gone until I called your cousin, who suggested you had come here. Why did you leave me? Do you not want me anymore? Have you withdrawn your love? What have I done to anger you?"

He left Valhalla? He'd been looking for me? "My God, Alrik! I was sitting here contemplating suicide because I thought . . . because you went . . . I didn't think I'd ever see you again—"

"You are my wife," he said, pulling me to my feet. His eyes were hard and bright, like the sun shining on a stream. "You thought I would leave you for the pleasures of Valhöll? I would kill a man for such an insult."

"But I saw you go in! You just left me, without even kissing me good-bye." I wrapped my arms around him, wanting to kiss every square inch of him, but he held me back, his face angry.

"I had to see the men to their reward," he answered, his voice hard. "I could not abandon them without ensuring that they were settled. I thought you understood that. I thought you would wait for me."

"But you didn't say that!" I wailed, new tears pricking behind my eyes. "I thought you were gone forever! I was heartbroken at the thought of never seeing you again! Oh my God, Alrik, how can you not know how much I love you?"

The angry expression faded as he pulled me back into his arms, his lips warm on my mouth. "How could you believe I would leave you, you who are my heart, my life?"

The floor beneath my feet reeled as I kissed him, every ounce of my body filled with joy. "I love you," I whispered as soon as I could speak.

"I know," he said, kissing me again.

I bit his lip. "Say it."

He laughed. "I am a Viking. We do not say such things."

"You are a former Viking. You are a . . ." I paused. "What exactly are you? An ex-ghost?"

"I am a Viking. I am your husband. That is all I could ask for," he answered, pinching my behind. "That is all you should want."

"It *is* all I want—assuming you're going to be around as long as I am."

"Do not fear, käresta, I will not leave you. I am allowed to visit the Midgard once every moon. You will not mind living in Asgard?" he asked, suddenly looking wary.

I hesitated, a worry of my own popping up.

"Asgard will not always be in Astrid Lindgrens Värld," he said quickly. "I have faith that Frigga will convince Odin to move it to less trying surroundings. Until then, I have secured us rooms in one of the halls. You will not mind living there?"

"I'd live with you in a shoebox if I had to," I answered. "Alrik, I know we both went into this marriage simply because of the curse, but—"

He pulled back a little. "You insult me again?"

"No, I'm simply pointing out that we didn't get married for the usual reasons, and that you might feel you need to carry on with it because of the oath you made Momo Hildi—"

His lips were forceful, demanding. I didn't argue, just accepted the happiness he brought me.

"I wed you because I wanted to, not because I was forced to. We will remain wed for the same reason," he said, his voice rough with emotion.

"Say it!" I demanded.

He gave a mock sigh, his hands warm on my behind. "Very well, but I do it only because I wish to foreplay you in such a way that will make you mindless with pleasure, thus forgetting that I have given in to your demands.

"I love you, Brynna. I will love you until the day I breathe my last. You belong to me, and I will make you the happiest of women. Now take off all your clothes, and pretend that you are a Celtic princess about to be marauded by an incredibly virile Viking studmuffin."

I looked up into his glorious, wonderfully changeable eyes, eyes that shone bright with love.

"That works for me," I said, and flung myself on him.

Epilogue

To: PaulHalvorsson@swedenhistorymuseum.se
From: BrynnaS@odinrocks.com
Subject: Happy New Year

New Year wishes from the sunny Bahamas! As you can see by the picture on the e-postcard, the new Asgard is pretty spiffy, although Odin still has his panties in a bunch over having to move. Evidently he can't get the same cable reception here that he had in Sweden. He gave Frigga hell about that for a while, until she whapped him upside the head with a swim fin. He stayed in his room pouting for a couple of weeks, but Alrik and I gave him a karaoke machine for Christmas, and he's spent every spare moment since then singing in Valhalla. He's got the warriors doing a cappella versions of Queen songs, which they seem to like.

The cabana on the far, far left in the picture is ours. Bardi and his wife are in the one next to us—he had to do some fast talking to get her out of Niflheim, where she was pretty happy teaching a class on henna tattooing, but even she now admits that oceanfront property is worth leaving Niflheim for. Torsten has fallen in love with another Valkyrie but she is giving him a bit of a chase. Jon and Grim spend most of their time in Valhalla, hacking away at each other during the day and boozing it up at night. They keep trying to get Alrik to join them, but he has other interests, cough, cough.

Did I mention that Gudrun has decided she needs to keep an eye on us until we produce a grandchild for her? She took a bungalow down the beach, and used to pop in unexpectedly to ask if I was pregnant yet until the day she caught Alrik and me pleasurably engaged. Alrik pointed out there would be no grandchildren if she kept interrupting, so ever since then, she calls instead of stopping by.

Alrik himself is just fine; thanks for asking. He sends his love, as do I. We used up our monthly visit to the mortal world today by going to Nassau for shopping, but we will come up to Sweden for a visit next month. And no, I'm still not smoking. Alrik manages to distract me every time the cravings get too much for me.

My new job is going well. I didn't know that Valkyries get to go into Valhalla, but evidently they can hang out with the warriors when they like. The Valkyries themselves are a bit intimidating—they bring new meaning to the word "intense"—but there's another new girl who evidently inherited the job from her great-times-however-many grandmother, too, so I'm not the only new kid on the block. I've only had to bring one warrior in so far, but it seems pretty simple work, all in all.

Oh! Did I mention I saw Momo Hildi? She's still in her young form, gorgeous as ever but raising hell (ha!) in Niflheim. It seems she didn't go to the good part, like Alrik's mom and sister. She went to Hel, and was assigned as Hel's personal assistant (that's the woman Hel, who runs the place, not Hel itself . . . oh, you know what I mean). Anyway, she's Hel's PA, and Momo Hildi is trying to get Hel ousted and herself put in charge. My money is on her.

Anyway, that's all the news from us. I've got to run—Alrik is waiting for me in our own private little cove. The man has discovered the joy of nude snorkeling in balmy Caribbean water, and I have to admit, his new hobby gets no complaints from me.

Hugs to Maja, and have a fabulous new year!

                        Love,
                        Brynna

FINALLY
A WEBSITE
YOU CAN GET
PASSIONATE
ABOUT...

Visit
www.SimonSaysLove.com
for the latest information
about Romance from Pocket Books!

READING SUGGESTIONS

LATEST RELEASES

AUTHOR APPEARANCES

ONLINE CHATS WITH YOUR
FAVORITE WRITERS

SPECIAL OFFERS

ORDER BOOKS ONLINE

AND MUCH, MUCH MORE!

DISCOVER DESIRE AFTER DARK

WITH THESE BESTSELLING PARANORMAL ROMANCES FROM POCKET BOOKS!

PRIMAL DESIRES SUSAN SIZEMORE

Only one woman can satisfy this Vampire Prime's every hunger…

THIRTY NIGHTS WITH A HIGHLAND HUSBAND MELISSA MAYHUE

Transported back in time, a modern-day woman falls in love with a Highlander descended from the faerie folk—who can only be hers for thirty nights.

IN DARKNESS REBORN ALEXIS MORGAN

Will an immortal warrior stay true to his people—or risk everything for the woman he loves?

SOMETHING WICKED CATHERINE MULVANY

Wicked desires lead to insatiable passions—passions no vampire can deny.

THE LURE OF THE WOLF JENNIFER ST. GILES

Be lured by a seductive shape-shifter whose dark allure is impossible to resist…

DESIRE LURKS AFTER DARK...

BESTSELLING PARANORMAL ROMANCES FROM POCKET BOOKS!

NO REST FOR THE WICKED KRESLEY COLE

He's a vampire weary of eternal life. She's a Valkyrie sworn to destroy him. Now they must compete in a legendary contest— and their passion is the ultimate prize.

DARK DEFENDER ALEXIS MORGAN

He is an immortal warrior born to protect mankind from ultimate evil. But who defends the defenders?

DARK ANGEL LUCY BLUE

Brought together by an ancient power, a vampire princess and a mortal knight discover desire is stronger than destiny…

A BABE IN GHOSTLAND LISA CACH

SINGLE MALE SEEKS FEMALE FOR GHOSTBUSTING…. and maybe more.